THE NEXT WIFE

KAIRA ROUDA

WHEELER PUBLISHING
A part of Gale, a Cengage Company

GALE
A Cengage Company

LIBRARY OF CONGRESS CIP DATA ON FILE.
CATALOGUING IN PUBLICATION FOR THIS BOOK
IS AVAILABLE FROM THE LIBRARY OF CONGRESS.

ISBN-13: 978-1-4328-8945-6 (hardcover alk. paper)

Published in 2021 by arrangement with Thomas & Mercer.

Printed in Mexico
Print Number: 01   Print Year: 2021

CHAPTER 1
TISH

Despite popular notions to the contrary, it isn't easy being the next wife.

I mean, sure, I have the benefit of his success without struggling through the "early days," whatever that means. But I also don't get to enjoy the open spaces of possibility — the opportunity to create a life together, baggage-free. So as we gather in the conference room to celebrate EventCo's big news, baggage invades my space.

I note one of the pieces of baggage standing just outside the conference room door: Ashlyn, the opinionated and overly dependent twenty-year-old daughter. For the most part, we have an amicable relationship, one I've worked hard to cultivate, and she understands the parameters. I used to babysit her, and we have a certain bond since she told me so many secrets. She thinks I have done likewise.

Next to her stands the steamer trunk of

baggage: Kate, wife number one. People say I'm the spitting image of Kate when she was young. And I am. We are both slim with shiny brown hair and big smiles. She is simply older by more than twenty years, a worn version of me. In her, I see my future. Sort of. She can't seem to stop wearing business suits to the office. I mean, the 1980s are calling, and they want their clothes back. Today she's wearing all white, meaning she's either a suffragette or pure as snow. As if.

Despite our differences in age and style, that cliché about men having a type is true. I mean, men aren't that original. They're simple beings, easy to figure out. Keep them happy, well fed in all areas if you get my drift, and voilà — a happy life.

Especially after they've had success.

Why would you let them slip through your fingers then? That's when you hold on tight. Sure, they're more work as they get older, and more successful, but that's just part of the deal. Some of us know how to keep our men, and some, well, they just don't. I will hang on. There will not be another wife.

Kate and I make eye contact, and I grin, reveling in the fact that I'm here inside the conference room seated next to John while she's milling around outside, trying to figure out where to be. Where her place is. Awkward for her, I'm sure.

Oh good, there's Jennifer, our beautiful vice president of marketing, going out of her way to make Kate feel welcome in the conference room. She's gushing over John's past family as if she were a long-lost relative. I should never have allowed her to be hired. Jennifer meets my eye and then quickly finds something to stare at on the floor. I wonder again why I am forced to work around someone who could be ripped from the pages of a fashion magazine: long blonde hair, impossibly smooth skin, big green eyes, and other enhancements. I'm a fool, that's why. Heaven knows I don't need John's attention divided any more than it already is.

The conference room door opens again and in walks Lance Steel — our COO — bald, brilliant, and gorgeous. He slides into a chair two down from me.

"Hey, boss," he says to John. Lance's jaw is drawn, intensity radiates from him. He's always thinking, from what I can tell. John says we were lucky to lure him away from a tech giant, and maybe we were, but I'd appreciate a friendlier COO if I had a choice. I sense Lance watching me, as always, and I meet his stare. I'm not sure if he's attracted to me or if it's something else. I assume we're about the same age, Lance and I, so I'm not interested. I like older men. I squeeze John's thigh under the table, but he pivots his chair away.

I force a smile as Kate and Ashlyn settle into their seats in the conference room, selecting chairs on the opposite end from me at the large glass table. All the officers and key employees fill the room now — the stakeholders, as they say — numbering twenty-four of us. Ashlyn stares at me across the table, her entitled confidence misplaced. She has no power here. If she had behaved, been a friend after John and I married, maybe things would be different for her. But it's too late for that. We act like we have a relationship when John's around, but it's a lie.

I break away from the brat and look around the table. Almost all the people at the table have been here since the beginning. Their tension and excitement are palpable. Beside me, I feel John shift in his seat. He's never quite gotten used to this — all of his family being together in one place, despite the fact we all worked here together in ignorant bliss not so long ago.

John stands, commanding the room. He's wearing a black polo shirt with *EventCo* stitched in red on the sleeve, black pants, and a big smile. We both dressed Steve Jobs-style, all in black. We planned it this way. Serious. Techy. My hair is pulled back in a low ponytail. My pants and black T-shirt display my curves. Bright-red lipstick completes my look. I know the men in the office notice what I wear, and I enjoy the attention.

John wears a leather bracelet, the one with a metal peace sign on it, a gift from me that I know makes him feel young. We're ready. The lines beaming from his blue eyes like sunlight convey warmth, experience. I think I fell in love with his eye crinkles.

The sheen on his forehead is the only sign he isn't feeling 100 percent. I fight the urge to hand him a napkin. Sweat is so unappealing.

"So, how does it feel to be rich?" John begins the applause, and the rest of us join in. My heart pounds in my chest. I for one think being rich is the only way to be. And now, we have so much more, John and I.

John continues, and I feign devout attention. "I know it's been a tough couple of months, with the quiet period and those nuisance lawsuits, but just look at those shares of EventCo popping!" John points to the television screen in the corner of the sleek conference room. It feels surreal. On a typical business day, charts and dry-erase marker scribbles cover the walls of this room in various bright colors. One of my jobs used to be wiping these walls.

Today, someone else wiped the walls clean, stark white, like a blank piece of paper. John and his black attire stand out more than usual. I decide to stand up next to him, enjoying the frowns from Kate and Ashlyn.

I smile at them both and wink at Ashlyn before turning my attention back to the TV screen in the corner. It's tuned to *Market Watch.* The stock market never mattered that much to me, but now, with EventCo going public, it matters. It matters very much.

"Look at her go!" John exclaims. I jump before realizing he's talking about the stock. Jeez, I'm not sure why I'm so on edge. I guess it's just the excitement of today. The last day before everything changes.

John glances at me, a look of concern but mostly of *what the heck are you doing standing next to me?* in his eyes.

"This is so exciting, honey." I kiss him on the cheek and whisper, "You should wipe your forehead." I push a tissue into his hand, but he ignores me.

14

John continues. "Before we go out there and join the rest of the company to celebrate, I wanted to gather you all here and thank you. Because of your hard work, Kate and I were able to build the company of our dreams. I hope you're happy with the results, and I hope you'll still come to work, even if you don't need the cash anymore."

I lean into John and smile, sharing the moment in the spotlight again. I wonder if any media are here to capture this happy scene through the glass-front conference room. If they are, it will be a great shot. Me and my man, all in black, standing in front of a white background with an entire team around the conference table staring up at us with pure adulation. A business success stock photo to be sure.

But I don't see any cameras, unfortunately, even though they should be there. This is a huge moment for EventCo. John started the company with Kate twenty years ago, and it's grown to become one of central Ohio's most prominent and well-respected companies. We're the all-American success story based in the all-American city in the heartland. Come on, you can't make this stuff up. We processed more than $1 billion in gross ticket sales last month. Successful beyond our wildest dreams, we offer online invitations, party supplies, and a one-stop shop for the hottest concert tickets all rolled into one. When I say "we," I mean they. My only job since I arrived was to keep John organized and happy: first as his executive assistant and then as his wife. I guess I did my part.

I'm satisfied when John finally wraps his arm around my waist and pulls me in close. That's better.

"Special thanks to Tish, who has put up with a very stressed-out CEO for these past few months. I know it hasn't been easy keeping my schedule organized. And to all of you, I know I haven't been the easiest person to work for lately."

Was that a slam? I mean, I am officially his executive assistant, but I'm so much more than a scheduler. We're married, so half of his half of this now-public company is mine. My chest thumps again with the bigness of it all. John's right, though. To say he's been stressed out is an understatement, but I smile and turn to the EventCo team.

"I'm so proud of you, John. You worked hard to make sure this IPO would be good for everyone. As for me, I just can't wait to whisk you away for a much-needed vacation this weekend."

Even though this is the first John has

heard about our trip, he doesn't react. That's fine. We leave tonight after the festivities. I've packed toiletries. The private plane waits for us at the airport. It will be nice to have a little weekend together in the mountains.

We have so much to talk about.

CHAPTER 2
JOHN

I take a deep breath and wipe my brow. My heart pounds in my chest as I realize it's all over.

I stand in this familiar conference room and look at the team — my team — and remember all we've accomplished. I spent my best years growing this business, and now, with the IPO, it's a bittersweet moment. Going public will change everything, that's what everyone tells me. I smile at Ashlyn, who narrows her eyes and glares at Tish standing next to me. I'm now aware that Tish is talking and that I should be the one doing so. I snap out of my reverie and jump in.

"Anyway, thank you from the bottom of my heart, to each and every one of you. I hope you're happy with your stock holdings. It's too late if you aren't," I add, noticing the ripple of tension zipping around the table. You can't please all the people all the time. But I tried, I really did. "And I know you know there is a lockdown period for the next ninety days, so no selling any stock before that. I predict three months from now our employee parking lot will be filled with shiny new cars."

A wave of "wow" and "no" flows through the room, and tense expressions give way to wonder. *What does it mean for me?* each of them is thinking. I know the feeling when reality sets in. Jennifer walks around the conference table handing out the rules and regulations packet governing initial public offerings and company executives. She's such an asset.

I note with relief that Kate seems at ease, too. I never meant to hurt her, and I've tried to tell her so lately. I'm not sure she believes me, but I have been making progress in repairing the mess I made. I hope so, at least. She tucks a strand of hair behind her ear. I love that habit. And I love that white suit. I wonder if she wore it today because it was my favorite.

My heart thumps loudly in my chest again, and I clutch the conference table for support while I continue watching my ex-wife. I hope her astronomical net worth will make her happy. Soften her heart a little. I can't really count it as my penance, though, can I? We built all this together. EventCo was our baby along with Ashlyn, our greatest achievement.

I remember my promise to my daughter: dinner tonight with her friend Seth. I can't wait.

Lance raises his hand as he stands. He's been a key part of our management team. He took a leap of faith to come to work here, leaving a publicly traded firm. Now, he's about to go full circle. "Are you and Kate staying on board?"

Kate leans forward and addresses her answer to me. "Of course. I'm not going anywhere. We have more innovations to roll out. Game-changing products. Isn't that right, John?" This has been our biggest fight of late. My ex-wife begged me to release her new product before the IPO. I refused.

Kate's Forever project is innovative, but we didn't need it for the IPO. It is expensive, and, well, I guess truth be told, I didn't want to share the IPO spotlight with a product launch. Does that mean I didn't want to share the spotlight with her? Of course not, but that's how she took it. Her instincts about what our customers want are on point and have been since day one. Despite the tension my decision caused, I hope she's happy now. Look at the stock climb.

I smile at Kate. Her eyes soften, and she winks at me. My shoulders drop with relief. We're still on the same team. Lately, more than ever.

I say, "Kate, I know you aren't going anywhere. And I can't wait to roll out the Forever project. It's brilliant. Like you."

"Thank you." Kate leans back in her chair and folds her arms across her chest. "I'm in for the long haul at EventCo. At least until Forever."

A ripple of laughter cuts through the tension in the room. If Kate can joke about her product launch being pushed back, we can all relax. I'm glad she understands. She's been so kind this week.

Kate adds, "EventCo is my life's work. My other baby, so to speak." My daughter rolls her eyes. Even so, I know she's proud of her mom and dad. "I'm glad we'll launch the Forever project soon. The market and our new investors will be impressed, along with our customers." Kate smiles at me, the gorgeous grin I first fell in love with all those years ago. It was her best feature and still is.

I forgot how much that smile could make my day.

Sandra Nguyen, our HR director, raises her hand. "I just want to say I'm here to review the rules regarding IPOs if anyone needs clarification."

A sigh rolls through the room.

I jump in. "Yes, there are rules as you all know. Be careful, but enjoy yourselves."

It used to be fun coming to work, but lately, I feel like I'm slowly dying. I need air, I need out of this conference room. I stare at the glass wall separating this room from the atrium, and I feel trapped. Like I'm an animal caged at the zoo. Look at him, the model CEO. White. Middle aged. I'm a cliché in so many ways and mostly by my own doing. Look at me, wearing all black as if I'm super hip when I'm not. And Tish keeps touching me, reaching for my hand, patting my thigh. It's annoying, unprofessional. The black leather bracelet she gave me feels like a handcuff.

Maybe her actions are especially annoying because it's a reminder of just how unprofessional I've been myself. I know she's doing it to anger Kate and Ashlyn. I used to return the affection, even in the office, in front of my family. I'm ashamed of myself.

My daughter stands by my side, a scowl on her face. I can't help but sigh.

"Dad, what did Tish mean about taking you away this weekend? We have dinner plans tonight, remember? With Seth? My back-to-college dinner?" Ashlyn says.

"Of course, honey. I'm not going any-where. When did she say that?" I ask. Maybe I missed something. I haven't been myself this week. Stress does strange things.

"She just did. Here in the conference room. She was standing right next to you."

"I must have tuned her out," I say. "Look, Ash, I'll fix it."

My daughter's expression tells me she doesn't believe me.

I clap Lance on the back and say, "Let's join the rest of the employees for a drink. We're not going to get any work done around here for a few days." I walk out of the conference room, wiping beads of sweat from my brow.

In my daydream, I just keep walking and disappear.

CHAPTER 3
TISH

Rude.

John departs the conference room with Lance, abandoning me — and Kate and Ashlyn, for that matter — to walk out to the party. Once the baggage leaves, too, I hang back, watching the scene. Unfortunately, now I'm stuck alone with Sandra in the conference room.

"So much change," Sandra says as she finally pushes away from the table.

"I know. I just want this to be over. Next phase and all." I smile at her and flip my ponytail. I guess that's nerves. I also know she hates it. If I had a piece of gum, I'd pop it in my mouth and crack it. I know how to do that, learned as a kid. The problem is Sandra doesn't have to be nice to me when John isn't around. And she's not.

"Next phase? What would that be, exactly?" Sandra folds her arms across her chest. A smirk spreads across her face. Why does she always wear brown? She leans toward me and whispers, "Seems like you should be satisfied with this phase."

Really, Sandra? John and I have been married for three years now. I'm not in the mood for this. She's on my last nerve. So many people are today.

I lean toward her. "What is that supposed to mean?" Although I've asked the question, I know what she thinks: I am an opportunist. The beautiful, winning, young second-wife type. And she's right for the most part. Except John seduced me. He did. Although it seems nobody around here believes that. Sandra and the rest of them all think I worked some sort of magic on John, took advantage of the poor man, yanked him away from his family. I did not make that first move. He did.

But as I said, it's not all fun and games being in my position. Nobody likes you, nobody believes you. I stare at my huge wedding ring, move my wrist so it sparkles at her. "You don't know anything about me."

Sandra embraces her inner Sheryl Sandberg and leans in, too. I take a step forward. She says, "I know all about you."

"No, you don't. I mean sure, you're the one who hired me to be John's assistant.

So, thanks for that." I'm tired of her and her insinuations. I've dealt with them since I started at the company five years ago.

She was the first to catch on to the little something-something between John and me. She sniffed it, I could tell. If she could have, she would have fired me. But John was one step ahead of her. He wanted me, plain and simple. There was nothing Sandra or anyone else could do to stop it.

I look down at my sparkling eight-carat diamond wedding ring and hold my hand up, pretending to inspect it. I know she's looking at it, too, with a dart of envy. "You'll probably retire now, right? You're that age, aren't you?"

Her face contorts into an annoying grimace. "You mean old, don't you? I'm sorry, I'm not going anywhere. I'll be watching you."

"Enjoy the view." I walk out of the now-empty conference room and feel her eyes on my back. There's nothing she can do to me, but she should watch herself. She'll need to stay on John's good side if she wants to stick around.

And she should know by now that John runs everything through me. At least he did until recently. Another little issue we need to address on our weekend together. We really do have a lot to discuss: our relationship and other relationships in his life. I wish I didn't have to pretend to be enjoying myself at this stupid party. I'd rather fly away with John and take stock of where we stand now that the IPO is launched. And we will soon. I check my watch.

I reach the atrium where the celebration is in full swing. The DJ is the best in the Midwest, and the catering company is central Ohio's finest. Waiters in white jackets circulate with silver trays laden with signature cocktails and appetizers. There should be no complaints from the crowd about this bash. On the walls, gobo lights tell employees to use the hashtag #EventCoIPO.

Kate has thought of everything.

And there she is. Standing with John and Ashlyn. I make my way through the crowd without much trouble. Ever since I married the boss, chitchat with fellow employees has been awkward. I get it. I'm so far above them all now: untouchable, wealthy, in command. I'm isolated at the helm. I told you it isn't easy being me.

"Nice shindig, Kate." I slip my hand into John's as I sidle up beside him. He's mine, ladies. John squeezes my hand but then pulls away. I need to get him out of here, away from all the temptation of his past.

"Ashlyn did a great job helping out," Kate says, and Ashlyn beams. In a new development, Ashlyn would like to be in marketing someday, and Kate thinks she's brilliant at it. How wonderful. It's especially wonderful because she won't be working for EventCo. Not if I have a say in things. And I do. This gravy train is all over, dear. Too bad. But you'll always have the memories from this summer's internship. She graduates college next summer, and hopefully she'll move far far away.

"I loved helping. You're amazing, Mom." Ashlyn finishes gushing over Kate. I fight the urge to say what I really think to the brat. Ashlyn and I have a détente, I suppose. Most of the time, I stay out of her way, and she stays out of mine. We were friends before I married her dad and for a time after. I was her slightly older BFF, a glamorous buddy to confide in, and a saving grace for a teenage girl who hated her mom. But things change.

Now I'm not so sure where we stand. I'll deal with her later.

John is speaking. "I'm going to miss all of this. I hope things don't change too much with the IPO."

Is he drunk? I can't tell. He's definitely

emotional. More emotional than I've ever seen him. His forehead is still shiny, too, and his face is pale.

"Did you eat?" I glare at him, but he ignores the question.

"I have dinner plans with Ashlyn tonight," John says.

"You'll need a rain check, I'm afraid."

Lance appears, serious as usual. "John, it's time to address the employees."

"Ashlyn, will you come onstage with me?" John motions to his daughter, and they walk away from me toward the front of the room.

I'm seething. John should call me up there. I should be by his side. My face flushes. Lance watches me.

"What?" My hands ball into fists by my side. *Calm down,* I remind myself.

Lance says, "John will be right back. It's just a speech. This is Ashlyn's family business, too, and she's the only child. It's important for the employees to see her. After all, they watched her grow up."

He's so annoying. "I know that. I'm the wife. I'm important, too."

He shrugs and walks away. I remind myself that in an hour we will be wheels up, free from these people for the weekend. I turn my back to Kate, who has been ignoring me anyway, and try to tolerate the show.

29

I suppose she isn't up there, either, so that makes me feel good.

John and Ashlyn stand side by side on a stage brought in for the event. He whispers something in her ear and she stares at me, shaking her head. The music stops, and John holds up both hands. The employees clink their glasses with cocktail forks until the room is silent.

"What a day! I just want to take a moment to thank you for your service to the company. Whether you've been here with us for twenty years or six months, we're family. I wish you all well with the IPO. Thanks, too, for welcoming Ashlyn into the family business. She's enjoyed her internship this summer and will be back after she graduates."

Ashlyn smiles and waves. She loves all this attention. I didn't really think it was in her, but it is. Disappointing, really. In high school she was so reserved. A bookworm. Easy to love, simple to understand, predictable, and malleable. I miss those days.

"I'd like to take a moment to thank Ashlyn's mom and my business partner, Kate. EventCo wouldn't exist without her. Kate, please join us." John waves at Kate to come to the stage.

"Come up here, Mom," Ashlyn says into

30

the microphone. She thinks she's some sort of emcee or something.

Oh, barf. *Really?* I feel my jaw clench as the whole room turns to watch Kate. She's wearing chic high heels. She smiles broadly, and tears shine in her eyes. The lights from the disco ball bounce sparkles of light across her white suit. She seems to glow as she walks to the front. Damn it. Meanwhile, I'm brooding among the masses. Ignored and forgotten. Alone and angry.

"Kate really helped pull us through these last few weeks. Thank you for everything," John says from the stage.

I watch in horror as the crowd parts. John takes Kate's hand and pulls her up to stand between them onstage. One little happily divorced family.

The applause from the company employees is loud, over the top if you ask me. Maybe they're all drunk.

Kate holds the microphone. "Thank you all for believing in us and our vision, some of you from the very beginning." She's at home in front of a crowd, in the spotlight. I know that already. I want to gag, but I'll keep up appearances. Of course I will. "It hasn't been easy lately, being one step removed from all of you as we worked through the S-1 filing and the quiet period, but now I couldn't be more excited for the future. And for EventCo, *the best is yet to be.*"

How clever of Kate to work in the company tagline. The crowd roars and yells, "The best is yet to be!"

Thunderous applause. They're lemmings. All of them.

"It's an honor to stand up here, with my family, and take this time to celebrate what we've all worked so hard to achieve. All of Ashlyn's life we've been creating EventCo. It started as an idea in the middle of the night and grew into a start-up in the basement of our first home." Kate smiles. "Ashlyn cooing in the playpen in the corner."

"Oh, Mom, really?" Despite her protests, Ashlyn seems proud of her mom right now. I thought they didn't like each other? Maybe they're both faking it in front of me. Or maybe things have changed? No. It's a show. It must be.

We all know what Kate really is: a bitter has-been dried-up divorcée who drinks too much and fights with her daughter. That's what John told me when we first started hooking up. That's why he left her. Her best has already been. I'm the new Mrs. Nelson. The beautiful, elegant, young Mrs. Nelson.

I need to get up there onstage. This is my

time to shine. This is my company, too. Ashlyn is my daughter, too. I can deliver a good speech. Just watch.

I start working my way up to the front of the crowd as Kate drones on.

"Thank you, each and every one of you. For believing in me, and John, and EventCo. Now, back to the party!" The happy family steps down into the crowd, Ashlyn between Kate and John, holding her parents' hands. I watch stunned as John kisses them both on the cheek. That's about enough.

If I still smoked, this would be the moment I'd go have a cigarette. This little display of unity also makes me realize I shouldn't have agreed to retire after the IPO announcement. John told me it would be the best for the company, that the stress of having Kate and me at the office was bad for morale. But how am I going to keep track of things if I've been pushed out the door? Unacceptable, really.

I won't be forced out, not when there's so much, let's call it abundance, right here. These employees need bosses. They need Nelsons to lead them. I'm the newest Nelson, but I'm the cutest. Take that, Kate.

I lean against the wall and watch the other Mrs. Nelson work the crowd. I grab a drink from a waiter passing by with a silver tray, the glass cool to the touch. I'm not going anywhere. Well, except on a quickie vacation with John.

Then I'll be back, whether she likes it or not.

CHAPTER 4
JOHN

Light pours through a crack in the curtains, and even with my eyes closed, the brightness pokes through and hurts my head. There's one thing I know for sure: I don't want to be here. Telluride is beautiful — don't get me wrong — but the last thing I needed after the week I had was to get on the plane and fly to the middle of nowhere for a "relaxing, romantic weekend."

No, what I wanted was to be at dinner with my daughter last night. And this weekend, I wanted to hang out with my friends, guys who can understand what it's like to sign over your life's work to the whims of the "public" and the stock exchange. Play some golf, some cards. Hell, I had to leave my own party early last night just so we wouldn't miss the flight on my own plane.

And Kate. I wanted to spend time with her, too, celebrating what we accomplished.

I'll never forget the look on Ashlyn's face when Tish told me it was time to go.

"You're leaving your own party? Now?" Ashlyn asked. "Why would you do that? We have dinner plans, Dad. You don't want to go, do you?"

I swear my daughter sees right through me.

Tish shoved her arm through mine and addressed Ashlyn. "The party was over half an hour ago. You should leave, too, so maybe all these people will get the message. Someone should cut off the bar. It's almost nine."

I know I should have stood up to her, but I was tired. Drained. I felt Kate watching us as we made our way out of the office. I wanted to say something to her, share a final IPO toast, but I had no choice. I had to leave with my wife. Tish and I need to talk. And we will. But I fell asleep on the plane only to wake up when we landed. Next thing I knew, we were at the house in Telluride, and I was climbing into my bed.

It's my fault, I know. I haven't dealt with things with Tish. I have plenty of excuses. I've been busy working on the IPO, for one, and avoidance has been my tactic. I've allowed myself to be put in this position. But it can't last.

My phone lights up with a text. Where are

36

you? Are you coming into the office?

I look around, guilty, which is ridiculous. I text, No. I'm in Telluride.

The little dots tell me she's typing. Why? There's so much to do here. And what about your heart? Do you have your meds? Did you want to go?

Before I can answer, the bedroom door pops open, and my lovely bride stands in the doorway. She's wearing tight-fitting yoga clothes, although I doubt she's been to a yoga class. She's in all white. She looks good. Young and, dare I say, virginal. She's not, of course, but she is young. She could be my daughter. I know what everyone says. I'm not deaf. I slip the phone under the covers.

"You're finally awake, sleepyhead!" She bounds to the bed and plants a big kiss on my cheek. "It's gorgeous outside! I thought we could go for a hike and soak up some of this fresh mountain air and sunshine. Columbus is so hot and stifling, and here it's just crisp and wide open and blue. I've never seen a sky this blue."

"And dizzying." I roll out of bed, and as my feet hit the floor, I feel it. Altitude sickness worsened, no doubt, by dehydration. I drank more than I planned at the party.

"I turned on the oxygen in the bedroom.

Thought that would help. Take it easy." Tish is so concerned that she helps me into the bathroom. I have a history of terrible altitude sickness. When we were here three years ago, on the day I proposed in fact, I fell sideways into a wall walking down the hall to our bedroom. It hits at the strangest times.

"Thanks, I'll be fine. I can handle a day or so. We're just here for the weekend, right?" The nice thing about having my own home to travel to is that everything is where I left it even though I haven't been here in a year. Each of my homes is stocked with the same clothes, books, and creature comforts. You name it. I grab my medicine and toothbrush — or in this case Tish must have grabbed them — and move from home to home effortlessly with everything I need waiting for me upon arrival. Kate made it happen first, and now Tish does her best to imitate.

Ah, Kate. I see her smile, her flash of wit as we cut the ribbon on our tiny first headquarters for EventCo all those years ago. It was just the two of us, a programmer, and a big idea. We'd fallen in love at UCLA, and she'd followed me to grad school in the Midwest. She was a California girl who gave up everything to build a company, and a life, with me.

"We can do this, John. I've researched it. There's a market. People want an easy way, a new way, to invite friends to parties. If we add in tickets to local events and concerts, we could really create something here. A marketplace for fun." She'd come bursting into our apartment, big brown eyes shining and the frigid air outside providing the rosy cheeks. "We need to do it before someone else does."

I tossed my book onto the floor and pulled her onto my lap. "Let's do it." First we'd made love, and then we'd written a business plan. Two months later we were up and running — in our apartment — but she made us cut a ribbon anyway. Before I knew it, we were married, buying a house, and she was pregnant with Ashlyn, all while growing the company, too. We set up our offices in the basement, painting the walls bright shades of yellow, orange, and blue to give us energy, Kate said. We celebrated every milestone, and we hit every one we set. That's Kate. The overachiever. Celebrations mean a lot to her. Heck, she built a company around celebrations.

"Earth to John." Tish stands behind me in the mirror. Clearly I should finish brushing. I open the medicine cabinet and find my blood pressure medicine just where it should be and beside it my bottle of herbal supplements from the naturopath. These pills keep me calm under stress and help with restful sleep. I look in the mirror and see an exhausted middle-aged man. Maybe I should take double the dose today. In the mirror, Tish watches me. I drop my eyes back to the medicine cabinet and remind myself to get a backbone. It's time to make a change. I swallow the pills with a big gulp of water before turning to my bride.

"What hike are you thinking about? I should take it easy day one." I move into the walk-in closet and find my hiking attire. I pull on khaki shorts with so many pockets you could never fill them all and a comfortable white T-shirt, then walk into the bathroom. I slide the rest of today's pills into my pocket. I'm supposed to take them throughout the day, and from the tension between us, I suspect today I'll need them more than ever.

"Let's do the meadow. That way we can enjoy all the wildflowers and pick some for the table."

The meadow isn't really a hike. It's a stroll. "Perfect." I should be able to stay upright for it.

"Breakfast is ready. Let's eat first." Tish

40

leads the way out of the bedroom. A bedroom designed by Kate, unchanged by Tish. Is that strange to her, I wonder? Does she care that my first wife's handprints cover this room? I find the continuity strangely comforting: a reminder of a beautiful past.

I'm such a fool.

On the way to the bedroom door, I slip my hand inside the sheets and grab my phone. I delete the incoming texts once Tish starts down the hall.

She turns around. Did she catch me?

She says, "I have a big surprise."

Oh no. All I can think with dread is: Now what?

41

CHAPTER 5
TISH

John follows me to the breakfast nook and sits. I pour him fresh-squeezed orange juice from a sparkling crystal pitcher. On his plate, I've arranged a European breakfast of sorts: a hard-boiled egg; toast and strawberry jam; hard, sharp cheese; and some prosciutto. Cherries shine in a bowl. I saw the whole setup in one of my lifestyle magazines. We're living the life.

"Lovely surprise. Feel free to do this every morning. Or any morning," John says before shoving a bite of toast into his mouth.

Cute. He's pointing out my lack of domestic ability. A backhanded compliment. He should watch it. When's the last time he made me breakfast? Never. "I guess I'll have the time to prepare this sort of feast since I'm now in forced retirement from EventCo. I still don't think it's fair. I like working with you better."

"That topic is settled." John's voice has an

edge to it today. I decide not to push the issue at the moment. But it is not settled. Not with me.

"I'm not sure I'm meant to be a housewife. It seems unfulfilling. But I'm glad you like my attempt. Eat up." I pull out my chair and sit across from him.

I still remember the moment a month ago when John called me into his office and told me to have a seat.

"Ooh, so serious and boss-like. What's up?" I asked. I made sure to cross my legs, showing them off from the side slit in my tight black skirt.

"Our consultants have told me that the new investors won't accept an ex-wife and the second wife working at EventCo once we're a public company. They say it will scare off potential shareholders. That it's bad for our IPO. It's negative optics."

I'll give you some negative optics, I thought at the time. "Maybe Kate should retire, then. Isn't she almost that age?" I glared at him, challenging him. "I've been here almost five years. It's not fair. She should leave. I'm the wife now."

"Of course Kate will not be leaving. This is her company." John stood up and walked around his huge desk. My mind flashed to the moment he'd seduced me, right there, on top of that desk. I'd had no idea our flirtations meant anything to him, no idea he was unhappy in his marriage. "Unsatisfied" is the word he had used then as he pushed me back onto the desk.

I shake my head. His office took on a whole different vibe a month ago. That's when he told me I was out.

"It's my company, too," I said. "I've been a good employee. A great executive assistant. You can't replace me."

"Of course not, honey. You're irreplaceable, but I'll need to. Sandra's working on it already," he said. His hands found my shoulders, massaging the tension, trying to make me agree to his stupid decision.

"Whatever." That's all I said. It wasn't really an agreement; it was a pause, time to think through my options and to appease John. When it comes down to it, for John, it's all about appearances. And, on the surface at least, Kate and Ashlyn's comfort and needs come first. Always have. I was such a fool.

When we first married, I thought it would be different. I thought I would be more important to John than Kate. But I never was. And Ashlyn? I thought she'd have her place, meeting us for dinner out once a week. He made a lot of promises to me back

44

then. He's broken them all. I just can't trust him.

As for Kate and Ashlyn, I'll deal with them later.

Focus, Tish.

And I do. First on John eating and then, behind him, the hideous curtains hanging in the living room. Kate has terrible taste in decor. Probably another reason he picked me. I was what he wanted. He said he wanted to escape from the failure of his marriage, the constant demands of a never-content Kate. I was his soul mate, his solution. Now, I'm not sure what I am to him. I need to get his attention.

John cracks the egg, hitting it too hard with his spoon. Shell fragments skitter across the table.

"I'm so excited for our day, aren't you?" I ask.

John's mouth is moving, as if he wants to say something, but he doesn't. I reach across the table and hold his hand. He allows the touch for a moment, before his phone buzzes.

"There's no need to jump every time your phone pings. Not anymore. The IPO happened. Isn't that great?" I hope, for his sake, he keeps the phone in his pocket. I stare at him, daring him to disobey me.

He ignores my warning and pulls the phone out, glances at the screen quickly before sliding it away.

He hears my exhale, and we lock eyes.

"It's not like it's over, Tish. I have friends calling, employees who need advice. The IPO happened, but there is still a lot to do. People have questions. That's why I can't believe I'm here with you instead of back home with them."

Really? "Oh, John, you used to love being alone with me, don't you remember? I saved your life. Rescued you from the hell of your first marriage, or something like that. Remember? You wanted me, you wanted a fresh start," I say.

He tilts his head, considering his next words. "Yes, I took the first step in our relationship. At work. It was wrong. I did fall hard for you. I did," John says. He picks up a shiny red cherry and pops it into his mouth.

"It has a seed," I say, and watch as he puts the pit on his plate. Good boy. "I've missed you lately. You've been so preoccupied." I bite my lip, a move that used to turn him on. "We really need this weekend to reconnect."

He pats my hand, placating me like I'm a child, before he slides his chair out from the table and carries his plate into what can only be described as a country mountain kitchen: loads of wood, carved moldings, and heavy tile. Ick. You can almost smell the old fashioned.

"I want you to enjoy this, our little weekend getaway, to celebrate and relax. I haven't had any attention lately. It's already Saturday. We'll leave tomorrow evening. You can get right back to whatever it is you're up to, OK?" Appeasement makes the heart grow fonder, I'm telling you. "Whoever's texting you on a Saturday morning can wait until Monday, can't they?"

John glances at me before gazing outside. It is beautiful out the window, sun shining on green mountains, a rainbow of wildflowers in bloom. Cue the *Sound of Music* soundtrack. "Right. It's not important."

He's lying.

It's her.

Too bad I'm one step ahead of you both.

But we'll just leave that alone for now. I have a whole day for him to come clean. He can tell me what's not right about our relationship, and I'll fix it. He needs me in his life, I just have to remind him of that fact. It shouldn't take much, nothing a little romance can't smooth over. I mean, men are simple creatures. We all know what they

47

think about most of the day. So first we'll enjoy a hike in the sunshine, followed by lunch and an open, honest conversation. Assuming everything is sorted out, we'll come back here for a little afternoon delight, as John calls it.

It's a day of new beginnings. The company is public. We're rich, and we're so in love. And no one is going to ruin this relationship. No one will come between us. I'm going to get to the bottom of everything. I'm a problem solver.

"Ready to hike?" My voice is light and airy, warm and friendly. I'm the perfect wife.

"I'll give it a try. Just can't promise much, stamina wise. I'm exhausted from the deal and the altitude." John drops onto the rustic bench by the front door, rummaging around for his hiking shoes. He sounds like an old man. Our twenty-five-year age difference usually doesn't bother me, but just now he's whiny.

I pat him on the head like a child, returning the favor. "Fresh air will do you good. You've never had a problem with your stamina, not that I've noticed." Yes, I'm overtly flirting now, but this is what the male ego needs.

I wonder what *she* sees in him. Sometimes I wonder if I should just bow out and let her have him. But then I realize: I'm not a quitter. And I like the crinkles next to his eyes and the way he looks at me when he remembers our love. He's stuck with me, whether he likes it or not. Or he'll be left with nothing. No one. It's his choice. I'm sure he'll come around today.

He'd better.

CHAPTER 6
JOHN

As I trudge along the well-worn path
through the meadow of wildflowers, I remind myself I used to love it here. The clean
air, the soaring mountains, the sense of being so far away from the flat, corporate,
contained world. This is the West, where
dreams come true, where anything is possible.

That's why I proposed to Tish in this very
meadow. Was it really only three years ago?
It seems like a different lifetime. I know I'm
tired, and this damn altitude gets to me. It's
hard to catch my breath. I need time to
adjust to everything.

Tish is trying her best to make me happy.
I realize that. As I follow behind her on the
path, I remind myself of all the fun we've
had. How she makes me laugh, how she
makes me feel young. How I told myself it
was against all the rules to fall for her, but I
did anyway. She is so pretty, so uncompli-

cated. I was overwhelmed with my life, with Kate and our constant fights about how to grow the company, how to raise Ashlyn. Tish was a beautiful escape. As if she senses my thoughts, she turns and gives me a smile.

"Isn't this just perfect?" she asks.

"It is," I manage.

It's really not her fault at all. She never stirred the pot with Kate. No, she kept this thing between us quiet and discreet until I spoiled it, bragging about my new love to the wrong guys. Tish was great with my daughter from the get-go, making sure Ashlyn knew she had a friend. She didn't have to be nice to Ashlyn — she did it because it was the right thing to do. And she helped smooth things out. At least, for a while.

It was so easy to fall in love with Tish. And she needed love. I could tell something was missing, something happened in her childhood in the backwoods of Kentucky. She won't talk about it, but you can sense it, want to fix it. I thought I could fill that hole, and in return, she would bring me the peace I lacked in my life. We didn't have all that history between us, not like Kate and me toward the end. Kate and I had nothing but fights, and company problems, and a teenage daughter tearing us apart.

And Tish? I suppose she pulled us apart without trying. Being there, being so damn there with her perky breasts, short skirts, always just smiling at me no matter how terse I was, no matter how frustrated I was with Kate. Tish was like running away to a private Caribbean island in the midst of stress and grown-up problems. A temptation I was too weak to ignore.

It's not her fault. It's all mine.

"Look at that waterfall." Tish points into the mountains, and I pretend to care.

"Pretty." I am such a fool. I threw everything I had away for *pretty*.

I remember telling Ashlyn I'd found true love. I'd moved out of our home, away from Ashlyn and Kate, and into a flashy condo on the sixteenth floor, overlooking the city. Tish loved it. Ashlyn hated every inch of the space.

"This is what people live in when they're young, just starting out," she'd scoffed, all sixteen years of wisdom looking at me with disdain as she walked in the door. How could she possibly know anything? She didn't. I mean, the condo was no starter pad. I'd been there, done that with Kate, complete with cockroaches and mice in the kitchen drawer.

I'll never forget that moment. Kate's

scream was so loud and urgent I thought someone was in the tiny kitchen murdering her. I ran from the front room into the kitchen to find my newlywed wife frozen.

"There's something in there. With bright-red eyes." She pointed to the closed kitchen drawer, her finger trembling.

I yanked the drawer open, revealing our measly collection of thrift shop silverware and nothing else.

"It's gone." I smiled. The hero.

"It'll be back," she answered, still shaking. "We have to move. Find another apartment. Or never use that drawer. All of those drawers."

Kate was like that. Take charge. All or nothing. Black and white. Fearless in life and business. She went from top of her class at UCLA to running one of the best start-ups in the country. She was successful in everything she touched.

Until we started fighting about everything. Until I began to resent the fact that she was always right. Until I couldn't bear it. Until I betrayed her.

Back then, I was her knight in shining armor, even though she didn't need one. Except to handle the mice.

"We can't afford to move. I'll tape up the drawers." I knew better than to come up with a solution that involved pesticides. She'd never agree to that. Or to a trap. And so we'd lived there another year, with taped-up drawers and hundreds of mice running throughout the old apartment's walls. And we were so happy. Some days we'd be working so long, so intently, we'd forget to eat. Who needs silverware when you're in love and building a business?

I had three drawers of real silver in the new penthouse Ashlyn stood inside that day. I shook my head, indignant at the time. How could she understand? She was only sixteen.

"This is a sophisticated penthouse, the finest on the market downtown. It's certainly not a starter apartment, Ash."

"You're clearly having a midlife crisis."

I held my ground. "No, that's not true. I found my soul mate. I hope you're as happy for me as I am. Tish and I are moving in together." I didn't even have a doubt as I told my daughter this. Not then.

Ashlyn had been seated on the sleek white leather sofa facing the view of the downtown skyline, but she stood and yelled: "Your *soul mate* just happens to be your assistant? Come on. You looked far and wide, not really of course, and suddenly your soul mate materialized at that desk. It was karma, is that it?" Ashlyn was angry, sure, but I wanted her to understand. To realize how happy I was. "Your soul mate babysat me! She's four years older than me. Oh my god."

When Ashlyn left, slamming the door behind her, I didn't worry. We had a great father-daughter relationship, and it would be fine between the two of us. Ashlyn and I were close when she was growing up. I was the fun parent, the one who said yes when Kate said no. The dad who volunteered at school, who went on the sixth-grade camp-out. The dad who stuck up for his daughter when she was accused of cheating on a test. "My daughter would never," I'd said to the prune-faced principal. Ashlyn's face had been streaked with tears, afraid. I didn't even need to ask her if it was true. I would make it false.

"This is preposterous," I'd said, and watched Ashlyn relax against the chair. "I'm taking her home." And I did. We even stopped for a scoop of Jeni's ice cream. Lavender. Our favorite. The next morning in class, her teacher apologized, and Ashlyn's straight-A record was intact. I always wondered if those grades were for her, for me, or for her mom. Doesn't matter, I guess.

Just like back then, I knew how to win

over my daughter. She'd be happy for me. She would come around. Ashlyn and Tish had fun together. I'd witnessed it firsthand. Once she was over the shock of it all, she'd be fine.

And I was in love with a beautiful young woman who adored me. *Win-win,* I thought.

I shake my head at the memory. That day, like many others, did not go as planned. I've been so wrong.

"Earth to John." Tish stares at me. What did I miss? What did I mess up? A neon-blue butterfly floats between us and glides away through the deep grass of the valley. I wish I could follow.

I need to take a break. From everything. "Can we sit? There's a picnic spot just around the bend."

Tish turns to keep walking in the lead. My phone vibrates in my pocket, and I pull it out.

Text: I'm worried about you. Call me?

Well, that's sweet. My heart thumps with excitement.

I text: I'm fine ☺ back tomorrow.

"What are you doing? Texting during our hike? Who is so important?" Tish grabs at my phone, but I delete the texts and shove the phone into my pocket. I'm tired of her snooping, of her trying to get into my business. She tries to control everything.

"It's none of your business!" I yell too loudly, and now I'm dizzy. Damn it. I feel my legs buckle and I hit the trail with a thud, landing on my knees before sitting down. That'll be two big bruises on my kneecaps, but I learned my lesson last time I toppled over up here. Bend your knees and drop. It's more than nine thousand feet.

Tish's shadow falls over my face. "We are a team. We're married. We're in love. We worked together until yesterday. We share everything. You are my business. I don't appreciate sharing your attention during our romantic weekend."

I don't appreciate her tone. I must admit I don't appreciate her much at all anymore. I force myself back to my feet, dusting the trail dirt off my shorts. "You're right, dear. We are married." For right now. But not for much longer. Suddenly it's all clear. I'll make it through this weekend and then beg Kate to take me back if she'll have me. Will she?

No, stop, I'm getting ahead of myself. First things first. I need to calm down. I take a deep breath and gaze at the top of the majestic mountains, jagged blue peaks against a forever sky.

I wish I were alone, with time to think. I

would take a leisurely stroll through the old town of Telluride, a town wedged into a box canyon surrounded by cliffs. Or go white-water rafting, or relax in the golf clubhouse after a round. But I'm not alone. I just need to get through this weekend with the least amount of stress. Once we're back home, I'll make my play. I'll move out, get some space.

Fix things with my real family.

In the past few weeks, Kate and I have been laughing together again. We've even sneaked away to a couple of lunches, couching them as business appointments. I've been swinging by her office, catching up, making plans. We've reconnected, I think.

Was it too much to hope for that Kate might even forgive me one day and take me back?

I remember our last meal together. Kate and I sat in the corner of what used to be our favorite restaurant, almost like nothing had changed although everything had.

"John, you don't look good," Kate said.

"Why, thank you," I answered. "I'm fine, really. I do appreciate your concern, though. It's nice to know you care."

Kate tilted her head and leaned forward. "I always did. It's you who stopped caring. But anyway, just promise to get enough sleep. I hear that's the secret to a healthy life."

"Yes, I read the study, too. Thanks, Katie." I wasn't allowed to call her that, not anymore. And yet, she allowed it.

"You're welcome. Make sure you're taking your blood pressure meds, too. Don't forget. We only have one more week until the IPO. I'm worried about you, even though it's not my place now."

"I want it to be your place. Thank you," I said, my heart pinging with guilt and renewed love. She still cared about me. She and I both knew how much stress was coming our way with the IPO scheduled. That's why she gave me a bottle of relaxation pills from her naturopath. She was taking them, too. Said it helped her, and she knew I needed it more. We both felt overwhelmed. But only one of us had an unhappy, demanding spouse. My heart was taking a beating, and much of it was self-inflicted. I was such a fool.

When the waiter appeared, we both leaned back. The moment was over, but I knew our love wasn't. I felt something reconnecting between us. It's like finding a favorite sweater that was at the bottom of your drawer, and you pull it on, and it feels just right. In fact, it felt great.

Kate probably wouldn't appreciate the old-sweater analogy, but we were so comfortable together, our lives still woven together. We'd even started collaborating outside of work. Kate suggested combining our real estate portfolios again, all our homes, and placing the properties in a trust for Ashlyn. I'd agreed happily. It felt good to be building trust again, literally and figuratively. A big step toward a brighter future together, I hope.

I pull myself into the present, taking a deep inhale of clean mountain air. I keep my tone light and reach for Tish's hand. "I'm all yours, babe. What's next on our itinerary?"

See, I've still got it. I watch her face flush. She believes I'm still in love with her.

CHAPTER 7
TISH

He's such a liar. I mean, I guess I am a little bit, too, since I'm grinning at him right now like he's telling the truth. I know him better than that.

How dare he talk to her while he's hiking with me in the very place where he proposed? I stop on the trail and turn back to John. He'd better realize where we stand.

From the look on his face, he does. "Oh, honey, I just realized this is the spot. Come over here."

My heart melts. He loves me, just me. Only me. I run into his arms, and he swings me around. I laugh. We are a Lifetime movie. It's wonderful. He's everything I dreamed about all those years ago. Everything I never had. Everything I always wanted. A loving man, a happy home, and a successful career: all the things girls in my hometown never thought they could have. I knew what I wanted. I found it. The perfect job. And then the perfect boss turned into my dream husband. I worked hard to get it. I am not going to let this all go.

"Ah, shit," John says as we topple to the ground. "Sorry about that. Got carried away."

I am cradled in his strong arms. I'm fine. We're fine. The grass is warm and soft and tickles my cheek. I pick a bright-yellow daisy and stick it behind my ear. "I love you, John."

It really can be this simple again. When Sandra in HR offered me the executive assistant job five years ago, I didn't know who I'd be supporting. I had some experience, albeit embellished. Everyone does it. I didn't have any interest in school — I just wanted out of my hometown as fast as possible, and so I left.

There was nothing for me in Pineville. No one had ever been there for me, not really. And once stepdaddy number two died, Momma just about died with him of grief, locked sobbing in her bedroom for days. He hadn't laid a hand on me in a month on the day he died. As for my dear old mom, soon she'd be finished grieving, and she'd focus on me. I knew the pattern. I was gone before I could feel her wrath again. And I never looked back.

A few months after I moved to Cincinnati, I realized the fastest way out was up, through a man. I met Ron the dentist while I was waitressing. He sat in my booth, morning after morning, at Bob Evans. A few weeks into our flirting, he slipped me a card and told me he'd love to fix my smile. How romantic. But I needed my crappy teeth fixed, straightened, whitened, and whatever else. And he was lonely, so it worked, for a bit.

Another way up was through an executive. Mr. Howe was my first corporate boss, a big step up from waitressing made possible by my newly straightened teeth and a Ron-sponsored professional wardrobe. Mr. Howe was grossly overweight and headed a real estate company. He thought he was god and acted as such. I showed him respect and a lot of thigh, and he doubled my salary.

The one good thing he did was talk me into getting my GED, said I'd look more professional on my résumé. And he was right, I suppose. I probably would have stayed there longer if his wife hadn't been such a Bible-thumping, mean-spirited, white-pantyhose-wearing bitch. As if I'd want to touch him. I wouldn't. But I had two long years there, learned all the computer software an executive assistant needs to know about, and earned my GED before I cashed my very generous severance check, hopped in my car, and moved to Columbus.

Truth be told, I googled John Nelson after I read a list of the hottest CEOs in the city. Yep, that's shallow. Guilty. But I'd already worked for a beast of a man. I wanted to have somebody good to look at all day. Sue me.

So there I sat in front of Sandra's sleek glass desk, hoping for an offer to support the cute guy I'd googled, or any good-looking executive at EventCo because I didn't know who was hiring. The job description simply read: administrative support for an executive. That was something I knew I could do. I liked the vibe of the office, the company's mission. When I walked into the soaring lobby, I felt nothing but possibilities. I mean the lava lamps everywhere were a little much. Everyone said they were Kate's idea, some sort of environmental branding. Whatever. The place was trendy, cool. Like me. I'd met all the executives, except Kate, in a series of brief speed-dating sessions. I still had no idea who needed help.

"We would like to offer you the position as John Nelson's executive assistant." Sandra pushed a white folder across her desk. "The details of the offer are in the packet. We'll need an answer within the next twenty-four hours."

"Mr. Nelson?" I was pleased I'd rocketed to the top of the résumé pile and landed the job. But surprised? Of course not.

"Yes. Any other questions?" She glanced at her phone, signaling my time was up.

I opened the folder, saw the offer, tried to keep from screaming, and said, "I'll take it."

I didn't know at the time that I'd take him, too, although I must admit the thought did cross my mind. Look, men can only be dislodged from unhappy relationships. Period. If they're happy with the first, there will be no second, I'm telling you. But I didn't start this. He did.

John rolls to his side. My head still rests on his arm. "It was a nice idea for you to bring us here. I know you meant well."

I did. Sort of. "Finally glad we're here? This is our special place." I kiss the tip of his nose and snuggle into his chest.

"I am, but there are a lot of loose ends to tie up. With going public and all the employees, it's a tough time to be away." John pushes himself to a sitting position, effectively ending our cuddle time. "I'm just not sure this is working."

I stare at him as we both turn to see another group of hikers coming our way.

What did he just say? "John? What's not working?"

He blinks. "This vacation. But let's make the most of this. We're here. Let's enjoy today and then we'll go back home."

"Sure. I just thought you'd wrapped everything up. I thought all you needed was time with me." I am right. He knows it. I wonder if he knows that I know what he's been doing with his extra time.

"It's been busy, crazy busy." John pulls at a clump of prairie grass and rubs it between his hands. He nods at the group of hikers who pass by us. He waits until they're a few feet away before speaking. "It was the biggest deal of my life. It needed all my attention. It was for everybody — you, Ashlyn, Kate, the employees."

"Whatever." It comes out of my mouth before I can stop it. "I wanted it to be about us, you and me."

He chuckles. "Of course you did."

This isn't a joke. "We need to get going. I have lunch reservations at the Chop House."

I'm kicking myself for letting my anger recede. I was lulled into complacency by his arm around me, by a cuddle in the meadow

66

and a trip down memory lane. I was transported to our engagement: the warmth of the sunshine, the bubbly zing of champagne, the huge diamond ring he slipped on my finger. Like a dream. It really was.

A dream I made come true. Let me tell you, though, it wasn't easy. Again, there's this misconception that the next wife just has it so easy. We bat our eyelashes and like magic, a successful husband appears.

Don't believe it. It was work getting to that meadow moment. At first I was happy with my new job in the big city. I found a charming apartment in German Village, leased a new car, and was feeling pretty empowered. I was a young professional woman launching her career in a new city, far enough away from my old Kentucky home that the past was just that. I was Rachel from *Friends,* Carrie Bradshaw in a smaller city. And I had a couple of dates those first few months in town. I did. With men, or boys really, who were all just out of college, self-centered, and sex driven. Blech.

I went to work at EventCo the next morning, happy to have escaped the clutches of yet another gangly twentysomething boy, and there sat John. Bespoke business suit. Hair graying at the temples. Blue eyes framed with crinkles. He'd smile at me like

I was a burst of sunshine or a hidden treasure, not like a girl he'd like to fuck. And that's when I knew. I needed to find someone just like John. He was my type, only unavailable.

After about a month on the job, I asked him if he had any single friends he could connect me with. I stood at the door of his office. Waiting for a response.

He looked up from his computer and tilted his head. "For what?"

"For a date, silly. I'm new to the city, and all I've met on my own are gross young guys. I want to find a successful older guy. Like you," I said.

"Like me, huh?" He smiled. And I felt it. A zing, a current running between us. "I'm one of a kind, Tish."

"OK, well someone almost as handsome and successful as you then," I said, laughing. "Will you think about it? Please?"

"Oh, I'm thinking about it," he said as I ducked out of the room.

With his wife working away on the other side of the office building, John began thinking about me. At least, that's what he told me despite the fact the framed publicity clip hanging above my desk declared Kate and John Nelson were "Mr. and Mrs. Incredible." The *Columbus Monthly* magazine article by the front desk read: John and Kate Nelson started EventCo with a big idea, long hours behind the computer in their first apartment in Columbus. Today, it's the world's biggest online event company. How did they do it? It's an incredible story. They're our own local superheroes. And they're still in love after all they've been through.

So when John made his move eight months after I started working at EventCo, our flirtation had been going on for months. I never thought anything would come of it. I wanted someone like him. Not him. I knew it would be a huge challenge with John. See, it wasn't like I was just replacing the first wife. This was an empire to divide and conquer. I had to become more vital than a superhero to John.

It turns out I did have an in, a superpower I didn't know I possessed. I understood Ashlyn and had an instant connection with her. Teenage daughters, something I'm quite familiar with personally as I recently was one, can be big trouble, a lurking villain in a superhero household. And Ashlyn was playing her role to perfection, the little monster. John and I became close because I could help his relationship with his daughter.

John confided in me shortly after I started

working at EventCo, hands on his hips, a worried frown spread across his handsome face. "Maybe you can enlighten me, Tish. I just don't get Ashlyn. We give her everything and yet, she treats her mom and me like dirt. All I asked was that she get a summer job. But 'nobody does that,' she tells me. I've raised an entitled, spoiled brat, that's what I've done. And Kate protects her as a way to get on her good side since she feels mom guilt about all the time she spent working while Ashlyn was growing up. Of course, Ashlyn just walks all over her mother. Always has. As for me, Ashlyn and I used to be so close, but now, who knows?"

You see, the crack had formed before I arrived. Ashlyn was a little ice pick chipping away at their relationship at home. Meanwhile, at the office, there was more than just me with the chisel. But let's stick with Ashlyn.

"John, why don't you let me talk to her? I could come over, maybe hang out with her? *Babysit* isn't the word, but I can, you know, try to relate. How old is she?" I asked, but I already knew the answer. The brat had just been given a shiny new BMW for her sweet sixteen.

"She's sixteen, going on thirty."

"I've got this. I'm almost twenty-one." I

70

watched as the shock washed over him.

"What? You're not even legal to drink yet? I had no idea." John shook his head, no doubt thinking about the company picnic the weekend before. He and I had bonded over a couple of glasses of rosé.

"Don't worry. I won't tell on you for providing booze to an underage girl." I winked. Oh, give me a break. It worked in the moment.

"Sure, yes, why don't you come over and hang out with Ashlyn. See if you can talk some sense into her. Kate and I fly to California this weekend. It's Kate's high school reunion. Not sure how long I have to stay, but I do need to make an appearance like she did at mine. Quid pro quo."

"I would rather die than attend a high school reunion." In fact, I wouldn't be caught dead in my hometown ever again. "But go enjoy. I'll watch Ashlyn. We'll have fun."

John nodded his agreement and said, "Kate will be relieved. She didn't want to leave Ashlyn alone. I'll go tell her. Thanks so much for the favor."

Kate may have been relieved then. But that's because she didn't realize what was happening right under her nose. And now I face the same threat. I don't know how John thought he could keep things from me. He knows I read his texts, have his phone password. I am watching his every move.

Just now, John and I walk side by side when he stops, puts his arm in front of me, and points at the trail. "Stop! Snake!"

I jump back, my heart pounding in my chest, as an eight-foot-long brown snake with an intricate diamond pattern down its body crosses the path in front of me.

"That's a rattlesnake," John adds help-fully.

Danger lurks around every turn, as they say. Nice of John to save me just now, wasn't it? Not smart, but nice.

CHAPTER 8
JOHN

It's a relief to be back in the bustling heart of Telluride instead of trapped in the condo with Tish or alone on the trail. And I cannot believe I almost told her that this isn't working. I can't be in this relationship anymore.

It's the truth. I must tell her. Soon.

We're eating outside at the Chop House, a restaurant on the patio of the New Sheridan Hotel. This place has been in business more than one hundred years. If the walls could talk, I bet they'd say they've seen a domestic dispute or two. That's the thing. Tish and I aren't having outward obvious fights, no name-calling; no plate throwing is going on. That's not my style, though if you asked me right now, I would tell you it's hers. I can feel her rage building like a summer storm. I haven't really paid much attention to us, to her, not with everything else that's going on.

But I feel it between us now like a live grenade. I don't know what will happen if one of us pulls the pin.

I don't like it. Not at all. Kate and I were never like this. I take a bite of my Cobb salad. Keeping my mouth busy chewing right now is for the best. For both of us. I don't want to start a discussion here that won't end well. No, that's best left for when we get back home to Columbus. And I have it worked out. I just needed some clarity, some help. And I got that. It's the juxtaposition between what I had with Kate and what my life has become with Tish. The difference is stark, once you see things clearly. And I've put some things in place, just to be safe. But I still need to do the right thing.

This is not working.

I'll sell the house we share. I'll give her half. She can keep her car and the jewelry, and she'll be set. With the stock I've given her, she's a wealthy woman. She's young. She can start over. She has plenty of options.

As for me, I just want to get away from her. Sad, isn't it? How love can so quickly turn to something so painful. Kate and I, we fought, sure, but it was to be expected. We had a teenager, the stress of the business. We didn't take care of our relation-

74

ship. This thing with Tish is something much worse. I don't have a name for it, but it makes you feel like there's a vise around your chest, and it's being tightened minute by minute. It's silent and far more deadly. We don't yell at each other, we simmer. It makes you want to run away, far away.

"How's your salad?" she asks, watching me closely. Ever since I saved her from that rattlesnake, she's been nicer. I guess we just need to come across a snake every few hours to keep things on an even keel.

"Good," I manage to respond before shoving another bite in my mouth. Tish has ordered a bottle of rosé and is in the process of drinking the whole thing alone. That's not healthy. I'd help her, but my altitude sickness is worse with alcohol. I'm saving myself for tonight. I'll need a few drinks to get through until tomorrow.

"You sure you don't want a glass of wine?" Tish asks. She's slurring a bit. She holds up the bottle. "Oops. Looks like there's only one glass left. Ha!" She pours the rest of the bottle into her glass. "Cheers! What else do you want to do today? What would make it special for you?"

I want to say "take a nap," but I don't think that's what an old guy tells his young wife on a romantic weekend. "Whatever you'd like."

She smiles at that. I am proud of my smooth answer.

"You know, I could use some retail therapy. A little shopping sounds good. You should get your daughter a gift. She loves Telluride, right?"

Ashlyn does love Telluride. She learned to ski here. We spent many happy Thanksgivings and Christmases here, just the three of us. I swallow. The last time I asked Ashlyn to come to Telluride with me, she told me I'd ruined it by proposing to Tish here. I'll admit, it wasn't well planned. But Ashlyn will come around. She's had a wonderful life all in all.

Tish, well, I know she had it tough as a girl. She hasn't told me much — it's what she doesn't say that lets you know it was bad. Tish never had anybody taking care of her until I came along.

Or, rather, she came along, and I thought with my dick instead of my brain. I swallow the pang of guilt at the memory and remind myself Tish will be fine. She'll be rich and never need to worry about anything. She'll be fine.

I don't say what I think. I keep it in, and then things turn ugly.

Like now. It looks like we are a happy

couple who shared a shockingly expensive lunch at one of the best restaurants in Telluride and are now out for a stroll through town. But we're not. Not really.

"What's Ashlyn's favorite store?" Tish asks.

I've managed to finish my salad, pay the bill, and escort Tish out to Main Street all while lost in my memories. Good question. "Last time we were here was almost five years ago." That revelation leaves a lump in my throat. Time is racing by, and my daughter and I grow further apart by the minute.

"That's too bad. Well, Two Skirts is cute. I'll find a little something for Ashlyn and something for me. You can wait out here." Tish points to a bench, and I do as I'm told. With all the wine she's had, I'm surprised she's able to walk straight, let alone shop. I take that back. She can shop in any condition. That I have discovered firsthand.

Kate never went to a mall. She'd browse the windows here but preferred to be outside enjoying the fresh air. Of course, Kate has a stylist who refreshes her wardrobe every month. Somehow, though, that seems sophisticated, sensible. She doesn't have the time to shop — she runs a huge company. But she always looked great. Still does. Kate would laugh at me if she saw me now, sitting on a bench like a scolded child in time-out.

Just an old sugar daddy waiting for his lady. Fuck. I pull out my phone. There is something I can do. Despite the fact I'm "not allowed," I push Kate's number. I have her in my contacts under Mabel, but I doubt we're fooling anyone. Too bad, Tish. We have things to discuss that no one else needs to know about.

She answers on the first ring. "Are you OK? What's going on? And are you alone?"

Let me unpack that for you. She's worried because I'm calling her on a Saturday during my romantic getaway. That is because Tish has made a rule that Kate and I cannot communicate directly without her approval and supervision, especially outside of the office. I never call Kate when Tish is within earshot. That would cause an explosion at my current home. World War III.

I've come to realize this is all ridiculous. Kate and I run a company together. We have a daughter, we have — had — a life.

Shit.

"I'm stupid. I let her whisk me away." I watch the front door of the boutique, ready to hang up if Tish appears.

"You're leaving me to handle all the questions." She exhales loudly. "Sorry, it's just

78

that it's a lot. I'm at the office, fielding calls from employees. I wish you were here to help me. We're so good together. A team. At work, I mean."

"I know, Katie. I'm home tomorrow. I'm sorry. For everything. I'm going to fix this." I don't know why I added that, but I did.

"Where is she right now? How are you getting away with calling me? Won't you be in trouble?" Kate is worried about me. But she's right to. I'm beginning to think Tish is crazy.

"Tish is in a store, buying something for Ashlyn, after she buys twice as much for herself."

"Shocking. She is good at that, so maybe just let her shop for the rest of the weekend? Don't worry. I can handle things here until you're back. It's fine." Kate is so nice to me.

"No, it's not. I feel terrible about leaving you," I quickly add. "I promise, I'll pick up my share as soon as I get back tomorrow."

Kate laughs. "Are you sure you'll be coming home tomorrow? Doesn't seem like you're the one in charge. But I hope you're right."

"Look, things will change just as soon as I get home. I promise. I'll make you proud again, Katie, I will." I wonder if she'd consider reconciliation, but it's hard to justify asking that question. Not yet, at least. I have a lot of work to do to earn Kate's trust back. I know that.

I see Tish at the cash register inside the store. The saleswoman is wrapping pink tissue around a pile of items. I'm running out of time.

"Enjoy Telluride. And be careful. Remember getting lost on the back side of the mountain?"

I laugh at the memory. We had been terrified at first but found a lift five minutes later. We always laughed about our mountain survival skills. "I remember. Quite the rugged mountaineers."

Kate laughs with me. The sound warms my heart. "We should hang up so you don't get in trouble."

"Kate. Wait."

I know she's gone. I shove the phone in my pocket as Tish walks out of the store with two shopping bags.

I kick the ground with my hiking boot before standing to help her with her latest unnecessary purchases.

This is not working.

80

He doesn't think I saw him on the phone. Talking to her. Sharing a private moment, a special laugh. I know that expression on his face. It's love.

"Looks like you did some damage," John says, taking the shopping bags from my hands.

Not as much as you've done. "Yes, I think Ashlyn will love the outfit."

"I told her you were shopping for her again. She told me to tell you thanks." He says it lightly, casually, the way you might say, *Oh look, there's a mountain,* despite the fact you're in a valley surrounded by them.

"Oh, you were talking to Ashlyn just now?" I chuckle a bit, despite myself. He's such a bad liar.

"Yes, I spoke to Ashlyn. She's my daughter. I should be able to do that whenever I'd like."

I'm a step behind him so I can't see his

face, but I know he's flushed. His face turns red when he's lying. "Of course you should. It's only when you lie to me about things, that's when it gets tricky."

We've reached the gondola station where we'll hop on for a ride over the mountain and down into the aptly named Mountain Village where our condominium is located. This was all so romantic before. Can't you imagine it? John and I, snuggled side by side on a date night, the town of Telluride blanketed in thick snow, twinkling below us like a dream. John slipped his hand inside my ski jacket. His touch made me dizzy.

Those were the days. Now we stand side by side, me fuming thanks to his lies, his deceits. Him smiling, thinking he's getting away with it. With all of it.

I think of Ashlyn, the beautiful outfit I selected in one of the bags. She won't like it, won't appreciate it, because it's from me. When we first met, she worshipped the ground I walked on. Kate and John flew off to California and left me and the terrible teen up to our own devices, which, of course, was mostly being on our devices. Kate was so thankful to have me there, keeping Ashlyn "company," as she put it. I wonder if she blames herself for any of this, for enabling my original entrée into their personal lives.

After a tour of the large and historic Grandville home — I'd already checked it out online and discovered it was formerly owned by a governor and was one of the most sought-after addresses in the city — Ashlyn had retreated to the family room to watch something on Netflix. While she watched her show, I snooped.

John and Kate's bedroom was bigger than any bedroom I'd ever seen. It was elegant, if old fashioned, with soft white bedding, blue silk walls, and a whole separate toilet and sink area for each of them plus a walk-in closet each. I mean, you could get up and never see each other. Fabulous.

Kate's dressing room, as they called it online, was filled with designer clothing, of course, but the most amazing thing was that it was divided into sections, with accessories from each brand displayed together with the clothing. I've never seen anything like it before or since. I could have moved into her Gucci section, seriously. And John always tells me Kate didn't shop. He's so clueless.

I forced myself to keep moving through Kate's closet and stopped in front of a family portrait of the three of them. Ashlyn looked to be about ten years old, and they were on Ponte Vedra Beach, where they have yet another house. Some folks just have too much of everything, you know?

I reached out and touched Ashlyn's golden hair in the portrait. Such a lucky girl, and she didn't even realize it. Still doesn't. But then again, you don't really appreciate things until they're gone, am I right?

"What are you doing?" It was Ashlyn. She'd sneaked up on me.

"Oh my god, you scared me to death," I said, clutching my chest. "What do you think I'm doing? What every babysitter does, always. Snooping around. Is your show over?"

Ashlyn grinned. She wore skinny jeans and a tight T-shirt, and her blonde hair was pulled back in a ponytail. She looked younger than sixteen. She looked like the girl in the portrait. "That's funny. You're right. They all do it, but nobody admits it. I caught my nanny in my mom's jewelry box once. She thought I'd tell on her."

"Did you?"

Ashlyn didn't answer. I followed her out of the closet and into the long grand hallway. She stopped at the top of the stairs, turned, and looked at me. "Not at first. But then, when she started having her boyfriend over during the day instead of taking care of me, well, that's when I told. When she betrayed

84

me, I betrayed her."

"I guess a girl's got to do what a girl's got to do. Listen, you can tell on me. It's fine. I grew up with nothing, so I guess I was just drawn into the closet like a moth to a flame. I've never seen so many beautiful things." I held her stare until she broke the gaze.

"How poor were you?" Ashlyn asked, bounding down the elegant stairway two steps at a time.

"Very. Poorest in my school. And all the kids knew it." I fight back the memories. The dresses with holes in the sleeves, the shame of pants too short for my long legs. The calloused hands touching my body, the hand over my mouth as I tried to scream. The knowledge that no one cared, no matter what he did. My momma's cold, dark, disbelieving eyes. No one ever believed me. No one ever became my friend. "It sucked. But I got out."

"How did you get out?" Ashlyn stood at the bottom of the stairs looking up at me.

"Well, first I moved to a new state and never looked back. Next I met Ron, the dentist I dated while I was waiting tables at Bob Evans. We were married. Everything was so wonderful. But then he left me."

Ashlyn's face contorts in shock. "He left

you? How horrible! You've had such a hard life."

"Yes," I said pretending to wipe a tear from under my eye. I did have a horrible childhood, but the part about Ron leaving me wasn't true. It made a better story, though. Ron had been good for about a minute. He had a fabulous apartment, a stocked refrigerator, and two cars. He checked all the boxes I needed for that moment. I needed him in Cincinnati. I needed the braces I'd never had and a soft bed with someone who loved me. But he was a means to an end — stability after the storm of my childhood. Once I got the corporate job working for Mr. Howe, I didn't need Ron anymore. When I left Ron, I never looked back.

"I can't believe you were married." Ashlyn's mouth gaped open. "You're just a few years older than me!"

"I know. It's been hard," I said. And then, seemingly overcome by emotion, I plunked down on the second to last step and let Ashlyn comfort me.

"Wow, well, at least you're here now. There are plenty of great guys out there, and I know you'll find one of them soon," she said. So sweet. She didn't know I wasn't looking further than her home.

86

And that's when we became BFFs. She really liked me, and I liked her. I could almost feel the love between us, the sense of family forming. Maybe I'd finally found a friend? Maybe more. Operation Ashlyn was a success. The rest of the weekend was fun and games, ordering in and staying up late. Pj parties and boys sneaking over. It was all a high school dream. Like it was supposed to be when you're a teenager, like it was supposed to be when you had a rich family. I was at once jealous and having fun.

And then, like a cherry on top, John came home early from the high school reunion in California, leaving Kate all alone across the country.

Of course, I needed to stay on and babysit. He had to work, so it was the least I could do. And Ashlyn insisted. It was thanks to her that we ended up together. I knew John flew home early to be with me. And I was right. The infatuation was so intense, I was surprised Ashlyn missed it. I didn't. But teenage girls only care about one thing — themselves.

It's too bad Ashlyn and I aren't as close as we once were. Jennifer slipped into that big sister relationship, and Kate, well, she's worked hard to get back into her daughter's good graces.

I have to watch all three of them at work every day. Well, I used to. It's disgusting. But I'll win Ashlyn back, just like I will John. We're family now, and that's the strongest bond. At least that's what my uncle George said last week when we got together in downtown Columbus, and I tend to believe him. I have to believe him. He's the only family I've got.

But grown women have a lot to worry about. That's why I'm here in Telluride focusing on my marriage.

I need to be in the moment and watch the scenery gliding by outside the windows of the gondola. It is electric here. Kool-Aid colors: bright blue, vibrant yellow, neon green. Telluride's best-kept secret is summer, that's what all the locals tell us. It might be true. There's something about the wide, deep blue sky, darkening each moment in the glow of the dying sun. The green grasses covering the meadows drenched in shadows. The towering pines. People who vacation here are the lucky few. Do they even notice the full moon peeking over the mountain? Do they notice nature at all, or simply believe they are masters of all they see? These people only notice the brand of designer attire the couples across the gondola wear. Is the fur real? Is her diamond bigger than mine? It's pathetic, really, but so fun to observe. I know because I'm watching them. I want everything they have, and more. Why play the game if you don't want to win?

I decide tonight the moon is an omen of some sorts. I don't believe in such things, typically. As a rule, I only believe in myself. Beside me, John gathers up the shopping bags. We're about to reach the bottom: our gondola stop.

Dangling here, in this glass box high above a pricey and pristine wilderness, you'd think everyone should be happy. I look at the other passengers on the gondola. Across from us is a young mom and dad with three small kids, the parents working so hard to keep everyone seated for the ride. The mom looks exhausted. These first wives do struggle. They have to give birth to the baby, or babies, and then devote themselves to the kids for the rest of their lives. That's the biggest thing. Us next wives waltz in after all the potty training, the shots, the school selection, the homework. I watch as she picks up the youngest, a baby who looks to be nine months or so, heavy but not yet walking. The baby arches his back and wails.

"Oh my god, Jill, can you get him to shut up?" says the young dad.

Jill bursts into tears along with the baby. I glare at the young dad. How rude. She's doing her best. She's a first wife. I imagine she lives not far from here, in a small one-story rural home. She has no help, no money for good clothes clearly, and vacation means babysitting her own kids with the extra pressure of making sure the children make the dad look good in public. Likely they saved money all year just to visit for the weekend, and now this. No thank you.

I like my men wealthy and broken in, and the kids, if they have to be around, happily away at college. That's why a man like John seemed so perfect. That's why I asked if he had any single friends.

Turns out, he didn't want to share me with anyone. His choice. And I felt like I'd hit the jackpot. He was trained by Kate, his first love, a strong woman who became his business partner. Check. He only had one child, and she was potty-trained and ready for college. Check. He dressed nice, but not flashy. He smiled easily and told corny jokes. He didn't make a move until he made sure I wanted him. Such a gentleman. Check, check, check, and check.

No one is going to take him away from me. I've provided the training on how to treat a young, gorgeous new wife. I'm the one who has created our exciting life. Kate will not waltz in and take it all back. She will not.

As we step off the gondola, away from the crying baby, I turn and face him. "Tell me what's not working? We need to figure things out."

He looks up at the sky. "Let's discuss this back home."

I shake my head. "No, let's discuss this now. How long have you been seeing Kate? Sneaking around behind my back? Tell me the truth. I will forgive you, of course. Everyone makes mistakes. As long as it doesn't happen again. You've been under stress. The grass seems greener, yada yada. And of course, she must resign. I can't have her working there with you. Not anymore." My hands land on my hips before I realize it. I tell myself to breathe. To calm down. I'm shaking with fury. There is a regular parade of gondola riders walking past us. I fake-smile at a couple, and they look away.

"What are you talking about?" John acts puzzled, but he's not. I guess he's just surprised I know so much.

"You know exactly what I'm talking about. Look, you and I did the same thing. Tell me the truth." My voice is a hiss. I poke him in

91

the chest for emphasis.

John blinks and backs away, hands held up like he's surrendering to the police. "The truth is that this isn't working. Us. You and me."

How dare he? He's tossing up his hands and trying to tell me it's over. Here? Like this? I stare at him, searching for an answer. He drops his head.

I'm so mad I can barely speak. "*We* are fine. You don't get to claim it isn't working. No, that's not how it's done. You just need to pay attention to our relationship again. Come back to me. Stay away from Kate."

"I don't know what you're talking about." John is such a bad liar.

I don't say another word. I turn and walk toward the condo. In my mind, the image of our perfect family, our perfect life, crumbles into dust. He seemed like just what I'd been looking for, and for a while he was. Now, he's a disgrace — weak and disloyal.

I stomp into the lobby of the condominium complex, aware I'm still shaking. I take a deep breath and calm myself. I can handle anything. That's why I've survived on my own for so long. I thought John was different, I thought I could count on him. I learned growing up that you have to keep your options open. It's time to pivot from love to revenge.

The elevator doors open, and I step inside, stabbing the button for the penthouse. John arrives at the elevator just as the doors shut, him on the other side. I give him a quick shrug but don't make a move to reopen the doors. I guess he'll just have to wait in the lobby for a bit. It will give him time to think about what he's done.

It's too bad he's turned into a liar. It really is a shame. The truth can set you free, I've heard. So what does lying do for you?

CHAPTER 10
JOHN

When the doors of the elevator closed, I almost left. I could have called the pilots and flown home. I did call Ashlyn and cheered myself up with the sound of her voice. I almost walked out, but I didn't. I promised Tish one night here, and I would keep my word.

By the time I walked into the condo, it was like nothing had happened between us. As if we'd never fought. Tish made a big pitcher of margaritas, and we're sitting out on the deck watching the sun drop behind the mountain. The air is turning crisp, and in a few minutes, I'll need a jacket. I soak up the beauty of the purple sky and take a sip of my drink. All I need to do is get through tonight and get back home. All the way home.

I inhale a deep breath. In my opinion, this is the best time of day during the summers up here. The light, the warm breeze that turns a little bit chilly once the dying glow of the sun disappears. It's gorgeous. I remind myself to take another breath. Since our little chat, I've been on edge, waiting for an explosion of sorts from Tish. But nothing bad has happened yet. She's been fine, calm and friendly even. Maybe she realizes it, too. The spark is gone. She'll be happier without me.

I sip my cocktail, enjoying the salt rim although I know I shouldn't be. I think the drink is a margarita, but from the stiff taste of it, she's added extra alcohol. It's a tangy, somewhat bitter version of a margarita. I love margaritas, so I'm not complaining.

I hold my glass up to her as she walks outside carrying a tray with guacamole, chips, and salsa. This is when I fell in love with her, why I fell in love with her. She's unexpected. Spontaneous. Unlike anyone I'd ever known. Kate and I had gotten into a rut, a pattern where neither of us had the energy to do anything but work and try to manage Ashlyn. We were just barely keeping it together. There was no fun, no laughter. Every day was heavy. Tish was light.

"Cheers! This is good." I lie and take another big sip.

"I wondered if it was too bitter. Glad you like it. I added a little something special."

Tish sits down across from me. I notice she's drinking wine.

"Can I pour you one?" I lean forward, reaching for the pitcher.

"Oh, no thanks, I overindulged at lunch. Gave me a bit of a headache, so I'm sticking with rosé. A little hair of the pink dog." She lifts her glass. "Cheers, though! I'm sorry for starting a fight. It's such a beautiful evening. Seems your altitude sickness has subsided?"

I shrug. "I suppose it has, or the drink is masking it." I dip a chip into the guacamole and enjoy the salty, lemony taste. "This is just about perfection."

Tish wears a fitted white sweatshirt with a lacy bottom. She has on jeans and the summer boots she bought at the boutique in town. Her hair is shiny and tucked behind her ears. Aside from the large diamond studs sparkling in each ear — last year's Christmas gift, among other things — and the oversize wedding ring, she could still be the same young woman who appeared at EventCo five years ago, fresh off the turnip truck from somewhere in eastern Kentucky. Or was it Cincinnati?

My mind has a pleasant haze gathering around it.

Despite what Kate thinks now, I didn't

hire Tish. Sandra from HR did. Actually, truth be told, the only folks I care to really interview are executive level, like Jennifer or Lance. Kate and I used to do those interviews together, making sure we both agreed before extending an offer. Thinking back on it, that sounds so simple, so functional.

Ah hell, we were good. We just needed counseling, or mediation, or meditation, or maybe a vacation alone.

We just needed to try a little harder.

I needed to try a little harder.

I should have tried harder.

I pull out my phone. Tish is somewhere inside, so the coast is clear. I take a photo of my margarita glass and quickly text it with a "cheers" message from under the table. All's well, my cheers is implying. Even though it's not, and she knows it.

My phone lights up: Looks delicious. Enjoy.

I text: It tastes horrible. I'm just trying to get drunk. It's working.

She texts: Ha! Xo

My heart swells. It's nice to have someone who cares about you. I hurry and delete this text chain so Tish won't see it when she snoops. She's always spying on me. I slip my phone under my thigh. This margarita is going to my head. I swipe the moisture away from under my eyes, quickly, before Tish

97

sees it. I grab a chip and dunk it into the salsa. I almost miss my mouth before gobbling it down.

She's filling my glass again. I probably should tell her to stop, but the drink takes the edge off this shit show. I've got nowhere to be, nothing to do, until I fly out of here tomorrow. "What time do you have the plane scheduled?"

Tish throws her hands in the air. "Why? Ready to get away from me?"

"No, of course not. Just a lot to deal with back home, that's all." I know my speech is slurring. I tell myself to talk slowly. I tell myself I'm happy to be here, drinking on the deck, watching the moonrise. Pretending everything is fine. Meanwhile, my inbox is piled high with emails. What does she expect? I just took a company public.

Then a word comes to me, the word to describe Tish: selfish.

"When did you stop loving me, John?" She's put sunglasses on, big black-rimmed sunglasses. She looks a little like a fly. Which is funny. I hear myself chuckle. I cover my mouth.

"What are you talking about, honey?" I gulp some more margarita as Tish's face blurs and then comes into focus. My phone vibrates under my thigh. I can't take the chance of looking at it, not with Tish staring at me. I need to say something. "I love you."

"I think that's past tense. You've made it very clear today that you've moved on, that our relationship isn't working. I believe that's exactly what you said. I know the signs, remember? You did this with me, too. It's a shame, John. You shouldn't go backward in life. Kate is a mistake. She's not as perfect as she seems, remember? You left her for a reason."

I left her for a stupid reason: to screw you. But I'm not talking about this. I'm too drunk. We will talk in the morning. I will leave here tomorrow, with or without her. And I will file for a divorce. All of this is clear, and then the deck sways.

"Do you remember why you left her?" Tish asks.

I won't answer that. "You think I have the bandwidth to sell my company, hang out with you, and start something up with my ex-wife?" I am too drunk. I need to stand up, get some blood flowing, but I'm not sure I could without toppling over. I try to reach for Tish's hand, but she pulls it away.

Tish stands. She's mad, I realize, really mad. "It's time to stop the lies. I know all about your plans to dump me for her after

99

the sale went through. Which it did. Yesterday. But surprise, I swooped you away to Telluride. One step ahead of you, John."

Tish disappears inside the condo, and I take stock of my predicament. It's funny. That's all I can think. How did she know? And when I think that, I start to chuckle. And then, before I know it, I'm laughing so hard tears spill from my eyes and roll down my cheeks. I'm laughing so hard now I can't catch my breath.

The deck sways under my feet again and I gasp for air as I stand, trying to follow Tish inside. I'll do it tonight. I owe it to her to tell her I'm finished.

Chapter 11
Tish

I pull the chicken dish out of the oven, an ugly flowery pot holder covering my hand, and poke at the center with a fork. All I need to do is reheat it, but I've been known to ruin a dish simply by giving it too much heat. I know, I'm intense about everything. Plus, I never cared much for cooking or for lingering around in the kitchen. I like food from cans and drive-through windows, and most recently, from my favorite gourmet restaurants in town. I mean, lobster dinner for two delivered to your door is a delicious option, especially since John thought I made it from scratch, the fool.

I hear him outside, talking to himself and laughing. I guess he's drunk. I do make a mean margarita, and with the altitude and the lies he's holding inside, he's probably a wreck. I should keep up appearances and get some food in him before he passes out. I can't believe he won't admit what he's done wrong, especially since he's buzzed. But he acts all innocent and loving.

"I'm starving out here. Something smells good."

Charming that he yells to me like a servant. For some reason the phrase *pretty please with a cherry on top* pops into my head. I chuckle.

"I'll be right out," I yell back. I grab the dish and shove it all into the microwave, push the reheat button, and close the door. I should have used it all along. The microwave dings, and voilà, a perfectly reheated chicken enchilada dish can be served. I'm glad I had the housekeeper freeze some meals. They come in handy at times like this when your husband gets trashed, fast, with a little help from yours truly.

I still can't believe I have a housekeeper — sorry, house manager — for each home. How far I've come since childhood. I think of my mom. Another woman in her house wouldn't have lasted a day. I barely survived.

I start to laugh, imagining my mom with a house manager of all things. But then I see my first stepdad. Just before he's going to throw something. Just before all hell would break loose. John sort of reminds me of good old Dad about now. Bellowing orders. I don't remember him much. Mom replaced him with another like she did my real dad. But I remember his anger, things breaking, me hiding.

I was always hiding when I was a child.

I place the glass dish on the island. I just want to stop this, stop John. Them. Back with Kate? How dare he? He will not humiliate me like this. *They* will not humiliate me like this.

I cut the enchilada and use a spoon to coat his meal with salsa. John should eat. I cooked dinner. He will have food in his stomach. It's date night.

I walk to the deck with a smile, enjoying the dark silhouette of the mountain, like a serpent guarding the town. I place the plate in front of John and note how he's sloping to the side. Gross.

He's on the phone. "John, who are you talking to?"

"Oh, hi, Tish. It's nobody," he slurs, still leaning to the right.

"John, it's time for you to say goodbye. It's time to eat something. You've had too much to drink." I use a commanding voice, and he snaps to it.

"Tish says I have to go now. Bye-bye." He stabs at the "End" button.

It's hard to watch as his fingers pick clumsily at the phone like a toddler, and his head tilts to the side. I wonder what he said before I caught him. Whatever it was, I'll deal with it later.

"Here, let me help you." I cut a bite and put it on the fork. Together we guide it into his mouth. Captain of industry, really?

I watch closely as he chews and swallows. It's time for another. Where's the bib?

"Thanks," John manages as he takes another bite. He leans back in the chair, midchew.

"Hey, wait, chew that. You'll choke." I slap his cheek.

John barely responds. I'm worried he'll fall asleep before he swallows his bite. "Hey. Hey!" I push his shoulders forward from behind, and he wakes up. "Chew, John."

I watch with relief as he does what I say. I can't have him die choking on a chicken enchilada on the deck. How embarrassing. Ashlyn would kill me.

As I watch him chew, I think more about little Ashlyn. She was a teenager when I met her, a spoiled only child. Meanwhile, I came from another world. I couldn't imagine the kind of gilded childhood she had. The organic packed lunch and a ride to school every day, even though school was just a block away. The kind of childhood where you earned ribbons just for being there, where praise flowed like a river, and the real world never intruded with problems like bad teeth or too-short pants.

There weren't any ribbons in my bedroom, but to be honest, I never really had a room to myself. There was a curtain hanging between my mom's bed and mine. It didn't seem to mean anything, not to anyone. A curtain isn't a locked door. It's something to be pushed aside, ignored.

I shudder. No, I can't blame Ashlyn for becoming the teenager she became. For being the woman she is today.

But you shouldn't blame me for who I became, either. We're all creatures of our environment. I'm the type of person who figures out how to get ahead. And it worked out for both of us. Ashlyn needed a little real-world experience, and I needed an ally in the office. So when I say that her little internship was all my idea, believe me, it was. If it weren't for me, Ashlyn would have spent another summer lying by the pool at the country club, flirting with the boys, and perfecting her suntan. It's too bad she turned on me once she started working at EventCo.

Shit. John's head is on the table. He's literally passed out on our deck. I cannot have anyone zipping by on the gondola seeing this. I mean, he's in the news now, with the IPO. This is unacceptable.

"John, John, wake up!" I shake him, but there is no response. OK, deep breath. I can handle this.

John moans. He's in there. I just need to activate him. He's drooling on himself. Ugh. His face is pale, but that could be the moonlight.

"John, look, we're going to go to bed. I've got you. Stand up."

He's doing it. We're walking inside. He's heavy, leaning on me with all his weight. It's all I can do to get him to the couch. I'll just let him rest here. That's what I'll do. I make sure he's settled across the couch and then cover him with the blanket.

He just needs to sleep it off. I wipe drool off his face. Nice, John.

While he's resting, I clean up the kitchen. I carry a tray out to the deck and clear all the glasses and dishes. I rinse everything in the sink with soap and pop it all in the dishwasher, setting the cycle to pots and pans. I like dishes extra clean, extra sanitized.

I didn't even know that was a thing until I married John. We never had one of these fancy dishwashers.

With the kitchen all tidy, I look around to

106

see if anything else in the condominium is out of place. John's phone is on the kitchen counter. I put it on the coffee table in front of the couch where John has passed out. I'd rather have him in the guest bedroom, in case the cleaning crew comes tomorrow. I've expressly asked them not to come tomorrow because of our romantic weekend. But you can never be too sure. Sometimes people just don't do what you want them to do. They lie. They cheat. I shake my head and look over at John.

The thing is, a lot of guys pass out on the couch watching sports or something on TV. I find the remote, and the screen flickers to life. I have no idea what channel has sports, or even what summer sports could be. I find two women playing tennis. Perfect.

John fell asleep while watching a tennis match. Happens every day. No one needs to know that he isn't a tennis fan.

I kiss him lightly on the forehead. It's slimy with sweat. I wipe my lips on the sleeve of my shirt. That was gross. This is gross. All of it.

I hope it's almost over. I look at his phone where I put it on the coffee table and see a text from her. How sweet! She wants John.

Call me when you can get away. Rather demanding, isn't she? And she's violating our private time by texting him. I feel my hands clenching into fists. I want to punch someone, something.

She thinks she's won. She thinks he can *get away* from me.

I drop the phone back onto the coffee table.

She's so wrong.

CHAPTER 12
JOHN

Where am I? Why am I so thirsty?

I roll to my side and fall to the floor, landing on a soft rug.

I just fell off my own couch.

Before I can make sense of it, my stomach heaves. I need to get to the bathroom. It's not pretty, but I'm crawling across the great room. It's dark, but I know I'm in Telluride, in my condo, and I'm headed in the right direction. Man, the altitude is really hitting this time. Oh, and the margaritas. Probably shouldn't have had so many.

Probably shouldn't have done a lot of things.

My stomach has calmed down, but I'm parched. I pull myself up to the sink and stick my head under the faucet, gulping water like I've just survived a desert trek. I relieve myself and limp back to the couch. My phone is on the coffee table. It's one in the morning. I just need to sleep this off, start fresh in the morning, but still I open my text messages and see there's just one. It came in while I was passed out.

Call me when you can get away.

I smile. She cares.

I hope Tish didn't see the text, but I'm certain she probably did. She's always nosing around in my business. I know it's late, but my eyes can't focus to text so I call instead. Her voice mail picks up. "Hey, listen I'm uh, really, really drunk but I uh, just wanted to call and you know, say hi and well, I love you. I'll see you tomorrow as soon as I can get out of here I, uh, I will. I don't feel so good. And, uh —"

Another wave of nausea hits, and I'm sweating profusely. I drop the phone on my stomach, force my eyes shut despite the feeling of being on a sinking ship, and will myself to fall back asleep. It's the only antidote for a situation like this one. It's my fault I drank too much. I've made my bed, as they say.

I don't know how long I've been asleep on the couch, or if I have slept.

Right now, I know I need help.

"Tish?" I think I called out my wife's name.

110

I wait for an answer, but there isn't one.

The vise that's been squeezing my chest clamps down. I can't catch my breath. My heart pounds against my rib cage.

I use my right hand to check my pulse on my left wrist, but the blood pumping through my fingers makes it impossible to count beats. My chest seizes.

And then I know. *Oh my god, I'm having a heart attack.*

I'm panting as I sit up and reach for my phone. It's fallen under the coffee table. I slide from the couch to the floor. With the last bit of energy, I reach toward my phone as my chest seizes again. I can't breathe.

My fingers wrap around the phone. My lifeline. My hope. I slide my finger across the screen, opening the text message: Call Me.

I want to. More than anything. I love you. I want to call you. I want to be anywhere but here, with anyone but her. I want to call, but my fingers aren't working. My hands are numb. I'm sitting on the floor as my head lolls to the side, my neck unable to hold it up. I have a big head. A heavy, big head.

My breath catches in my throat as panic washes over me.

Suddenly, a stabbing pain grips my chest.

I collapse forward, landing on my face, unable to break the fall with my numb hands. My nose is bleeding. I taste the rusty metal. Blood. I roll onto my back to escape the flood of blood.

The pain is unbearable, a million pounds of pressure and a bolt of lightning.

I can't breathe.

There is only darkness.

CHAPTER 13
TISH

I stretch and hop out of bed, taking my time as I walk across the wide-plank wood floor (heated, of course) and pull back the ugly floral (of course) curtains in the master bedroom. It's a beautiful, sunshine-filled mountain day. I slept like a baby with the bed all to myself. It's late, almost ten in the morning. I decide to shower and get ready for the day before making coffee. I know I need a little more time before I go downstairs.

An hour later, I'm looking good. I'm wearing a black EventCo T-shirt — for old times' sake I guess — jeans, and tennis shoes. I check my phone, and I'm surprised it's already 11:00 a.m. Time flies.

I pull open the double doors to the master bedroom and walk out into the still-dark great room. I closed all the blackout shades last night before going to bed, and even in the brightness of midday, they do a remarkable job. Small shafts of light escape from the crevices of a few windows, but for the most part, it's like a cave in here. Or a tomb.

"Time to wake up, sleepyhead." I walk toward the couch and notice a foul odor I can't describe, a smell unlike anything I've encountered. "John?" I find him sprawled on the floor, halfway under the coffee table.

"Oh my god." I run to the kitchen, my stomach lurching, and dial 911 from the landline. They answer immediately.

"What's your emergency?" the operator asks.

"It's my husband. He's passed out on the floor. Unconscious. Something is wrong. He's vomited all over, and I think wet himself. Oh my god." I think I'm screaming. I don't know. This is disgusting. Worse than anything I could have imagined. I'm shaking all over. My voice quavers, "Hurry, please."

"Help is on the way. The squad will be there in two minutes. You're at 565 Mountain Village Boulevard. What unit?"

"Penthouse 401. At the Plaza. Oh my god. Please hurry."

"Ma'am, is your husband breathing?" the operator asks. "You need to try to perform CPR. Do you know how to do that?"

"No. I meant to learn, but I was too busy."

114

I'm sobbing now. I know she is trying to help, but I can't go over there, touch him. It's too awful. I won't do it. I grab a dish towel and drench it with cold water. I ring it out and hold it on my forehead.

"Keep talking to me and walk to his side. Now!"

I do as I'm told, pinching my nose with my fingers. I can't see John's upper torso, it's under the coffee table. Why is he under the coffee table?

"I'm here. By his side. Oh god." I pull on John's arm. On TV they put their finger somewhere on the wrist, right?

"Is he breathing?"

"I don't know," I answer. I lean over and wipe his face with my towel, cleaning him up from the mess he's made.

There's a loud, hard bang on the door. "Paramedics!"

"Let them in, ma'am."

I jump up and rush to the door, flinging it open as a team of four medics push past me and invade the living room. Without my directions, they've found John and pulled him out from under the table. One man is pushing on his chest while another starts an IV. I watch in horror until a woman emergency worker approaches me.

"Ma'am, your husband is in cardiac ar-

rest. We're going to have to transport him."
We watch together as John is rolled onto a
stretcher.

"I need to go with him. I'm his wife." I'm
chasing after the stretcher when someone
grabs me. "Take your hands off me."

"Ma'am, I'll drive you to the Telluride
Regional Medical Center where they'll
stabilize him before transporting him on.
Come with me." And then he starts the
questions: "How long have you been in
town? Does he have a heart condition? Did
he overdo it yesterday? Activity and altitude
increase the risk of a heart attack."

I'm numb. I don't have any answers. I
don't want to talk to this stranger. As we
step off the elevator, everything starts flash-
ing black and white. I drop to the floor as I
hear, "She's passing out."

I wake up in the lobby of our condo building, aware there is a crowd gathering around
me. I couldn't have been out for long. I
stand up quickly. "Take me to John."

The EMT doesn't say anything as he leads
me out the door. Once we're outside, the
sunshine is blinding. I blink. He stops and
touches my shoulder.

"We need to hurry. What are you doing? I
need to get to my husband. Now," I de-
mand. I love him.

"I'm so sorry, Mrs. Nelson. Your husband died en route to the hospital."

John's dead?

My mind goes blank as a tiny thought makes its way through to the surface. Is this real, true?

"I don't believe you. Take me to John."

■ ■ ■ ■

PART 2:
TISH, KATE,
AND ASHLYN

■ ■ ■ ■

mind races through a million scenarios. The stock steered selling, someone ran a negative story on Evan.io. Some scandal, made up but credible, had taken us down.

"Are you alone?"

"No, Ashlyn is here. What the hell is wrong," I yell into the phone.

"It's John. He's ... he's dead," Lance sobs into the phone.

CHAPTER 14
KATE

I stand at the kitchen sink and look toward the fountain gurgling in my back courtyard, birds splashing in the water. It's going to be a good day. Ashlyn and I had a late breakfast together. We managed to enjoy a full meal without an argument and without a harsh word. I chalked it up to her hangover. She'd been out with old high school buddies, a last fling before they head back to college.

We're getting close again, my daughter and I. It warms my heart. She is my life. Her, and the company. They are all I care about.

My phone rings as I'm rinsing the dishes. I check to see who is calling. It's Lance from the office, so I answer.

"Where are you?" he asks.

I don't like the frantic sound of his voice.

"Um, I'm talking to you from my kitchen. What's wrong? What's happened?" Deep down, I think I was expecting this call. My mind races through a million scenarios. The stock stopped selling, someone ran a negative story on EventCo. Some scandal, made up but credible, had taken us down.

"Are you alone?"

"No, Ashlyn is here. What the hell is wrong?" I yell into the phone.

"It's John. He's . . . he's dead." Lance sobs into the phone.

My knees buckle, and I slide down the cabinet onto the kitchen floor. "No, this isn't true."

"I'll come over. I'll be there in twenty minutes. Oh my god, I'm so sorry, but it's true."

"How do you know?" I wrap my arms around myself. I am shaking.

"Tish called me from the hospital. They just declared John dead. I don't know what else to say. I'm so sorry."

I knew John's heart was trouble. I pinch myself. This is real.

"Kate. Are you there?"

"Yes," I manage.

"I'm coming over." Lance hangs up.

John's dead. My brain is having trouble accepting the fact of it. Not yet. So far it's just Lance's words.

My mind shifts to John, nervous, on one knee, proposing to me. We'd been dating

122

and living together, working on the company. We were in Maine, at a small bed-and-breakfast he'd heard about from a mutual friend. It was private and isolated and tiny. At Small Point Inn, I learned how to properly eat a whole Maine lobster, how to appreciate a purple lupine, how to dress for a forty-degree temperature shift. And on the last evening of our visit, before we joined the other guests for cocktail hour on the screened porch, I learned how romantic John could be.

"Will you marry me, Katie?" he said as he dropped to one knee on the moonlit path outside the inn.

I was stunned. Not because he was proposing, but because he was proposing here, in this strange place full of history that wasn't mine and never would be. Here, and yet, it was magical, out of time, out of place. A place we didn't belong and would never visit again.

I looked into his twinkling blue eyes and knew he was the one. It wasn't about where we were, it was about being together, always. I knew we would build a big life together. He'd already proven his work ethic. EventCo was better because of him, because of our teamwork.

"Yes. Of course I'll marry you." I was

drinking a strange cocktail, something traditionally East Coast, something pink. An old-fashioned? I remember the promises of forever, and loyalty, and until death do us part.

The doorbell rings.

I push myself to stand and walk on wobbly legs to the front door.

"Mom? Do you want me to get it?" Ashlyn calls from upstairs. It's too soon. She can't know this. Not yet. Not until I have more details.

"I've got it. It's Lance. Work stuff," I yell. The lie rolls off my lips easily.

"Of course. Work stuff. It's always fucking work stuff!" Ashlyn slams her door.

My mind flashes back to the dinner when John told me he was moving out, leaving me for Tish. That night changed my world forever. Changed me forever. I push those thoughts away and focus on now. John is dead.

I hold Tish responsible for this, even as part of me sees it's what he deserved. He left me for a woman half his age, a woman who used the oldest trick in the book to seduce my husband, right under my nose. So yes, I hold him responsible, culpable. Liable. Lie-able.

But it's my fault, too. Why didn't I see her

coming? See the threat more clearly? Was I so blinded by ambition, by our race for success and the promise of big money on the horizon, that I didn't care enough about our personal life together any longer? I mean, when John stood up and walked out of that restaurant, we hadn't been intimate in months. Nothing but quick kisses, brief hugs, promises of tomorrow night, or the agreement that we needed a date.

He was trying to work his way back to me, to his family. I just know it. He was seeing me again, and he liked what he saw. John was ready to reconnect. He wanted to come back home. That's what he wanted.

It's time to let Lance inside, as much as I want to avoid this moment, the reality of what has happened. I take a deep breath and open the door.

Lance embraces me. "God, Kate, I'm so very sorry."

I lead him into the living room. I'm in shock, I know. I also know I need to tell Ashlyn. John's death is news. Our company just went public.

Lance drops into a chair in the family room. "We're in trouble. The IPO. John."

I ignore Lance for the moment. I open my laptop and scroll to the news. And there it is. EventCo CEO dead at age fifty. Apparent heart attack. News travels fast. Bad news, faster. Tragic news, the fastest. We need to get in front of it. Stay in front of it. We cannot allow this tragedy to ruin the company. It won't.

I take a deep breath. "I'll be right back. I need to tell Ashlyn."

I climb the stairs slowly, thoughts racing through my mind. I need to bring John home. I need to be the one in charge of his body, of his proper burial. We'd had it planned, morbidly I suppose, for years. And now, it's my role as the mother of his only child, as the wife — his first wife, with whom he spent twenty-three years.

I say a silent prayer as I reach the top of the stairs. *Don't worry, John. I'll handle everything. You've done enough. Rest in peace.*

I knock on Ashlyn's bedroom door, knowing after I walk across the threshold, John's death will be real. And things will never be the same.

"Mom, what's wrong? Are you crying? You never cry."

"Oh, darling." I fold her into my arms. This will be the hardest moment in her young life. I take a deep breath. "Your father has died."

"Mom? What? No!" I hold her tight. I'll

126

help her through this. She'll need me more than ever. The company will need me more than ever.

I kiss the top of my daughter's head as she sobs. "Shhh, Ashlyn. I'm here. I'm so sorry. It's going to be all right." As I say those words, I resolve to make them true.

My daughter is shaking. "Dad missed us."

"I'm not sure of that, honey, but I'm here. I'm always here for you. We have each other," I murmur, knowing it's not enough in her mind, but it will have to be from now on. Was John's plan to attempt to reconcile? Maybe so, but it doesn't matter now.

The house phone begins ringing downstairs, and I hear Lance answer in the hallway.

"No comment. Please respect the family's privacy." I hear the phone drop back onto the cradle. The media wants a comment from me about John's death. I wasn't there, what can I add? We'll need to prepare an official statement.

Ashlyn leans against me, sobbing. "Have you talked to Tish? Was she there, with him? Did he suffer?"

A gruesome image of John dying burst into my imagination: bug eyes, foaming mouth, choking sounds. Accompanied by the vision of Tish standing over him. I shake my head. "I don't know, honey. I don't have any details, but I'll get them. I will find out what happened. I promise."

CHAPTER 15
ASHLYN

I fall into my mom's arms. I can't stop shaking. This isn't happening. My dad and I talked last night. My mom is wrong. She must be. It doesn't make sense. My heart beats so fast I think it might break.

"I talked to Dad last night. He was so sad. He said he was coming home to us."

"What do you mean? What exactly did he say?" Mom asks me.

"He was slurring his words. But he said he wanted to come home, he didn't feel good. And then she came out on the deck and made him hang up," I say, fighting to talk through my tears. "I hate her. I hate what she's done to our family. I hate what she did to Dad."

Mom pulls me tighter. "Yes, she's horrible. But Dad's an adult. He made his choice, honey."

"He made a bad choice," I say. There is a dark and angry pit growing in the bottom of my stomach. "What are we going to do now?"

Mom pulls away. "What do you mean? We'll be fine. We have been fine ever since your dad left us. Don't worry about a thing. I will handle everything."

"OK," I answer. I know Mom is in charge, she always has been. I guess I meant what will I do without my dad? He was the one in charge of fun. He used to be the one who could make me laugh. Since Tish came along, all he did was grow more and more distant. And now, he's gone. A sob shakes me to the core as my mom holds me tight.

"Listen, honey, come with me. We need to make arrangements. Lance is waiting," Mom says. "Doing something for your dad will help you feel better."

"No, hugging Dad right now would make me feel better. I need a minute alone." Mom nods and kisses the top of my head.

"We'll always miss your dad, of course, but we will get through this together."

We have already been missing my dad. Now, I guess we always will. I can't stop the tears as they spill from my eyes. My phone lights up. Texts pour in from college and high school friends. My dad's death is big news in Grandville and beyond. It's crazy to think that tragedy gets more attention than good news. I mean, not one of my friends texted about the IPO. But I guess that's true of people in general. They only see what they want to see, even when the truth is right in front of them.

I ignore all the texts, grab my teddy bear, and curl up in bed. My dad shouldn't have left home. We were all happy once, just the three of us. It seems so long ago that he and I were allowed to be alone together, to laugh together.

I knew they weren't happy together anymore. I saw it. He told me. But I never imagined this could happen, that he would die before he got away from her. Oh, Dad, why did you mess everything up?

Why did you have to leave me?

CHAPTER 16
TISH

Officer Taylor hands me a cup of coffee and tells me I don't have to go to the morgue if I identify John's body here, at the hospital. This place is bad enough. I can't imagine what the morgue looks like. I glance up at the officer, standing next to me like a guard dog. He's so kind and because he is, another round of tears springs to my eyes.

"They brought John's body here from our condo. They know who he is. It's already online everywhere. Tell them to google him." I take a sip of coffee. It's terrible.

"It's just a formality, ma'am." He stands up. His dark hair is slicked back and receding, creating deep V-shaped peaks on both sides. It works for him, I must say.

Focus, Tish.

"OK." I follow him down the hall and into the last bed in the emergency department. He pulls the curtain back, and when I nod, he pulls down the top sheet.

I cover my mouth. I haven't had to identify a dead body before, and I'd like to avoid it in the future. He looks terrible, his mouth frozen as if he's trying to scream. I turn away.

"That's him," I say, and feel my knees buckle.

Officer Taylor rushes to my side, helping me back to a chair in the waiting room. "What happens next is the coroner will collect the body, take legal custody. He'll want to talk to you, too. There will be an autopsy."

"No," I say. "Please. He wouldn't want that. He was under a lot of stress. He had a bad heart. It was a ticking time bomb. We all knew it."

"I understand. Nobody really wants a loved one opened up, not unless it's foul play or something. You can tell him your feelings when he calls, but it's Colorado law," Officer Taylor says.

The ER doctor on call comes by to give her condolences, says John was dead on arrival and that she's so sorry. I wonder briefly why an ER doctor is overweight. Isn't that a health risk? Lead by example and all. She probably stress eats french fries or doughnuts, like John did. Poor John. I sign some forms she hands me.

"The coroner will be here any minute. His

name is Dr. Welty. He's quite good, very compassionate." The ER doctor stands. She's finished with me.

I watch a lot of *Law & Order.* I mean, who doesn't? So I expected a pale, frail older man to play the part of the coroner. But no. This Dr. Welty is at least six feet, is tanned, and has perfect white teeth. Store bought. We shake hands.

"Mrs. Nelson. I'm terribly sorry to meet in this manner. Could we step into a conference room? I have a few questions," he says.

Officer Taylor and I follow him down the hall and into a tiny all-white room. I feel like a criminal in this room, pinned in by a cop and a movie-star coroner. But I'm not a criminal, I'm the wife. A tear rolls down my cheek.

"Did your husband have a heart condition?" Dr. Welty asks, typing notes on his phone.

"Yes. High blood pressure. He was on medicine," I answer. "Edira is the name."

"Any other prescription drugs?" he asks. "Recreational?"

"No. John enjoyed a stiff drink now and again, nothing else. But he was under a lot of stress. Our company just went public. We celebrated last night," I say.

My heart thumps in my chest. Do I sound

like I'm hiding something?

"Yes, I read about that. Unfortunately, news of his death leaked almost immediately. We have launched an internal investigation," he says, white teeth visible even while frowning. I wonder if he drinks coffee. No way.

"I was surprised by the media coverage, too. But he is, was, an important man. That's why I need to take John home, for a proper burial," I say.

"I understand. I'll perform the autopsy sometime tomorrow. It's standard in a sudden death like this, especially if alcohol is involved, section A.3," he says.

"I'd rather you not. It was a heart attack," I say.

"It's the law, ma'am. But I'm not expecting to find anything suspicious. Were you two perhaps drinking more than usual last night?"

I smile. "It was a special evening. Yes, we were celebrating the IPO, and well, our anniversary. It was our place. We were going to retire here." I drop my head, momentarily unable to speak. I am embellishing the purpose of our trip, of course, but John did propose to me right here in Telluride.

"Unfortunately, we see this happen quite often. Mountain Village sits at more than

9,500 feet. You combine drinking and altitude with a heart condition, well, it can be trouble."

"I didn't realize," I say. "He'd just been working so hard. I was trying to help him unwind."

"I understand. Mrs. Nelson, if you could provide me with the name of Mr. Nelson's cardiologist, I think I have what I need for now."

I write down the cardiologist's contact info. "When will I be able to take John home?"

"There's a process, ma'am," Officer Taylor says.

"Yes, indeed," Dr. Welty agrees. "Once the autopsy is complete, and as long as there is nothing suspicious, we try to release the body within a couple of days. You'll need to wait for the official death certificate before removing him from the state. Give us a week, Mrs. Nelson. We'll be in touch."

Dr. Welty leaves the room, and I slump into my chair. I'm trapped here, it seems. All I can do is wait and hope they don't find anything "suspicious" that holds things up. They won't, though, I'm certain of that. I start to cry, and across the table Officer Taylor shifts in his seat.

"Can I drop you somewhere, maybe with

a friend? You're not going to want to go back home until the scene is cleared and cleaned."

My mind flashes to John's body, the vomit, the smell. "I don't know anyone here. Can you take me to a hotel?" I ask him. I didn't realize I'd be stuck in Telluride, waiting for John. But it would look terrible if I flew home without him, so I will stay.

Officer Taylor opens the passenger door of his squad car, and I slip inside. I'm glad he didn't make me ride in the back like a criminal. As we pull out of the parking lot, I book a room on my phone. A suite. "The Peaks, please."

"Nice choice," he says. "Best place on the mountain."

Oh, I know. There are winners and losers in life. I like to stay where the winners stay.

CHAPTER 17
TISH

My phone rings, but I don't recognize the number. I almost ignore it but realize it's a Telluride number. I've been stuck here in my hotel room for three days waiting for news about John. Sure, it's a beautiful suite, but I feel trapped. I'm cranky and restless. Hoping for any information, I answer the phone.

"Mrs. Nelson. It's Dr. Welty," he says, and I see a big toothy grin.

My heart thumps in my chest. "Yes, hello. Have you, um, finished with John?"

"Yes, ma'am. I'll be releasing the body. The cause of death was cardiac arrest due to or as a consequence of hypertension and heart disease. The death certificate should be processed soon. Again, my condolences."

I realize I've been holding my breath. "Thank you."

"Any questions for me?" Dr. Welty asks.

"I just wait for the death certificate, and

then I'll take him home, right?" I feel as if the weight of the world is off my shoulders. I take another deep breath.

"Yes, that's all you need to do. Take care, Mrs. Nelson," he says and hangs up.

Well, that's not all I need to do, not by a long shot.

Here's another truth when you marry a man who is twenty-five years your senior: he will die before you. Everyone knows it. Not sure why there had to be any questions, any "investigations." Yet, according to Officer Taylor, that's what they have been doing since he died. Recreating John's last day, retracing his steps. It's absurd and gruesome. Maybe they don't have much action up here? I assume all of that nonsense stops now that the coroner's report is in.

I take a sip of tea and rub my tired eyes. Before he dropped me here, Officer Taylor handed me the business card of a company that specializes in cleaning up after deaths in the home. A gruesome way to make a living, but they were there this morning after the scene was cleared to "take care of things." Cleaned or not, I will never be able to set foot in that condominium again, I know as my stomach lurches at the memory. Not after what I saw.

Because John is dead. Cardiac arrest.

Underlying heart disease. Period.

His obituary is in the paper today in Telluride, Ponte Vedra Beach, and Columbus. That all happened seemingly by magic. A single call to handsome, helpful Lance at EventCo, and everything was set in motion. I didn't have to make any calls. Not to Kate, or Ashlyn, or to the rest of the company. Lance handled all of that. He said I had enough on my plate. He even offered to fly out, help with the arrangements.

The arrangements.

I am in charge of the *body*. Just thinking about it, right now, my skin prickles into goose bumps. I mean, it turns out there are a lot of decisions to make when you're the wife of someone who has died. In Ohio, where we live and where he'll be buried, the wife has all the rights. It is all up to me, no matter how much Kate and Ashlyn want to make it about them. And they do. They call me, or at least Kate does, every other hour. I've taken to sending her to voice mail. She leaves messages saying she just wants to help, blah, blah, blah. That she'll handle everything. To think of Ashlyn. To have some compassion.

No way. I'm in charge now. John was my husband, not hers. I told them not to fly here, that there was nothing for them to do.

140

They called me again, just this afternoon, together, in a wonderfully overwhelming show of strength and solidarity, and left a long voice mail.

"Please, fly the *body* home to the family mausoleum. John's parents are buried there. I know that is what he would have wanted. Let Schoedinger Funeral Home handle this, please. I've already talked to them, and they expect his remains. It's all been prearranged. Tish, please, I know — knew — John better than anyone. Better than you. Please." Kate sounded firm, but she was desperate. She always wants to be in control.

They don't know anything. I don't care what morbid plans John and Kate made when they were married. I'm in charge now. To me, cremation is the answer. It's good for the environment, and really, you become dust anyway. I found a good guy here. Funeral home directors are so helpful to us grieving widows, even though they pretty much have you at their mercy, don't they? They know everything, and you're just trying to clean up a gross mess.

Kate needs to understand what I've been through. I am the wife now.

My phone lights up. It's Kate. Again. She's such a bother.

I pick up the phone. "Look, I got your

141

messages, but you should know I've already lined up the funeral home here to take care of things. I'm in charge of his body."

"How dare you. John had plans in place for this with the funeral home here in Columbus. You should respect his wishes. I can handle it. For the love of god, it is what he wanted." Kate's voice is frosty through the phone.

I hear Ashlyn sobbing. It grates on me.

I'm tired of both of them. Kate is acting like she's the boss of me or something. I hate that tone. Where's the compassion for the grieving widow anyway? "John will be flown home on Saturday. It takes five days to get the official death certificate now that the autopsy is finished."

I hear her gasp at the word.

So I say it again. "Yes, he had an autopsy because it was sudden, and alcohol was involved, and he's prominent or something."

"You didn't tell me that was happening," Kate hisses.

"You never asked," I say. "Besides, it came back all normal. Nothing criminal. Just his poor heart stopping. So Kate, please do as I've asked and focus on the memorial service. I know it will be a big deal. You can be onstage, the way you like it." I'll admit that was a low-blow comment.

"You're unbelievable. You know that?" It's Ashlyn piping in. Aren't children supposed to be seen and not heard? "My mom and dad picked out the place where he wanted to be buried. They had a plan. Just honor that, why don't you? Why do you have to be such a bitch?"

Oh, silly Ashlyn. She's so clueless. I don't have the time to get her back on my side right now. "That plan was made when your parents were together. They are divorced, and I'm his wife now. You don't really expect me to bury your dad next to your mom's slot, or plot, or whatever it's called, do you? That just doesn't make sense. I know you're stressed, though, so I'm not angry with you."

"I'm pleading with you, please. We'll give you whatever you want, just send John home. To me. To his family," Kate says. "At least tell me what you're planning. I have a right to know."

I took a breath. We need to be a grieving team once I'm back in Columbus. A unified front, they call it. Just the three of us: John's women. I dig down deep for my last bit of sympathy for Kate, wife number one.

"I hear you. And I'm so sorry this has happened, for all of us. But you must understand that I'll need to make the arrangements for John, the way he and I planned. We discussed this, and he had specific instructions."

"You're lying." Ashlyn again. She is on my last nerve.

"You don't know anything. I'm handling things."

The only thing I heard on the other end was sobbing, so I hung up.

Of course Ashlyn is right. John and I hadn't discussed our death plans — I'm the second wife. I'm vitality and youth and light. We had years to settle into that type of morbid rumination. Years of luxury travel, adventurous sex, and second-, third-, and fourth-home shopping.

There's a knock on the door. Room service. I pull the fluffy white robe tight and answer the door to a handsome young server. He no doubt wonders how a woman his age could afford this suite. I walk to the sitting area of the room and take a seat. He places the silver room service tray on the coffee table in front of me and hands me the bill.

I leave him a big tip, and when I hand him the bill folder, our hands touch. He turns bright red before hurrying out the door.

As I eat my room service oatmeal, I reflect on the newly unified front. Does Ashlyn still hate her mom? I don't see it anymore. I mean, Kate seems so, I don't know the word, boring? So in control. When John told me he and Kate had never had sex at the office after building a company together, I was in shock. Who doesn't do it on the conference room table when you own the whole place?

And then, just when we'd begun to enjoy our new life, really settle into a routine, he started drifting away from me.

Unbelievable. Disappointing. You can understand my anger with this situation now, I'm sure. I let my guard down, that's what I did, and Kate the rat slipped back into his life.

I place my bowl of unfinished oatmeal on the room service tray and consider my next move. I have nothing but time as I wait for John's body to be cremated so we can fly home.

It's time to make an important call. I pull up Uncle George's contact, and he answers immediately. I knew he would. We've been spending a good amount of time together recently — on the phone and in person. We go way back. It is too bad Uncle George wasn't interested in helping me when I was a kid and being abused by my mom and her lovers. I suppose some of his overt interest

145

in my affairs now is due to that negligence. Or maybe he just smells money? I guess that's what all lawyers are good at: following the money.

"And to what do I owe the pleasure of this call, honey?" George's slow drawl pulls out the last word like taffy. I imagine he's in sweatpants and a size XXL sweatshirt with the Cincinnati Bengals logo printed on it, even though they never win, and nobody cares. He told me he doesn't get dressed up for any client but me.

I sniff. Tears pop into my eyes. I did love John. I do still. "It's John. He's died." And then the waterworks won't stop. I think of John's body on some slablike table, somewhere in town, waiting to be burned.

"I know. Saw it in the news. No need for tears. It's all buttoned up, honey. We took care of it all when I was in town, remember? I know you liked him a lot, but now, you can move on. You'll have all that money, everything you need. All the t's are crossed, all the i's are dotted, as they say." I hear George sigh and take a sip of something. The sounds of clinking ice cubes and a slow slurp fill my ear. I put the phone down and put it on speaker.

"You're right. I am fine, money wise." I blow my nose and look around the penthouse suite. I can stay in hotel rooms like this every day for the rest of my life if I'd like. There is so much I can do now with all I'll be inheriting.

"Even so, you should be careful. The IPO is fresh. You don't want to upset the investors. You want them to think everything at the company can run just fine without John. Get it? It's called a controlled company — you and John controlled fifty percent; his ex-wife the other fifty percent. Now, with what's happened, you have sole control of his fifty percent. But you're going to need to be sharp."

I stretch and touch my toes. "Yes, I know." George has taught me a thing or two — about business and life. And he's discreet. He didn't even ask me what really happened to John.

"There will be a lot of sharks in the water. Make sure you keep yourself on solid ground. You're going to be on the cover of some big working women's magazine, I just know it." Mixed analogies aside, a shiver of dread runs down my spine.

"Should I be worried about anything?"

"No. Right now, everything is handled," George says.

I take a deep breath. I imagine Ashlyn and I will grow closer again. I'll be the fabulous,

147

young, rich co-CEO of EventCo. One of the city's top businesswomen. As for Kate, I don't really care what happens to her, do I? I mean sure, she'll still own half the company and will be co-CEO for a bit, but maybe I'll figure out a way to take that, too. She'll be heartbroken, too sad to come into the office, perhaps. It's all a dream come true.

I pull myself out of my daydream and remember George is on the phone. "OK, well thanks. For everything."

George chuckles. "Sure thing. But remember, blood is thicker than water in times like this, sugar."

He said the same phrase when he came up to Columbus a week and a half ago. It's annoying, especially if you're a person like me without any relatives — except George, that is.

"We'll see. We'll see." I am drumming my fingers on the sleek sofa table by the door. I'm feeling a bit trapped, even in this large suite. I needed George to represent me and make sure I'm covered legally. But all my life I've made a point of never relying on anyone, so this role isn't comfortable.

"Do you need me to come help you? Where are you anyway?" George doesn't believe in social media, so he has missed my posts featuring the beautiful meadow, our romantic lunch, the rustic beauty of this mountain town.

"Telluride. And no, I don't need your help. His body will be cremated as soon as I get the death certificate." The last thing I need is George here.

"Oh goodness. Are you sure you want to do that? There? It might not look good for you, you know?" he asks. He's pretending his proper fundamentalist Christian cockles won't approve of cremation.

"Fire and brimstone, George. Ashes to ashes. You know." I add, "I've got things handled here. The memorial service is next Saturday. Why don't you come?"

"I'll be there. Whatever you need," he says before we hang up.

As the only person from my past I trust, I need to keep him on my good side. He didn't help with what happened at home, but he told me I'd be fine once I got out of my hometown. Out of my home. And he was right. And despite his slow southern drawl and meandering walking pace, he's a cutthroat attorney. No doubt he'll be the only one on my side in the entire room. Sort of the way my life has always been.

My phone buzzes in my pocket.

"Mrs. Nelson? It's Curtis, over here at the

149

funeral home. They expedited your husband's death certificate once you called and told them who he was. I didn't know he was a famous man. Got celebrity treatment from the coroner."

I sniff. "He was." I didn't make that call. I suppose Lance had someone handle it.

"Everything is as it should be. We can go ahead with the cremation then, all right?" Curtis sounds at once impressed by John and sort of sad to be burning up his body.

"Yes, please do. Thank you." The call ends, and my heart pounds in my chest. I tell myself this is the storm before the calm, something I'd promise myself often as a kid. Right now, John's body is being burned.

That's enough to keep you on edge, wouldn't you agree?

My team rented the best ballroom in the city, complete with sparkling chandeliers and soaring ceilings. They had it decorated tastefully in John's memory with blown-up photos of highlights of his life featured on easels throughout the room. But as I look around, I realize it doesn't matter what the setting is for a memorial celebration of life. If you're part of the family, it's awful, claustrophobic, depressing. Despite the air conditioning, the large room is sticky and hot as the summer air blows in each time the doors open. I wipe my forehead with a tissue and take a deep breath.

Ashlyn and I stand side by side at the front of the ballroom, awkwardly greeting John's "friends." Most are coworkers, employees, people who have depended on us for their livelihood. John's real friends will be at the funeral: his golf buddies, his wine buddies, the couples who all followed him after the divorce because he's much more fun to socialize with than I am.

The people in line now are random life connections paying respects, whatever that means. I lean forward and look past Ashlyn to watch Tish. This is the first time I've seen her since John died, although we have struggled through many frustrating phone calls. The left side of her mouth tilts up in a smirk.

She can smirk all she'd like, but she will soon learn the truth: she better not get in my way. I'm not sure why, but I hold eye contact with her until someone touches my arm and I jump.

This is all quite awkward. When a perfect couple with everything going for them suddenly implodes, there are shock waves. I know the rumors as well as anyone else. I should say I know now. I wish someone had warned me, but no one did. I didn't pick up on a clue, a telltale lipstick stain on the collar, or too many late-night meetings. Once I found out, it's all I thought about. But even then, I was convinced it was a fling. Turns out I was very wrong.

"How could this happen?" My best friend, Christine, had paced across the floor of my kitchen, distraught, but more to the point, bummed she didn't discover the truth about

John first. Her blonde bob shook back and forth with her stride. "I know everything that happens in this town. This is unacceptable."

"It is." I took another drink of the French burgundy she'd brought with her when she rang the doorbell unexpectedly. As soon as I saw her face at the back door, I knew everyone had heard about John's affair. "They say the wife is the last to know. They are right."

"Damn it. You two are perfect. Everyone says it. Look at what you've built. And I mean *you.*" Christine stopped, grabbed her wineglass. "I'm writing a story about the true brains behind EventCo. It's time, beyond time. I'll place it nationally. You'll have guys lining up to get in your pants."

"Honestly, the last thing that attracts men is a woman who seems smarter, savvier, and more powerful than they are in business. Trust me." I know from experience. The only way we could grow EventCo was through John's good-old-boy network. Sure, banks are supposed to treat women-owned companies equally. Sure, private clubs and investment bankers are supposed to, too. But just like women earn on average seventy cents to every dollar a man makes, women-owned businesses have a long way to go to be equitable when it comes to financing. We decided together to have John take the CEO title. Telling that story now would just be spiteful. "I'm not sure anybody would care."

Christine stared at me. "You're afraid to step into your power. That's the problem. We need to expose him. I can write it."

"No, you can't. I won't let you. It would hurt the company. And maybe, maybe this is just some phase he has to go through? Maybe he'll wake up?" I sipped my wine and realized my hope sounded about as realistic as snow in Columbus in July.

"How old is she?" Christine was pacing again.

"Twenty-two." I touch the limestone countertop, willing myself not to cry. The fact that John moved out two nights earlier still seemed crazy. Really, John?

"Unbelievable. What a shit head. And you didn't see any signs? Completely blindsided, even though you all work together every day."

"I was busy, you know, running a company." I sounded lame. But that much was true. I didn't have time for an affair. But John did.

I turn my focus back to the line of mourners and take a deep breath. John left me more than three years ago now. I still cannot fully believe he actually married her. I thought it was a fling. That it would end. I never imagined another Mrs. Nelson.

But still, I held my head high. I survived, bided my time until he realized his mistake. Because I knew he would. How could he not?

I watch Tish hugging a mourner, a large man with an old fedora on his head, and wonder who it is. He does not speak with me before hustling away.

As I watch the stranger recede, my thoughts crystalize. John was leaving her. He told me as much over lunch. But did she know they were over? Maybe she did? The realization zips through me.

I look at her again. Tish's bracelet is too much for this place — the diamonds sparkle in defiance of the sadness in the room. She's a walking billboard for the phrase *money can't buy taste.* I cannot wait until she is out of our lives forever. I remind myself we just need to make it through this ceremony, and the funeral tomorrow. And then she's a bad memory.

"Mom," Ashlyn says. "What are you doing?"

She caught me staring at Tish. "Nothing, darling. How are you holding up?"

Ashlyn shrugs. *Focus on the present, on*

the mourner in front of you, I tell myself while my brain searches through scenes when John, Tish, and I were together at the office. Before I knew the truth of their affair. Did I miss something? A lingering touch, a secret smile? No, there was nothing. They were sneaky.

She was the mastermind, I'm sure of it. The woman always is.

Ashlyn tugs on my sleeve. "Mom, you're holding up the line."

I look at the next person in line. "Hello, Bill," I say to the man who manages our country club.

"I'm so sorry, Kate," he says.

"I'm sure you are, Bill," I reply. I do not care for the man. He's a sexist and an opportunist. A horrible combination.

Bill turns to Ashlyn and grabs her hand with a big shake. I fight the urge to push him away from her. She lets people in too easily. The wrong people.

"Hi, Mr. Oyster," Ashlyn says, but she isn't smiling. Maybe she knows what he is, too? Good girl.

Tish stares at me. She has nothing to do but wait until Ashlyn escapes Bill's grip. I can't believe just over one short week ago we were all in our conference room together — Tish viewing me with disdain as if I were some old has-been relic, and her looking smug and in charge with her all-black outfit that matched John's. The memories of that day trigger a rush of strong emotions despite another mourner touching my shoulder.

I'll never forget how out of place, how uncomfortable she tried to make me feel in my own office, standing there preening in the conference room with John by her side. As if she had anything to do with the company's success, as if she belonged there in the spotlight at all. Absurd.

"Kate, darling, I'm so sorry for your loss. Standing up here like this must be horrible. How are you holding up?" Christine, my closest friend, whispers in my ear. She looks chic as always, and as always, she's concerned about me. She thinks I'm a workaholic, and I think she's right.

I lean into her hug. "Why did all of this happen?" I manage to ask as if she can tell me why our marriage cracked and allowed a horrible person to climb in. Why my daughter used to hang out with the horrible person. Why John married a woman practically his daughter's age.

"I'll come over later," she says, squeezes my hand, and moves on to Ashlyn.

A tap on my shoulder brings me back to the never-ending line. It's my executive assistant. "The Lord works in mysterious ways. I'm praying for you all," Nancy murmurs as she pats my back. "You and Ashlyn. John's real family."

With that simple phrase, Nancy is on Team Kate. She's made that clear from the get-go. "Thank you."

"Can't believe she is even standing up here, next to you, like she's family." Nancy pats my shoulder one last time and moves on to Ashlyn.

I can't believe it, either, I realize. Even now. Even with all of this. I don't want to believe it, but it's true. John's dead and I'm hosting a memorial service with his young wife.

I wish I'd taken two Xanax.

Why did I agree to a shared memorial? She should have had a service with her friends, and Ashlyn and I would have this one with ours. Tish and John were a blip on the radar screen, a nonsensical affair for a married middle-aged man with an expanding stomach, high blood pressure, an avalanche of work responsibility, and a teenager.

This situation is a joke. I'll find comfort in the fact that after today, I will never be in the same space with that pathetic young woman again. I will never have to share my family, my husband, my daughter, or my company with her. Not ever again.

I will take charge of EventCo, and she will dissolve into a bad memory.

I take a deep breath and remember. It's all mine now. I'm the only one in charge. I know what to do, and I know how to keep growing the business. I also know who Tish really is — a scrappy junkyard dog. I can't erase the fact that she came into our lives, but once John is buried, she will be out of our lives forever. Our assets are protected from Tish, and Ashlyn's future is more than secure, thanks to the property John transferred to her trust and the shares she owns in EventCo. We are both set for life.

And that thought is the only reason I can handle all this.

It's almost over.

She's almost gone. And she will leave with as little as possible. I will see to that.

CHAPTER 19
ASHLYN

More than standing here in this receiving line, more than anything in the world, I realize, I really hate her. I don't believe a word she says anymore. I will find out all I can about her, where she came from, why she ruined my family. And if she hurt my dad, she'll be sorry.

Another stupid stranger mumbles "I'm sorry" in my direction. He better not try to touch me. Good, he stays back.

"Thank you," I tell him.

Tish's purse is on the ground between us. In between talking to strangers, I check out what's inside. I am learning a lot, standing here between two adults who hate each other. I learn about my mom's strength, about Tish's flashy confidence, and I learn something else, too. I'm a little bit of both of them, I suppose. And because of that, neither of them really sees me as my own person. I'm more of a reflection, I suppose.

160

And that's just fine.

I look at my watch. My dad would have hated this whole morbid procession, I know he would. It's all so fake. None of my friends are here, and from what I can tell, only people who worked for Dad showed up. I know he had friends, at least he used to before Tish came along. Maybe she cut him off from all of them, too. Or maybe it was his decision? I know it was awkward for them to go to dinner with couples who knew Mom.

This whole thing made life awkward for all of us. I look up, and Seth is standing in front of me. He's made an effort to tame his blond hair, and he's even wearing a tie. He looks good in his dark-navy suit.

I fling my arms around my best friend and whisper, "Thank you for being here. Did you cut the whole line?"

"Sorry, my bad," he says. "I wanted you to know I'm here. I'll wait outside. Text me if you need anything." He kisses me on the cheek and slips away.

And because of him, I will tolerate this ridiculous line of misery for a bit longer. As another mourner touches my arm, I move my mind to the last time I talked to my dad. And it makes me angry. Angry he picked her over our dinner plans. Angry he was in

161

Telluride against his will.

Angry he is dead.

There is so much I don't understand.

I make myself a promise: I will get to the bottom of this.

CHAPTER 20
TISH

A quick glance at my watch lets me know I have about another hour to suffer through this memorial service.

And I do mean suffer. Ashlyn stands next to me, and she is a mess. I guess, in most people's opinion, she's got it the worst. Her father's dead. She's going to miss out on all types of important events with her ever-doting daddy — college graduation celebrations, assuming she graduates on time now; an elaborate and expensive wedding of her dreams to a young titan of industry; the birth of her first child. Too bad. But she had him for twenty-one years. That's seventeen more years than I had with my real dad, before the first awful stepdaddy came around. She should consider herself lucky, but I know she doesn't.

I'm too far away to hear what Nancy, Kate's red-haired executive assistant, the office busybody who thinks she's everyone's mom, whispers in Ashlyn's ear. But I know it was something about me. They both turn and stare at me, and I decide to meet their glares. I mean, really? You haven't scared me away yet, so where do you think I'm going now?

Ashlyn doesn't realize it, but she works for me now. She'll be fine with it. We'll be buddies again. I am much more fun than her mom.

I'm the new Kate. The younger, better version. Ashlyn already likes hanging out with me more, so she'll get used to the arrangement. Or, rather, she will for a bit before she goes back to college. Bye-bye, Ashlyn. Then it's just me and Kate. What a team. That thought brings a quick smile to my face. I drop my head and pretend to cough.

Nancy walks toward me. I suppose she must save face and murmur something kind in my ear, too. It's only right. I am the grieving wife and the co-owner of EventCo. She'll report up to me. It's Kate and me in charge from now on. Won't that be fun?

What? Nancy just wagged her finger at me, turned, and walked away. She didn't come over to me to express her condolences. How dare she? As I watch her slow retreat, I fantasize about all the ways to fire her. I'll get awful Sandra in HR on this immediately.

Sandra is ruthless, I know from firsthand experience. She tried hard to force me out of the company after John and I were engaged. She'd pleaded with John to have me quit. But I told him I loved working with him, promised him some more after-hours fun on the conference table, and I won. I always do.

I glance at my purse sitting on the ground beside me. John's phone is in there. I pull it out and hold it in my hand, although I'm not sure why I'm still carting it around. I tried to get into all his apps, but he never gave me a password to anything but his phone. And that doesn't work on any of the apps — an extra layer of security that I find completely annoying. What was he trying to hide? I tried Ashlyn's birthday, my birthday, our anniversary, and all the usual suspects. Nothing. I've kept it charged, hoping I'll think of something.

I was able to clean up his texts, delete a few sweet notes from Kate, who calls herself Mabel for some reason. She was a little flirty but nothing overt. I suspect there were more that he deleted to hide them from me, and I have no way to retrieve them. The ones that weren't deleted covered basic logistics of their sneaky affair: lunch dates, call time reminders, and the like. I can see how many calls John made to her. He even called her the night before he died, but she is the only one who has the voice mail messages if there are any. Not that any of it does her any good now. Or him. The cheaters. Kate likely reads the texts over and over again, pining away for what might have been. Too bad. She lost. How desperate to go after a guy who dumped you for a younger model.

It's a shame Kate has no spine, trying to weasel her way back into my man's life.

I look at John's phone. Odd, isn't it, how his voice mail has outlived him.

I drop John's phone into my purse and grab my phone. I quickly check for messages. There aren't any. I'm beyond bored. It must be time for this thing to end already. There's nothing left to say. John is dead.

I, for one, am ready to go. There is so much to do now that I'm back in town.

CHAPTER 21
KATE

Nancy's words of support give me the energy to handle the last of the mourners. I see the end of the line, some twenty people deep. Jennifer pulls on the heavy doors to seal off the ballroom and to keep anyone else from joining the line. She knows we've had enough. I nod thanks in her direction, and she offers a brief wave.

"How are you holding up?" Lance has tears in his eyes. He's so much more than our COO. He's family. Lance folds me into his strong arms.

"You must be exhausted, Kate." Jennifer is behind me, patting my shoulder. "Have a seat. Drink some water."

I do as she suggests and remind myself to breathe. I sip the cold water, not minding as condensation runs down my hand and puddles in my lap. I'll never wear this dress again anyway.

Ashlyn is hugging someone I don't recognize, engulfed in a conversation she doesn't want to have. Tish is alone. She smiles at me and shakes her head at what she thinks is my weakness.

I want to jump out of my chair, grab her, and shake her. Hard. She has no idea how strong I am.

"Feeling better?" Lance asks. "You looked really pale for a minute, like you were going to faint or something."

"I'm fine, thank you. Do I need to speak to anyone else?" I'm shielded from the remaining mourners in line by Jennifer and Lance who stand side by side to create a sort of protective screen blocking the view of what they decided was my near fainting.

"You can be finished. You're not feeling well. You've done enough," Jennifer says. "We'll tell the rest to send you a note of condolence. They're happily joining the celebration of life cocktail party."

My shoulders relax. I glance up just as Tish darts down the center aisle of the room and out of sight. Ashlyn stands alone, staring out at the now-empty ballroom. *Don't worry, Ashlyn. We'll be fine.* I make that silent promise to my little girl as I watch her. Ashlyn and I will come together. We're family. We'll reconnect. She just doesn't realize that everything I do, I do for her. She'll understand. It will just take time. I'm all she has now.

As for Tish, I know her type. She'll take the money and run. I am almost Tish-free.

"Ashlyn, ready to head home?" I don't tell my daughter that I have a lot of work to do making sure this IPO doesn't fall apart with John's death. I know she doesn't understand. She'd call me work obsessed.

Ashlyn stands frozen at the front of the stage, alone, staring at her phone. When I call her name, she blinks, as if she'd forgotten where she was.

My heart is heavy for my daughter. There is no telling what effect all this will have on her. John and I tried our best to be great parents. He couldn't help his shortcomings, I suppose. But over time, I'll help her see things clearly.

"I have some stuff to do, Mom. I'll see you back at the house later." Ashlyn picks up her purse from the floor. It looks just like Tish's purse. The bags were like twins sitting side by side. Likely from one of their girls' shopping trips. Another thing Ashlyn faults me for, my complete lack of interest in shopping. She can't believe I outsource it to my stylist. I'm pretty much a big disappointment.

She's practically running down the aisle

of the ballroom. What is so important? I hope she isn't meeting up with Tish. She wouldn't do that, of course not.

It's nice to be outside, away from those ghoulish people who wanted to touch my shoulder, hug me. Yuck. As I begin to walk to my car, I stop in my tracks when I see a surprise. Ashlyn walked out the door, too. Maybe she wants to make up? We'll have a mother-daughter parking lot chat. How wonderful. Or not. She's giving me a strange look.

Interesting.

"Hey, how are you holding up?" The poor little rich girl and I have barely spoken since I flew home with John's body. Not his body exactly, his cremains. Strange word, isn't it?

"Fine." She crosses her arms, a smirk on her face. The designer bag I bought her hangs from her shoulder.

"You know I loved your dad. More than anything. And I'll always be here for you." I take a step toward her.

"He didn't want to go to Telluride. You

know it," Ashlyn proclaims. "He was dreading it. He was supposed to have dinner with me. Why'd you make him go?"

"He needed a getaway. A break. You wouldn't understand all the pressure he was under. The IPO was overwhelming, among other things that were taking up his attention. But I won't fill you in on that adult stuff. He was overly stressed."

"This doesn't make sense. Dad was happy. He loved working on the IPO. And once that was finished, he was going to dump you." Ashlyn takes a step toward me. "I think you knew it, and you did something to him."

"Oh, stop being dramatic. He had a heart attack. Look at the death certificate. You should be nice to me. I'm running EventCo now." Am I yelling? No, just speaking with conviction.

Ashlyn steps back, shaking her head. Over her shoulder, I see Jennifer hurrying toward us.

"Everything good, ladies?" Jennifer says, stepping into our standoff like an annoying watchdog.

Jennifer places a hand on Ashlyn's shoulder. "Where's your car, honey?"

"Over there," Ashlyn says, still staring at me.

172

"Why don't you get going, Tish?" Jennifer says.

"Good idea. Glad this is over. Is there anything else we're supposed to suffer through?"

"The funeral?" Ashlyn spews out the words as if I forgot or something.

"I know that. It's tomorrow. I planned it. I'll be there, of course. But today? I'm outta here." I check my watch. I'm not busy, but I'll pretend to be. "I have an appointment." I blow a kiss to Ashlyn, just for show, and walk to my car, swinging my hips.

I sense the dagger eyes of the two women behind me slicing into my back. Whatever. I stop, turn around, and wave toward them. Ashlyn and Jennifer ignore me.

I'm surprised how bright the sun is today. The windowless ballroom, with its artificial light and heavy, tearful mourners, would make you think it's dark out.

I slide behind the wheel of John's beloved silver Audi. It must be 150 degrees in here. I turn the air-conditioning to high as I inhale the smell of his aftershave, still very much present in the leather seats. His aura, his scent, is all around me. There's a sour feeling in the pit of my stomach, a feeling like dread. I shake it off. It was all his fault, what happened to him. He couldn't take

173

the altitude, the pressure at work, the pace of a younger wife. But it was everything he wanted. I was everything he wanted. Until he didn't. And then, well, RIP.

I pull out of the parking lot and turn into traffic. For John, I drive fast, even though I'm on a suburban street, weaving in between cars just like John does. Used to do. I need to stop dwelling on John. I need to move on, move forward. I smile as I scoot through an orange-yellow light and drive into the matching sunset. Poetic, isn't it?

This day is finished, and it's a relief to be heading home. I have one more ceremony to suffer through, and then on to my new life. I thought I'd be so happy being Mrs. John Nelson. I imagined myself a younger version of Kate, a hip parent to Ashlyn. But then he turned his back on me, on our life.

It's time to recreate myself. I'll become a powerhouse, like Kate. I turn up the radio. It's John's favorite station, classic rock, most recorded before I was born. I push the button for "Today's Hits." It's almost time to leave the past behind. Before I know it, I'm pulling into the driveway, and the garage door opens as if by magic. Technology is really something. Our home is what they call "smart," which makes me laugh.

I teased John about the system when it

had been installed, a five-day project that cost tens of thousands of dollars.

As I watched the crew of tech guys climbing around our home, I said to John, "I picture our house with a big cap and gown, its degree tucked proudly under the copper gutter downspout. So educated."

That word *educated* rankles me. People think they're better than you when they have degrees. The more degrees, the more superior. Most of the people around here pay big bucks to get their kids into the best schools, through the back door with their big donations and named buildings, or sometimes through the side door of cheating and bribes. I didn't try any door, not that I'd had the option or inclination. I do have my GED. I don't need anything else. I mean, look where I live.

"Honey, the house isn't educated, it's sophisticated. Technology to protect you if I'm out of town, that sort of thing." John had pulled me into a tight hug. I could tell what he wanted. "I'll always protect you, babe."

"Actually, the house will, right?" I'd teased, wriggling away.

"Let's go upstairs, I'll show you what's new."

Back then, when we'd first married, all he

wanted was sex.

It wasn't his fault. I am pretty irresistible. I push the garage button and watch as the heavy door drops before I step into the house. The alarm warns me to disarm it, and I punch in the numbers.

It's still beeping. More frantically. My fingers fumble over the digital keypad, retrying the code we've had since we married: John's birthday.

Focus, Tish. I take a deep breath and press 0517*.

The beep stops, and the robot voice says, "Disarmed."

It's been a long day. Relief washes over me as I step inside my house. But only for a moment. I realize I expected to see John sitting at the counter. The only things that greet me are my breakfast dishes from this morning, tossed hurriedly in the sink, unrinsed.

Unwanted, my mind flashes to another kitchen sink, this one cracked and stained, rust circling the drain. My momma stands at the sink, her back to me, a pile of dishes stacked on the counter on either side of her. I was seven or eight years old, and I remember standing behind her, watching, wanting to help but not knowing how. On good days, my momma was fun and playful, and I knew

176

she loved me. On bad days, she was the opposite. I didn't know what today would bring, so my body began to tremble when she turned and spotted me.

"Terry Jane, what the hell are you doing? You scared me." Momma held a dirty wooden spatula in her hand, and before I knew it, she'd swiped at my bare leg, leaving an angry welt on my thigh. "You're in my way. Get out of here."

Shocked by the sudden attack, I froze, my back against the kitchen cabinets. Tears filled my eyes, and the dishes and Momma's face blurred. When the next swipe of the spatula stung my shoulder, I finally ran from the room. It was a bad day.

I shake my head. Enough of the pity, enough of the past that I've left far far behind me. I pick up the phone and call the cleaning lady. She'll get everything in here all sorted. She loved John. She'll be happy to help me. Well, maybe. A little argument we had a few weeks ago comes to mind, but I push it away. She'll come over; she needs the money.

"Hello, Sonja?" I am using my friendliest tone.

"Hi, Mrs. Nelson." She sighs.

"I need you to come clean the house, please. Like ASAP."

"No, Mrs. Nelson. Remember, I quit." Big sigh.

"You didn't really quit. You just left in a huff. I need you. Now with John gone." I pause and sniff.

"I am very sorry for your loss." Sad sigh.

She's cracking. "I don't have anyone else to turn to. Please. The funeral is tomorrow, and my home is a disaster." I run a finger along the kitchen counter. It's spotless. But I hate dishes in the sink.

"I will come one last time. Tomorrow. OK?" Resigned sigh.

"Perfect. Thanks. I'll likely be at the funeral. So, can you let yourself in? I'll mail you a check."

"I know the code. Leave me cash, Mrs. Nelson. Three hundred dollars."

Sonja is so demanding. So untrusting, too. "Fine. Make sure the sheets are pressed."

Nothing on the other end. Silence.

"Sonja?" I sound like I'm yelling. Of course I'm not. "Gracias!"

She hung up on me. She has some kind of nerve.

No one treats me that way and gets away with it.

CHAPTER 23
ASHLYN

I wave goodbye to Jennifer and walk to my car. None of this makes sense. My dad was healthy, happy the last time I saw him. Proud of EventCo, proud of my mom. He didn't want to go on a trip with Tish. He didn't want to go anywhere at all with her.

I slip into the car and lock the door. I toss my purse on the passenger's seat and rummage inside until I find it.

My dad's phone. I saw it in Tish's purse as we stood together in that terrible line of sorrow. She doesn't need his phone anymore. I do. I unlock it and see all his apps, everything he used to run his life. I open Find My Friends and watch as Tish's dot speeds through her neighborhood and pulls up to her house. She's home already, likely counting all her money. She thinks she knows everything, thinks she's in charge of everything when it comes to my dad. But she's wrong. He and I had our secrets, too.

179

"Oh, Daddy," I cry as I hold his phone close to my heart and the tears come again.

I jump as someone knocks on my car window. It's Seth.

I roll the window down.

"You OK?" he asks. What a friend.

"I'm fine, sort of. I just need a little space," I say. What I need is a little time to investigate some things.

"I get it. Call me. Or come over. Anytime. I'm here, whatever you need," he says. He squeezes my hand before he walks away.

I wonder if my mom felt like this about my dad in the early days, and vice versa. They had to. How did they let it slip away?

Or maybe it didn't slip at all. Maybe it was destroyed by a hurricane named Tish. Did she target my dad, is that why she ended up as his assistant? How did she find him, anyway? It seems like such an unlikely coincidence that she would apply for a job at EventCo. Her previous job experience, she says, was in real estate.

Maybe Tish had a plan from the minute she drove into town. And maybe that plan was to marry John Nelson, no matter that he was married, no matter who got hurt along the way. That sounds like Tish.

I decide that I need answers, and I'm going to get them.

CHAPTER 24
KATE

The sun has set, and I'm alone on the couch in the family room. I can hear the neighborhood kids outside, riding bikes, playing hide and seek, jumping on trampolines, their sweaty summer faces tanned and so joyful.

Meanwhile, my house is silent and dark. I still cannot quite believe the way all of this has unfolded, all that has happened. I tried to pretend my life with John was perfect. But sure, there were issues. I never did anything to him like he did to me. I never pushed him aside for a younger model, never flaunted a new version of him in front of the company.

I stand up and shake myself out of the past. I tried to do some Pilates this evening, my home reformer usually provides stress release. But tonight, I didn't have the heart. I touch the top of a silver picture frame. I know the photo all too well: John, Ashlyn, and me at Disneyland, smiling, holding hands. Ashlyn's grin is as large as the lollipop in her hand. We did have fun together. It wasn't all business.

I hear Ashlyn walk into the family room. She's dressed in a tie-dye T-shirt and jean shorts, her long blonde hair spilling over her shoulder in waves.

"Mom, what are you doing in here in the dark?" Ashlyn pushes a button on her phone and the room is alight — the oversize chandelier, the sconces, the table lamps, and the ceiling track lights, all at the perfect evening brightness.

The light hurts. Everything about the past week haunts me when I am alone. The regrets, the decisions we are forced to make. It was all so simple before that woman tore us apart.

Her hand touches my shoulder. "I'm sorry Dad left you for that . . . that woman. Left both of us. I understand now how hard it must have been for you." Ashlyn is being kind. Maybe she's beginning to understand the truth.

I look up at my daughter. I pat the hand on my shoulder with my own. "I was just reminiscing. We were good together. I'll always —"

Ashlyn interjects, finishing my sentence. "Always love him. I know. Me, too."

"Honey, we need to discuss our next steps."

"What do you mean, next steps?" She gives me a look like you would a child who has surprised herself by saying her first word, half disbelief and half wonder.

"You and I are business partners now. You receive your dad's shares in the company with his death. I made sure everything was sorted during the divorce, and Dad and I made a few other moves to protect your interest a few weeks ago. Tish may have stolen your dad away, and some of his money, but she won't get anything else." An image of John dissolving into ashes fills my mind. I shudder.

"Tish said she's running the company now. She told me that in the parking lot after the memorial service," my daughter says, repeating what Tish must have told her. I would never let that happen. Tish has no role here. I've made sure of it. I would never be wrong about something this important. I'm much too careful.

"She's crazy. The law says she is only entitled to whatever he made during their three years of marriage, any property in her name, and personal items like jewelry. She'll get a lot of money but otherwise, we're finished with her. I have a copy of your dad's will and trust. It's in the safe. I can show it to you. The shares go to you. We both made that a stipulation of our wills. He wouldn't change that. He gave me his word. It's all taken care of. The company and more."

"I hope so. I'm going out. I won't be late." Ashlyn holds up her hand as I'm about to remind her the funeral is early tomorrow. "I won't miss the funeral. Don't worry. Are they sliding Dad's ashes in a drawer or something? How does it work? This is all so stupid. So gross."

Her words are sharp, but tears swim in her eyes. I really don't know how it will all work tomorrow — the funeral arrangements were handled by Tish, the interloper.

"It is." I turn away so my daughter cannot see the fury on my face. Even though John and I spent twenty-three years together, I'm not the one planning his funeral. It should have been me. I cannot wait for this to be over. It's time to get back to work.

"I'll see you in the morning," I say. "I love you."

"I love you, too. And don't wait up. You need some sleep." Ashlyn walks out of the room without saying another word. Which is probably for the best. For years we've been fighting, or as my therapist explains,

Ashlyn has been asserting her independence. I think it's more than that. She's independent but confused. She feels abandoned by her dad, confused because when she was sixteen, he chose to leave her for another life, another woman not much older than she was. That's tough. And as she would say, it's gross.

I thought I would simply outlast Tish, truth be told. Once I found out about the affair, I decided to ignore it. I thought it was a phase John was going through and that he'd realize his stupidity in a couple of months and then we could deal with it through counseling. I was in denial, I suppose. And I also was wrong. Dead wrong.

I never imagined he would ask me for a divorce. I never imagined he would move out of our family home, never to return. I never imagined he would go through with it and marry Tish. That would be socially unacceptable.

Something in me darkened deep down inside when I heard about their engagement three years ago. It was like a part of my heart dropped to the bottom of a cold, black sea.

I didn't even know John had been drifting, but she did. And she grabbed him and held on tight.

I knew it wasn't a phase the night he told me he was moving out.

That's when everything changed.

I open a bottle of wine and pour a generous glass. It took a while, but about a year ago, my therapist and I celebrated my progress. I was no longer a victim, she declared. I had found constructive ways to channel my anger. I started developing the Forever project, a cutting-edge consumer portal for EventCo clients.

In the weeks before the IPO, John stopped by my office so often it was almost like back in our start-up days. He was eager to bounce ideas off me, and I was pleased to see him walk through my office door.

"Kate, do you have a minute?" He'd appear in my doorway without an appointment, Nancy frowning behind him.

"Come on in, John." I'd smile at Nancy and close the door behind us. He was in my territory, my office, asking for my support.

"I can't believe our luck. This thing is happening." John's glee was boyish and charming. Sometimes, Tish would walk past my office door, stalking him, somehow knowing we were together. John's phone would ring, and he'd have an "important meeting" immediately.

Despite Tish's maneuvers, I told Nancy to

let John in to see me as often as possible, especially if he was alone. She had a little tally going of his visits — proof, she said, he wanted to reconcile. I don't know what was in his heart. No one really knows another person, do they? I do know one thing for sure — if he hadn't married Tish, he wouldn't be dead. Of that I'm certain.

It must have been taxing, balancing Tish's many demands and the reality of working at the same office with me, all the while making plans to take the company public, his biggest project ever. There was just so much strain on his heart, already weakened by his high blood pressure.

All it took was a little something more to push his heart over the edge. The high altitude in Telluride was never good for him, it just wasn't.

CHAPTER 25
ASHLYN

I sit in my car, headlights off. I'm parked on the street across from Tish's house, the one she talked my dad into buying because she said the condo was too small, too bachelor pad. It was, I agreed.

This house is two story, four bedrooms. Painted white, with black shutters. It looks like a family home, like it should be filled with kids and laughter. But it's not. It never was. One of the bedrooms she called mine, but I never felt comfortable here. Well, I guess that's not true. At first, when I still thought of her as a friend, when all of this was new and shiny, I did like it at their house. It was decorated "soft contemporary" according to Tish, with all neutrals: gray, cream, and white. It was like walking into Restoration Hardware, Tish bragged. I liked my all-new bedroom, decorated for an adult in all white with a rattan headboard and cool woven lights. A thriving potted fern in the corner by the bay window and a cozy sheepskin rug on the floor. The golf course the house is nestled next to made the backyard seem to go on forever, especially at night and on Mondays when no golfers were out. So, that first year they were married, I did enjoy it there. But it got old fast. Tish would try too hard to make me talk, to connect, to be best friends. Meanwhile, my dad would have his hands all over her. It turned gross and uncomfortable.

I can't imagine how my mom felt at the office. I was only subjected to the PDA when I went to Dad's house, stays and visits that tapered off considerably by the time I left for college.

I'd been blissfully detached, consumed by college life: studies, sororities, and social life. Then, when this summer rolled around, my college adviser told me I needed an internship in my field, and Tish helped me talk Dad into it. I worked at the office all summer. I was watching, expecting to see gross displays of affection between my dad and Tish. But I didn't.

Things had changed between my dad and Tish, and between my dad and my mom.

Now as I watch Tish walking around in her bedroom, lights on but shades not drawn, a hot wall of rage surges through me. Who are you, Tish?

I remember back to when they got married. My dad was proud, and dripping with excitement when he showed me the marriage certificate. I just laughed at the name I saw there: Terry Jane Crawford. Birthplace: Pineville, Kentucky. Using that memory, I search Google. Nothing. From what Tish has told me, she left home in high school and never looked back. And then she was married to a dentist until he left her, and she also worked in Cincinnati for a bit. She's like a ghost, though. No electronic footprint until she became Mrs. Nelson.

I hit the steering wheel with my hand. I don't know of one single friend she has, not one other family member. It's like she just appeared. We don't know anything about her.

I type in "Crawford" and "Pineville." I find a forty-seven-year-old Betty Jo Crawford Roscoe listed. I smile. She could be Terry Jane's mom. She could shed a light on her daughter.

I punch in the number listed.

"Hello?" A smoker's voice answers.

I haven't thought this through, but oh well. "Hello, Mrs. Crawford?"

"Mrs. Roscoe. Who is this?"

"A friend of Terry Jane's," I say.

"Where is she?"

"I'll tell you if you help me with a few things. Has your daughter ever been violent?"

"What kind of dumbass question is that? Everyone is violent. Sure, Terry Jane can take care of herself. I taught her that much. She's not smart, but she can throw a mean punch," Mrs. Roscoe says. "Is she in trouble? Did she hurt anyone?"

"I think she hurt my dad," I say, and tears fill my eyes.

"Wouldn't put it past her, the ungrateful brat," she says. "Where the hell is she? She owes me. What did she do to your dad? Same thing she did to her stepdaddy?"

"What do you mean?" I swallow and lean forward. "Tell me."

"Well, it was funny, that's all. My second husband, rest his soul, dropped dead. Police came after me about it, but I knew who'd done it. Tish, that's who. The two of them hated each other, so I know she did something to him. They never did prove nothing. He died, and she was gone the next day." I hear her take a pull on a cigarette as my stomach lurches.

"What was your second husband's name?" I ask while I have her talking.

"Ralph, Ralph Dunlop." I can hear the

191

sadness in her voice, the pain. "I think Tish left just to make me look guilty, the little bitch. She tried to get me busted," Mrs. Roscoe says as I write her dead husband's name on a note in my phone.

"Has your daughter ever been married to a dentist?" I ask, searching my brain for things Tish has said, trying to find out what's true.

"Yeah. I heard about that, too. Ron Pleasant. Funny name. I didn't even know about it. He called once, looking for her after she split."

I type more notes into my phone. Tish acted so distraught when she told me the story. She said he left her. All lies.

"Look, hon, I need you to tell me where she is, or I'm not saying another word," Mrs. Roscoe says.

"I'm trying to figure that out. As soon as I find her, I'll be in touch," I say, and hang up. I'm not going to tell her where her daughter is. Not yet. I realize Mrs. Roscoe has my number now, but I'll block her unless I need her. My hands shake as I open my dad's phone. I fine-tune a few of the apps and close it again. It feels good to get a little revenge by talking to Tish's mom. There's a lot more to this mother and daughter story, that's for sure.

I type "Ralph Dunlop death suspicious Pineville" and instantly have news results. The first headline: Pineville Man Dies Under Suspicious Circumstances. The article from the *Pineville Union* goes on to report that Mr. Dunlop, age forty-five, had no known history of heart problems and dropped dead in his kitchen while drinking a cup of his morning coffee. According to his wife, Betty Jo, her daughter ran away the next day after they had what she called a small disagreement. The daughter has not been located. Authorities are investigating, but police sources tell this reporter the death will be ruled a cardiac arrest. My source says officers have been called to the residence regularly for domestic disturbances.

Sounds like Tish may indeed have had something to do with her stepdad's death, but this old news doesn't get me anywhere.

I type in a search: "How did Ralph Dunlop Pineville Kentucky die?"

All that appears is a link to his grave site. But a shiver of dread tells me more. I'm not giving up. One way or another, I will find out what happened in Telluride. My mom was right all along. She told me not to get close to her, told me not to trust her. I was an idiot.

But I'm not anymore. I don't believe a

word of what Tish told me.

I don't even know who she really is. I do another Google search: "Ron Pleasant Dentist Cincinnati." He is quite easy to find. I'll call his office in the morning.

Before I drive away, I find the Sonos app on Dad's phone, pick his Favorites playlist. And then I decide to go for something a little different. Metallica will do.

I can't prove Tish did anything yet, but I can dig into her past, among other things.

CHAPTER 26
TISH

I've picked out my outfit for John's funeral tomorrow, a simple, designer-label chocolate-colored dress. Sure, most people wear black, but I wear black almost every day. This little number is one of John's favorites. It's skintight, showing off my perfect figure. I'm also bringing photos of the two of us: our engagement in Telluride, our honeymoon in Rome, and a favorite selfie taken at the office with John leaning over my desk, just about to kiss me. So good.

That was the moment I got him. The precise moment I had won. He'd asked me to stay late at the office, to help him with a project. Sure, I thought he might have something else on his mind, but I was fine with that as long as there was an endgame. He was going to have to put a ring on it.

I'd locked the front door of the office, per John's request. I'd touched up my makeup and was picking leaves off the dying plant on my desk when the door to his office opened.

"Hey, Tish. Thanks for staying," he'd said, walking over to me.

I peered up at him through my thick eyelashes. "My pleasure."

Up to this point, he hadn't been too overt about anything. Sure, he never suggested a friend of his for me to date, but still, if he was looking, he could have any woman in town.

"I do need to send my mom a photo of me and my boss. She doesn't actually believe I have a job." That was a lie, but it worked. I would never send my momma anything.

"That's so cute," he murmured.

John leaned toward me, and I fought the urge to make the first move. All I had to do was lean up a little and kiss him, but I didn't. He had to make the first move. So, I pulled out my phone, held it out in front of us, and said as I took the photo, "Let's see that perfect smile."

I'm dizzy now, just thinking about it. There's nothing like that first kiss.

Oh, John. Why did you have to betray me? So frustrating. I stomp through the kitchen and notice the floodlights illuminate the backyard. A chill rolls down my spine. The lights only activate if they sense motion.

I hurry to the keypad and set the alarm. I know I'm being silly, a "scaredy-cat" as my momma would say, but I feel better now that I know no one can get in. Uncle George told me a lot of rich folks get robbed during weddings and funerals, and I for one am not going to lose any of this to anyone.

Outside, the floodlights have gone out. I take a deep breath, pour a glass of cabernet to take upstairs to my room. For some reason the heater has turned on, and it's pumping out hot air. I'm almost at the top of our grand staircase when the speakers hidden in every room of the house begin blasting some horrible heavy metal song. The wineglass crashes from my hand and red liquid flies everywhere, making splatters on the carpet and walls like a crime scene. I'm shaking as I try to remember how to turn it off, make it stop.

I pull my phone from my pocket and try to remember which app controls the music. The sound is piercing, so loud I'm sure my neighbors hear it, wondering who is throwing a party. Oh my god. I'm losing it.

Damn it. John loves all this smart home shit. I never paid attention to how to work any of it. Frustrated tears run down my cheeks, and I'm about to throw my phone down the stairs when I see the Sonos app.

I click on it, type in our usual password. "Your password has been updated. Please type the correct password." Fuck.

Now I do throw my phone down the stairs. The music gets even louder.

Just then there's a pounding at the door. "It's security, ma'am. Open the door." Damn it. The community's security guard has been summoned. I don't know how much he makes, but who would want his job? Hassling housewives and fining teenagers for driving their parents' cars too fast. Worthless sense of security, if you ask me.

I hurry and yank open the door, setting off the security alarm. Sirens blare all around us as the house is illuminated inside and out. My head is about to explode. Red wine is all over my yoga pants.

"Ma'am, calm down. Are you all right?" The community guard is looking at me like I'm certifiable.

"I can't get the music off. My husband controlled all of it on his phone. It just turned on. It won't stop," I cover my ears with my hands. I'm in a panic. I can't think. I need the music to stop.

The guard is in my face. "The alarm. You need to shut it off or you'll have all kinds of first responders here."

My phone rings. It's the security company. Oh my god.

"Mrs. Nelson. Are you safe?"

"Yes. I set the alarm off by accident. Please make it stop."

"What is your safe word?"

"Ashlyn." Ironic. His daughter is the safe word. If there is trouble, the panic word is "Kate." He thought that was funny, at the time.

"We've notified the authorities this is a false alarm. Thank you, Mrs. Nelson. Have a great night."

The sirens have stopped, and the lights return to normal nighttime setting, but the music is still blasting. "I don't know the password. John must have changed it."

"Can you call him? Get him to tell you the new one." He's yelling, and he looks at me like I'm an idiot.

"He's dead," I yell.

Just then the music stops. Thank goodness.

"Praise the Lord," the guard says simply while shaking his head. "You gonna be OK?"

"Yes, thank you." I close the front door. I turn to the stairs and note the wine mess everywhere. Sonja will be here tomorrow.

She can deal with it.

I'm beginning to hate my life about now, and that's not good for anybody. Just ask John.

It's one habit I cannot break. Every morning I roll to my right, and I'm stunned when I feel the cold sheets and realize John's side of the bed is empty. I have to remind myself John is gone. It's funny how much muscle memory guides us. I know, intellectually, he'll never be coming back. Ever. Yet I reach for him.

I don't want to imagine John as a pile of ash. But I can't help it. I do. I know he didn't feel anything, especially not the fire. I want to know if he felt the pain of a heart attack — the official cause of death according to the death certificate — but no one knows. Tish told us she was asleep upstairs. That she left John asleep on the couch downstairs, passed out because he drank too much. Poor John.

I make my way out of bed and into the bathroom. I avoid looking into his empty closet because it is a reminder that he is gone forever, the shelves holding only a thin layer of dust.

I'm brushing my teeth when I see Ashlyn's reflection in the bathroom mirror. She's already dressed in a black suit, her long hair pulled into a high ponytail.

"You're ready early," I manage before finishing up.

"I'm going to go over to the cemetery. I'll meet you there," she says, and there won't be a discussion.

"No problem. I'll catch up with you. I know it's a tough day, honey," I say, careful to keep my tone neutral. I don't want a fight, not today.

"You'll be OK getting there?" She is about to add something else but shakes her head.

"Yes, no problem." I check my makeup and decide to apply more. My typical minimalist approach doesn't cover the sudden loss of color in my cheeks, the circles under my eyes.

"I love you, Mom," she says, and then she's gone.

My phone vibrates on the bathroom counter. It's Bob Atlas, our corporate attorney and longtime friend to both John and me.

"Glad I caught you. We need to talk." Bob doesn't waste time on niceties. That is fine with me. Today, I welcome the business

202

distraction.

"Bob, John's funeral is in an hour." I take a breath and let out a sigh.

"Yes, I know. I'll be there." Bob sighs in return. "Can I give you a ride over?"

That sounds much better than driving and arriving alone. Corporate counsel seems the perfect escort today. "Sure."

"I'll be there in fifteen minutes. And Kate. I am so sorry. Heart attacks sneak up on people all the time. I just never pictured that could happen to John." He hangs up before I can reply.

John did have a heart condition, but he had been stable, on medicine for his high blood pressure. He was in great shape, and it was time to celebrate the success of the IPO. But none of that matters because the fact is, he died.

Everyone is sorry. Now he's just a memory.

Today, I'll likely be relegated to sitting in the second row of folding chairs at the service, I imagine, like a second cousin or a crazy aunt. But this will be the last time Tish hijacks my family's spotlight. That's a promise.

I pull on my black dress, add a strand of pearls, and slip on my sensible heeled black pumps. It really doesn't matter what I wear, I know.

This service is simply something to endure.

I'm surprised when the doorbell rings. Time seems to be slipping, speeding up, and then slowing down to a crawl ever since we received the news of John's death. Days pass slowly, but this, just now, the time between Bob's call and his arrival, seems to have happened in a blink of an eye.

As I hurry downstairs, I realize I'm grateful for the company, grateful for a friendly, familiar face who is on my side. I open the front door and a wave of summer air rushes in. Even this early in the morning, it's already a hot one.

Bob's salt-and-pepper hair is thinning but still covers his head, and his forehead is lined with experience, deepened with sorrow. I know he's going to offer the usual sympathy line, so I speak first.

"Thanks so much for driving me. I really wasn't up for going alone," I say, stepping out into the surprisingly warm and sunny summer day. Aren't all funerals supposed to take place on overcast winter days? There should be a rule about that.

Bob opens the passenger door for me, a black sedan that seems fitting transportation to a funeral. He slides into the driver's seat and doesn't say a word. I've found Bob to be a remarkably neutral business adviser. When John and I had disagreements, Bob would not take sides. Instead he would carefully weigh both points of view. I value his counsel.

I take a breath. I have told myself this will be the last time I have to see Tish, ever. After this, she'll return to wherever in the swampy south she appeared from, taking a large chunk of our fortune with her.

"How's Ashlyn?" Bob asks as we pull into the parking lot of the cemetery.

I've only been here once. It was when John and I picked out our burial sites. He thought it was practical not to saddle Ashlyn with any decisions should something happen to both of us. Like a plane crash on a business trip, he'd explained. I think, maybe, it had been Bob's idea. Something with the estate, but I don't know now. All I remember is the way it made me feel to be here, contemplating death in the middle of life, cementing us as a team for eternity, or so I thought. And now, we'll be using John's half of our crypt.

"Ashlyn came ahead. She'll be here." I answer logistics because I don't know how she is, not really. "Bob, was it your idea for

John and me to secure a burial place next to his parents? Are you the reason we reserved spots in the mausoleum?"

"Yes, they were going fast, and it's the best mausoleum in the city, but god knows I never imagined him needing to use it so soon. It's tragic. At the height of his success, this happens. Had he been having heart issues?" Bob asks the twenty-million-dollar question.

"You knew about his high blood pressure, but he was on meds, so it seemed under control. You'd need to ask his wife, I suppose." John never discussed his high blood pressure, never wanted anyone to know about it, likely not even Tish. He wanted to seem to be her age, not ours.

I clear my throat. "As you know, the last few months were very stressful, with the IPO. I think the stress, combined with the altitude in Telluride, was hard on his heart."

Bob shakes his head as he pulls into a parking space. "He never should have done it."

"The IPO?" I ask.

Bob pats my hand. "Married that woman. Such a fool. I told him he had it all."

It wasn't enough, though. I'm not sure what to say, so I just smile at Bob.

"Ready?" Bob asks. "Let's get this over

with. None of it is how John imagined it would be, I can tell you that much."

That much is entirely true.

Bob slips out of the car and opens my door, helping me out. I notice the parking lot is quite full, but I don't know if these are regulars visiting grave sites of loved ones or people here for John. I realize I don't know who was invited to the funeral. My parents wouldn't have come if they'd been invited, and all of John's family members are deceased. They're all here.

The cemetery has a parklike feel, if you don't focus on what's beneath. Mature trees, rolling green lawn, the oldest in the city. And the mausoleum where we purchased our his-and-her drawers are the most "requested" and "desired" in town, at least that's what the man told us when we reserved our slots. John's own parents have a similar setup. John and I had an awkward laugh about it afterward, the afterlife next to my in-laws. A girl's dream.

Bob is beside me, and while I'm grateful for his support, I'd like to step inside alone. Unsupported. Since John left three years ago, I've learned how to stand on my own. He forced the lesson. And I'm a quick study. I've practiced my eulogy speech in front of my bathroom mirror. It's short, sweet, and thankful: a reminder to everyone in attendance that EventCo is fine, even if our cofounder perished. Our *beloved* cofounder perished. I scratched both out. I'll say, "EventCo is in my capable hands, even as we mourn John's loss."

"I'm ready," I say.

CHAPTER 28
ASHLYN

On my drive to the cemetery, to take my mind off where I'm going, I call dentist Ron Pleasant's office. Dentist Pleasant has a nice ring to it. I'm surprised when his answering service puts me right through to him on a Sunday. It's not really an emergency.

"Look, I don't know what you want, Terry Jane, but you better leave me alone. Do you understand? The nerve of you, calling after all these years. Let me guess, you're in trouble again? Well, you've come crying to the wrong mark. I won't be fooled by you again. And I'm a married man," Ron said in rapid fire, like he'd been waiting to say this for years. He sounded anything but pleasant.

I suppose I do know why I was put through to him. I pretended to be Tish. I clear my throat. "Actually, Dr. Pleasant, my name is Ashlyn, and I'm calling because I think Terry Jane hurt my dad. Like she hurt

209

you, only worse."

I hear a big sigh. "Damn it. I finally got over that woman, and I don't want to hear her name again."

"She married my dad, and now my dad's dead," I say, and tears spring to my eyes. "I really need your help. You were married to her, too. Did she try to hurt you? Please help me. I miss my dad, so much."

"I'm sorry, I am. And I'm sorry your dad had anything to do with her. She met me, married me, I fixed her teeth, gave her a place to stay, new clothes to wear, and then one day she was gone. No note. Nothing. She didn't hurt me physically, but emotionally and monetarily, I was a mess for a long time."

"That stinks," I say.

"Sounds like I might have gotten off easy," he says.

"You didn't ask her for a divorce," I am speaking through sobs. I can't help it. I'm mad and sad all rolled into one. "That's what she said. She told me you left her. I felt sorry for her."

"No. It's the other way around. I had to get the court to give me an annulment. She just left," he says. The sadness in his voice matches mine, but the anger doesn't. Mine's more visceral, more raw. "I wish I could help you. But I can't. My advice. Stay far away from her."

I finish the rest of the drive to the cemetery wiping tears away. I'm mad at myself for falling for Tish's lies. And I'm mad at my dad for falling for her, too.

I park and look around. It's surprising how few cars are here. I make my way across the parking lot, my flats crunch on the gravel path leading up to the ornate mausoleum. Stained glass windows and heavy, dark wood architecture give the outside of the building a somber, church-like feel. If it was dark outside, I'd be freaked out.

I open the door to the creepy place where my dad will be buried and walk inside. Tish stands up front with a ghostly white guy. Behind her are drawers full of dead people, including my grandparents. I almost turn around. I feel sick.

Tish spots me first. "Ashlyn, darling, come in."

The first thing I think is she's wearing brown when she should be wearing black. The second thing I think is why did she cremate my dad. He has a drawer reserved. One of those right behind her. His whole body would have fit just fine.

"Can I talk to you? Alone?" I ask.

Ghoulish mortuary worker nods and disappears.

"How are you holding up? I thought maybe we could do some retail therapy after this?" Tish says. Her eyes sparkle. I don't know if she's serious or just messing with me. Or, worse, is she a psycho?

"Why did you cremate Dad?" I ask.

"We've been over this. It's environmentally sound."

"Why didn't you bring his body here? Have them do it?" I ask. "It all seems rushed."

"Well, it was rushed. Someone called the coroner's office in Colorado and told them your dad was a big shot, so they expedited the death certificate. It was such a hectic time it didn't matter to me who made it happen. I remember they thought I called. It was weird, but whatever," she says. She picks up a photo of the three of us and shows it to me. We're at Atlantis in the Bahamas. "This was fun, remember?"

"You didn't expedite it?" I ask, my heart beating faster.

"Nope. Not me."

The heavy door to the mausoleum opens with a moan. We both turn around. It's my mom.

CHAPTER 29
KATE

Bob pulls the thick wooden door open, and I step inside.

There's no crowd like I expected. The whole place is empty except for Tish, standing up front where the minister should be, wearing a ridiculously tight brown dress. Ashlyn sits in the front row. Rows of empty chairs face the wall of "drawers" where the deceased reside. I notice our two slots, *John Nelson* and *Kate Nelson* labeled in gleaming bronze, side by side. My blood runs cold as I focus on Tish.

"Where are all the people?" I ask. This is an important moment in the history of the city, certainly in the history of one of its most successful companies. This should be a state funeral, a moment to refocus everyone on the new head of the company. I feel my speech in my pocket. "Why is no one here? Where is the mayor?"

Beside me, Bob shifts. "Not invited. It's

private. Per Tish. It wasn't even announced in the paper. I only know because I still control some of John's affairs."

Bob's hand on my back propels me into action. I walk down the center aisle past rows and rows of empty seats and can't help but shake my head. John's friends would want to be here. This makes no sense.

"Sit wherever you'd like, Kate. This is going to be short and sweet," Tish says as I reach the front of the room. Ashlyn turns around, her face is grim, puffy. I slip into the row behind my daughter. Bob sits beside me.

I touch Ashlyn's shoulder as I turn my attention back to the front, the altar so to speak. I notice a row of four silver framed photos. Tish and John. Tish and John and Ashlyn. John and Ashlyn. Tish and Ashlyn. How sweet. Next to the photos is a blue ceramic pot. My brain registers: *that is John.*

Bob whispers, "Oh my god. Poor John."

I nod, my brain recalculating at the reality of it all, ignoring whatever eulogy spews from Tish's mouth. I can't listen to her. All I can do is focus on John.

In that pot.

He'd really hate that. I reach into my pocket and pull out my speech, my Dear John eulogy and company rally.

I tear it into little pieces and watch as they fall to the cold stone floor.

At least it's all over now.

CHAPTER 30
TISH

I watch Kate's face contract as I touch the urn. She clearly has a problem with cremation. I should have said more about it in my speech. I had quite the lesson working with the undertaker on this. Ashes to ashes and all. Oh well.

Oh, I almost forgot to bring up the brat. I say, "We all loved you, John. And now, Ashlyn has a few words she's prepared. She'll be the last speaker."

Kate looks at me and brushes bits of paper from her hands. She's feeling left out. Whatever. She's so dramatic.

Ashlyn stands and walks to the front next to me. She should kiss my cheek, hug me, show me some love. But she doesn't. Even so, this must be killing Kate, and I love that. I know I should not feel this way, but I do. She never was nice to me. Ever. And I tried, especially at the beginning. I mean, she didn't want to have sex with him anymore or else why was he so responsive to me? That's the thing. I did her a favor, really. What did she lose? Nothing. She has her kid, her company, her house, and her fancy life. She really needs to get over herself.

I pat Ashlyn's hand, a small but obvious gesture signifying our closeness, and take a seat in the front row. As I wait for Ashlyn to begin, I smile at the elegant simplicity of this funeral. I mean, the photos glisten in their silver frames, John's urn is masculine and respectful. The creepy drawers full of rich dead people throw things off a bit, but all in all, this is a nice funeral.

I remember I need to pay attention to Ashlyn's speech, or at least pretend to. She's reading from a piece of paper that's shaking between her hands. No composure. But that's to be expected. She's never had any adversity in her life until this. If you don't count the divorce. And you shouldn't. I mean everybody's parents are divorced these days. Her day-to-day spoiled life isn't even affected by it. She told me she considers it a blessing. She gained an older sister. Truth be told, she said that a long time ago, and I think her perspective has shifted.

She should stop talking. Tears stream down her cheeks. The speech is shaking in her hands. "I just miss you so much, Daddy.

I don't understand why you're gone."

I can't take it. I jump up and wrap my arms around her, preempting a move by Kate to do the same thing. I whisper, "There, there, sweetie. You're going to be fine. I'm here for you."

Ashlyn shakes harder. I hug tighter.

Kate is behind me. I feel her hot breath on my neck. "Let go of my daughter."

"I've got her. She's fine," I answer without turning around.

"Mom." Ashlyn shrugs out of my embrace and reaches for Kate.

Traitor.

"Step aside, Tish," Bob says. He's Kate's guard dog and for some reason, he is standing behind me. I didn't invite him here. He invited himself, I bet. To escort Kate. As if she's the poor widow, incapable of driving herself to this service when I'm the one who's the widow here.

When Ashlyn came early to meet me here for a special moment with her dad, I thought she was on Team Tish. Instead, she questioned what happened with her dad's autopsy. She should be thanking me for handling things so well and so quickly. Who cares how it was expedited? I thought she came early to spend time together, but really it was to question me. The nerve. I'm fuming. I really can't believe the little brat.

Wrong, stupid Tish, wrong.

It's my momma's voice. I hate that voice. I fight the urge to kick something since it wouldn't be appropriate here. I want to kick Bob, hard, in the shin.

"What did you say?" I ask him and can't help putting my hands on my hips. He makes me defensive, the jerk. Bob's probably just a sore loser. I mean, he still has Kate's business, but he lost the power couple of John and Kate. I know he bragged about that. I do my research. Don't let my looks fool you. I glare at Bob and lean into the fire. "Can you just leave me alone? You weren't even invited here. You are not wanted."

Bob stiffens. Behind him, Ashlyn and Kate are holding hands. I can't hear what they say, but I need to get over there. Bob says, "This is John's funeral. Everyone should have been included. Everyone."

I give him the stink eye. "Shut up, Bob." I push past him and reinsert myself into the Ashlyn and Kate lovefest. I'm beginning to feel I'm being unkind. But really, I'm just defending myself. Besides, it nauseates me when they are cozy with each other.

"Ashlyn, you did such a nice job. Your dad would have been so happy. I know he's smiling down from heaven right now, loving his girls." I smile and pat Ashlyn's shoulder.

"We should go." Kate takes a step away from me and then points her finger at me. "Back off, Tish."

Oh, Kate. So firm, so scary. I step to the side so she has the full view of John's urn, and our happy family photos.

I turn my attention back to Ashlyn. "Up to you, Ashlyn. If you'd like, we can go shopping or something, to cheer us up." See, I'm amenable.

Ashlyn looks from me, to her mom, and back at me. "I'd rather not. Ever."

Interesting. Seems she has turned on me.

"Let's go." Kate wraps her arm around Ashlyn, and they walk out the way they came, back down the center aisle without a word of thanks. Bozo Bob follows behind them like a lost puppy.

"Oh, you're welcome!" I call after them. "Lovely service, Tish. We are so grateful, Tish!"

Bob stops and turns around even though Kate and Ashlyn continue out the door. "You'll be sorry someday, young lady. This was pure evil, cremating John despite the objections of his family."

"He was my husband. My choices." My hands are on my hips. I fight the urge to walk toward him. I like being here, at the front, in the spotlight.

"Did you know he was going to leave you? He'd had enough of you and your games. He told me so himself."

A bubble of fear explodes in my chest, and I put my hand on my heart to calm down. He couldn't know that, could he? John didn't tell Bob anything. He's bluffing, trying to shake me up. It won't work. "You're crazy. John loved me. We were on vacation at our favorite place when he died."

"Oh, I know where you were. And I suspect John didn't want to be there. I mean, why would he go to the mountains in the middle of the biggest deal of his life? Doesn't make sense. Your *existence* doesn't make sense." Bob turns and walks out the door.

I'm shaking all over. It must be from the stress of the day. I feel a hand on my shoulder.

"Mrs. Nelson, we can handle everything from here." It's the helpful mortuary staff. Everybody is so pasty in this industry, doughy white like they never see the sun. It's creepy.

I smile. "Thank you, Elliott. I'm so exhausted. So sad."

"Would you like to accompany the cremains to the burial site?" he asks.

Just then, the door opens and Kate steps into the mausoleum. Maybe she forgot her purse or something. She is getting old, senile, and menopausal at the very least.

"I want you to know that you are not welcome in this town. Not near my business, my family, or me. Not ever again. Do you understand me? I am not playing around, Tish." She's pointing her finger at me again.

I'm tired of her drama. And she's kinda scary at the moment. But I'm not worried. I'm one step ahead of her. She really should just stop playing the game. It's over. He's not coming back to her, or to me.

"Let it go, would you? John's gone. I'm following his wishes. His new wishes. Cremation and burial in the meadow. I'm sorry he didn't tell you. That space next to yours in here, it's already been resold. Right, Elliott?"

"Yes, Mrs. Nelson. That's correct," Elliott manages to say.

"You are unbelievable." Kate stares down at me. I see the fury in her eyes, her face glistens with sweat. "You have ruined everything."

"Mom." Ashlyn comes through the door

and to the rescue. "It's time to go. Come on."

"Of course. I'm coming," Kate says, practically stomping out the door. Such a toddler.

I step from behind Elliott once Kate is gone. This whole time Ashlyn watches me, not her mom. I smile and mouth the word *thanks.*

But Ashlyn shakes her head and turns away.

Fine. Ungrateful brat. I'm finished with you, too. You're the one who should stay away from me.

Chapter 31
Kate

I finish washing my face and walk into my bedroom, dropping onto my bed. As much as I'd love to just sleep for days, I can't. I have a company to reassure. And I have a daughter to set straight. Ashlyn and I haven't seen each other since the debacle at the cemetery.

I've decided we will never speak to Tish again. That will be our rule. Our pact. She doesn't owe that woman anything. Neither do I. I stand up and head down the hall.

Ashlyn isn't in her bedroom. The door is open and the room is dark as I walk by. I find my daughter downstairs in the kitchen, drinking a glass of wine. She's become quite comfortable in her skin this summer. Confident in her young adulthood, in her place in the world even though she's still a college student. I never would have sat in my parents' kitchen sipping a glass of wine, not without being offered one first. We were a family of rule followers, we always did the right thing. I really cannot think of a time I didn't follow the rules, and it never occurred to me to rebel. Not until my husband left me for a woman half my age.

"There you are," I say.

"Here I am," Ashlyn says. Her fingers drum the kitchen counter.

I pull out a barstool and sit, resisting the urge to pour myself a glass. "Listen, I want to talk to you about Tish, about what happens from here forward. We can just ignore her. She has no relationship with us anymore."

Ashlyn smiles. "You've never had a relationship with her, so that's a pretty easy choice for you to make. She was my friend. At least, I thought she was. Now I know it was just an act. I was proud of you today, Mom. For sticking up for us, for Dad. I can't believe all you've been through because of Tish."

"It's been a lot. You know, she's not your friend. Never was. She's an opportunist, maybe worse. She used you to make it easier for Dad to leave."

"I'm starting to see that. She lies about everything." Ashlyn sighs.

"It's time to move forward, and with Tish out of our lives, it will be easier. Everything will be," I assure her.

"I hope you're right." She looks so sad, my poor girl. "I still think she did something to Dad. In Telluride."

I pull my daughter into a bear hug. We're a team now. "You're going to have to let it go. Dad is gone. We need to focus on the future. EventCo will be all yours one day. Everything I've done, I've done for you."

"Thanks, Mom. I know." I watch as her face crumbles with a wave of grief. "It just sucks. I miss him so much. And at the same time, I'm angry with him for falling for Tish in the first place." Tears roll down her cheeks.

I must admit this is something I've been dreaming of: Ashlyn holding John accountable for the mess he made in our lives. But there's no time to gloat, not now when Ashlyn is in such pain.

"I know this is all so hard. You and your dad had a very special relationship. I'm here for you, whatever you need. And just try to forget about Tish." I take a deep breath and exhale. That feels good.

"She's been my stepmom for three years. I know a lot about her. More than you even." Ashlyn stands up. She grabs a tissue from the box and wipes her eyes. "For some reason, Tish is convinced Dad was coming back to us, getting back together with you. It was kind of driving her crazy. I saw her unraveling at work. It was funny how she tried to sneak up on you and Dad when he'd be in your office. Or when you guys slipped out to meetings together."

I smile. My daughter is quite perceptive, I suppose. "Yes, your dad and I were talking again, building a relationship again, that's true. But getting back together? That wouldn't be something I would have agreed to, not likely."

My daughter's face falls.

"I mean, who knows. Maybe we could have gotten back together? There would have been a lot to overcome. But maybe." I lie, but it will make her feel better.

"It seemed like you were open to the idea," Ashlyn says. "As for me, I'm watching her. I don't think she's told us the whole story of what happened in Telluride."

"She's a liar and a fake. But you don't need to worry about her anymore. It's all over. We need to stay away from her. Just leave your dad's death alone. It was a heart attack."

"Was it? I'm not so sure." And with that, she walks out of the room.

My daughter and I are on the same page. She is more like me than I thought.

227

I slide back onto my barstool and reach for Ashlyn's unfinished glass of wine. I'm celebrating. It's such a relief the EventCo office will finally be Tish-free. I didn't realize how much I'd been holding my breath these past few years. How much I'd actually dreaded going into the office every day, knowing she was in the same space. Even if I didn't see her, Tish's presence was like a black cloud, bringing down morale. Employees feeling sorry for the president on a daily basis just doesn't make for a great atmosphere, or the best way to run a company. I tried to explain that to John, but he was blinded by love. Or lust. Or just blinded by Tish.

"Tish will be here every day, just like before we got engaged," John had stated, storming into my office after hearing "rumors" that I was hiring a replacement assistant for my ex-husband. "You just stay out of my affairs." He'd flushed at the word choice and then softened. "Look, I don't know if it was really you who wanted Sandra to hire a new executive assistant, or if that's just gossip."

"It's gossip," I'd answered, although I had been behind it. "It is the right thing, John. We cannot all three of us work here. It's too awkward."

John had shaken his head. "We've all *been* working here. Nothing has changed."

Everything, of course, had changed. "You are the CEO of this company, and you're engaged to be married to your assistant. Engaged, John, oh my gosh! I'm the president of this company and your ex-wife. It sounds like a sad soap opera. We are the laughingstock of the entire business community. I've never been so ashamed. Tell her to find another job somewhere else. This is ridiculous."

"You're ridiculous. Feel free to resign, Kate. Maybe a change will do you good. Tish's not going anywhere."

I still feel a stab down to my core remembering the conversation. He was committed to this folly, engaged to this young woman, enjoying his embarrassing midlife crisis. He was picking her over everyone else, and over our business interests. That's when I knew for certain our company was in danger, and I had to do something about it. I remember where I stood in my office, the smell of the lavender candle I had burning on my desk. I remember my stomach lurching and feeling as if I would be sick.

Most of all, I remember the smug look on John's face, the smirk on his lips. I'd never felt so enraged, and alone.

Back then I'd summoned up my resolve, balled my hands into fists, and said, "I will never resign from this company. It is half mine, most of the big ideas were mine. You won't drive me out with your stereotypical young fiancée prancing around with that obscene engagement ring. You are both a laughingstock. For the good of the company, you should get rid of her, or at the very least tell her to stay home and go shopping. I hear she's good at that. Spending."

Yes, low blow. I know now I should have attempted to stay as unemotional as possible. But the rumor mill, and my own daughter, brought me continual stories of Tish's excessive spending. It was an open secret. Still is, I suppose.

"You're a piece of work. Not sure how we lasted so long. But I'm glad we're finished." And with that, my former husband, the love of my life, turned around and walked out of my office, slamming the door behind him.

The War of the Roses, office-style, had begun.

CHAPTER 32
ASHLYN

I sit on the living room couch and search my dad's phone. It turns up a lot of useful information. The most stunning is the number of times my parents were talking, and what they were talking about.

I think they were falling in love again, despite what my mom just told me. He'd changed her name in his contacts to Mabel, an old nickname or something I remembered hearing. But it was Mom's number.

My mom's texts were flirty and supportive. They arranged lunch dates, and she asked about his health and made sure he was taking time to exercise.

It's sort of surreal. Their text exchanges were normal, as if my dad wasn't married to Tish at all.

But Tish was reading Dad's texts. Dad warned Mom as much. So of course Tish worried she was losing him. I would have.

I don't like how you're treating me. I know

231

you've been talking to HER. Tish texted my dad, just a week before he died. I won't put up with it. You've been warned.

And this, a few days later: How dare you John? I won't stand for this.

And about my mom, She's horrible. She's watching me. She's trying to break us up!

If I were reading these exchanges, I would have been worried about what my mom and dad were planning, too. My poor dad. He seemed so sad and stressed the last time we had any quality time together. It was lunch, a week before the IPO. We met for pizza, just like the old times. No Tish. No Mom. Just the two of us at our favorite table at Tommy's.

"You look terrible, Dad," I said as soon as I sat down. And he did.

"This thing should wrap up in a week, and then I'll get some sleep, some peace, have some fun again," Dad said.

"You and Tish, you aren't getting along, are you?" I said, and watched his reaction. He hadn't told me anything, but I'd been keeping an eye on everything at the office. When you're an intern, you have plenty of time to poke around. Tish and Dad weren't kissing in the hallway or holding hands in his office anymore. The horrible PDA other people in the office had told me about had stopped by the time I arrived for the summer, thank goodness. Whenever I stopped by to see Dad, the door to his office was closed. Before, it was open so he and Tish could flirt from her desk just outside his door.

"Oh, honey, it's hard. I have made some mistakes. I need to fix things, but I've got to get through the IPO first," he said.

My heart beat a bit faster, and I grinned like a he'd made a promise, because to me he had. I pull myself out of my memories when I hear the knock.

It's Seth. I open the front door and step outside, joining him on the front porch.

"Hey, how are you holding up?" We've been best friends since elementary school. His presence now means a lot.

"I miss my dad," I say, and a sob breaks out from deep inside me. "And I think Tish killed him."

Seth takes a step back onto the porch, pushes his thick blond hair back with his hand. "Uh-huh. That's a lot to unpack."

"You don't believe me, do you?" I ask, pushing the tears aside. I need to focus, find proof. I'll have plenty of time to cry for my dad.

"I do want to believe you, but that's a lot to process. I think you need a hug, Detective," Seth says.

The hug does feel good, but it doesn't change my mind. "Fine, don't believe me. I'll find proof. I'll outsmart her." I'm going to keep watching her, keep digging into her past. I need to keep pushing her until she cracks. And she will. I know it.

Seth shakes his head. "I didn't say I didn't believe you. If anyone can, it's you. But even detectives need to eat. Let's go."

I'll allow myself a momentary distraction. But I'm not letting this go.

CHAPTER 33
KATE

It's like any other Monday, arriving at the office before anyone else, having this place, all of this beautiful office space to myself. My space.

I turn the key and push on the heavy all-glass door. The familiar warning beep of the alarm system greets me, and I hurry to disarm the panel. That done, I inhale. Perfect. There are no morning office smells yet. No perfume fighting with aftershave. No roasted coffee beans competing with the scent of pressed juices and ginger shots.

Early in the morning, the office is my sanctuary. Even when John and I were married, when everything was still happy, or as happy as any couple working together can be, I'd leave home first. To experience this — a slice of solitude in the place I created.

Because when it comes right down to it, I created EventCo. It's my name on our first patent.

I reach my office and slip the key in the door. I didn't even have a lock on my private office, not until she came along. The locksmith rekeyed both executive offices again last week.

So much for listening to my own intuition: I protected my office, but not my marriage. There's likely something juicy in this statement for my therapist, but I'll tuck that away until later. I know what Dr. Ray would say: "Let's delve deeper, Kate, shall we? There's so much more to mine in that statement."

I remember the look on Dr. Ray's face when I told her John and I were having lunch together. And her worried brow when I told her I knew that when we were cordial, it was driving Tish crazy. I'd hoped a wedge between them would be enough to get her out of the office at least. It was just a week before he died.

"I need you to be realistic," Dr. Ray had said at the time, swiveling back and forth in her desk chair. "You can't control another couple's relationship. It's a dangerous proposition you're playing with here. You have every reason to stay angry, to *be* angry. You have every reason to move on. I'd hate to see you backslide here."

"But we do have business to discuss.

Sometimes we do it over lunch," I told her.

Dr. Ray shook her head. "No. That's a terrible idea. You'll never be able to trust him again. Stay distant. Professional, but distant. You share a daughter and a business, that's all."

"True. But what about forgiveness, Dr. Ray?" I'd asked.

"Yes, you should forgive John. But you also should never forget what he did to you."

I'd nodded but didn't say anything. Our session was over. And now I suppose I don't really have much more to talk to her about. I'm just not angry anymore. I drop my favorite pod into the Italian espresso machine and enjoy the familiar hum, the smell of the dark liquid as it swirls into the mug. Another simple ritual I enjoy in the morning.

Out of the corner of my eye, I notice a shadow down the hall beyond my door, and goose bumps tickle the back of my neck like a finger. My imagination has been having a field day lately. I'm jumpy, suspicious of the slightest odd sound. It may be because I'm haunted by John's death and especially spooked by the way she had him cremated. Was it John's ghost I saw walking down the hall? No, of course not.

It could be the unease of everything right

now, the tension in the air here at the office, everywhere. I take a sip of espresso to combat the chill spreading inside me. I can't fight the feeling of being watched.

When I turn around, Tish stands in the hallway just outside my office, looking at me with a deadly stare.

CHAPTER 34
TISH

Oh, hello, princess. Did I startle you?

I smile at Kate, and she looks, well, I can only say, terrified. I'm not certain why. I guess she's surprised to see me. She's standing so delicately in her fancy designer pants suit, sensible Jimmy Choo pumps, enjoying a perfectly brewed cup of coffee in her over-decorated corner office.

As for me, I'm dressed in my John-copying, business-as-usual all black. Black silk top, dress pants, pumps. I turn the handle of her office door and let myself in.

I expect her to jump back, but she doesn't. She eyes me over her coffee, sizing me up, challenging me. It's funny and appropriate, I suppose. Here we are, two equals, the two Mrs. Nelsons.

"Good morning. Do you have a few minutes to chat?" I ask. I'm accessible. Friendly. We're a team now, although I suppose she doesn't know that yet.

She holds her coffee cup with both hands like a vise. "I don't have anything to talk to you about. I don't know why you're at the office. Remember you resigned? Go back to wherever it is you came from."

Kate is feistier than I expected.

I take a step forward, my hands on my hips. Power position. "Everything has changed with John's sudden death. I'm not going anywhere. I'm family."

"I need you to leave. Now." Kate points to the open door behind me.

"Fine. If and when you decide you want to be civil, I'll be in my office." I'm about one step toward the door when she explodes.

"You don't work here. Do you understand? Get out." Kate slams her coffee cup down and splatters coffee all over her desk. I know it's hard for her to yell. She was raised in a *nice* family where children were to be seen, not heard. I know this because I had the opposite upbringing. My family is all about rage.

Therefore, unlike Kate, I know how to mask it.

"Oh, what a mess!" I say on my way out. I hurry down the hall of what I like to think of as Kate's World, her half of the office building where all her loyalists are housed

240

— sales and computer geeks mostly — and into the lobby atrium, the beloved Ping-Pong table's space.

I cover my mouth and stifle a yawn. It's hard to sleep without John in bed next to me. As soon as I closed my eyes, I'd see him, foaming at the mouth, fist clenched on his chest. I bolted upright, wide-awake, and stayed that way. During the night, my heater turned on and went haywire, too, adding to my misery.

My house went after me again when I was getting ready for work. This time, some ridiculous hick music switched on in my bedroom suite, blaring Johnny Cash's "Ring of Fire" at 6:00 a.m. The expert at the A/V and security company who stopped by for an emergency visit this morning can't seem to come up with an explanation.

"Ma'am, we've checked the system. Everything is as it should be. Are you sure you're not just imagining things? You have suffered a big loss. The mind can do powerful things. All the stress." He shoved his hands in his pockets with a shrug.

"I am grieving the loss of my husband, but what I'm more upset about is the loss of control of my house. I expect answers, not lame sympathy. Understand?" Had I been too firm? I think not. My house is haunted.

Focus, Tish. Lance's office is next door to John's, and I knock on his closed door and pop my head inside.

"I need to get into John's office. Can you help?" I blink, a damsel in distress.

Lance furrows his brow. "Yes, sure. We changed the locks last week, ah, after he died. You're just stopping by to clean some things out, I assume?"

"Sure, yep." I don't feel the need to explain myself. I step into John's corner office — my office now, the mirror image of Kate's except mine is larger — and close the door behind me.

As I pull out the black leather desk chair to sit down, there is a knock on the door. It's not Kate, of course not. I smile through the glass at Ashlyn. What a surprise.

"What are you doing here?" she asks, walking into my office without permission. She pulls the door closed behind her before leaning against it. "I want to make it clear we won't be hanging out anymore. We aren't friends. I don't even know you. Everything you ever told me was a lie. Remember your sob story about your marriage? Remember how you told me the dentist dumped you?"

"Yes, of course," I say, pulling open John's desk drawer and rummaging around.

"A lie. Ron says you left him. Without so much as a goodbye. He really hates you," she says.

What? How does she know his name? How did she find him? I slam the desk drawer closed and stand up.

"I don't even know what you're saying." I am furious. She spoke to Ron? I'm livid. I let out a deep breath as my stomach turns. "Can you just go? Get out of my office."

"Oh, I talked to your mom. She wants to know where you are. Should I tell her?"

"You what? How dare you." I walk to the door and face her. She has gone too far.

"I just thought I should learn a little more about you, Terry Jane," Ashlyn says. "Your momma was very helpful. She wants me to connect you two. Says your stepdad died under mysterious circumstances, sort of like my dad."

"Your dad died of a heart attack." I feel my hands clench into fists. I tell myself to take a breath. "She can't know where I am. She's dangerous."

"It's not fun when people mess with your family, is it?" Ashlyn asks. "How about you leave now, get out of town even, and I won't tell your mom where to find you."

"You wouldn't dare. And I'm not leaving. I have worked too hard to get here," I say.

Ashlyn laughs. It's guttural, cruel. "You've worked hard? You're delusional."

I don't care what George said. I'm beginning to realize I'm better off without her. Good riddance. I smile and touch my heart to feign compassion. "I know you're still getting used to the notion that your dad is gone, and you're lashing out like a child. But you're not calling my momma again. As for this office, it's mine."

She crosses her arms. She's digging in. I'm surprised. I didn't think she had it in her, not against me.

"You're wrong. You'll see. The thing is, Dad left the company to Mom and me. That was part of their divorce deal. You get your jewelry and some money."

Think again, sweetheart. "Actually, your father revisited his will just before he died. He had complete faith in me, and you're so young, too young to handle a company like this. He named me co-president, with your mom, should anything happen to him. And shockingly, it did. You're picking the wrong side here."

"You're only four years older than me. Don't tell me I'm too young to figure things out." Her voice wavers. I've outmaneuvered her. She knows it.

"You did something to my dad. I'm going

to prove it," she says, pointing her finger at me. "Your own mom says you're capable."

"She's crazy. She'll say anything." I need to soften my tone, even if she is accusing me of things. She's just confused, and sad. "Look, it's hard, I know. I miss John, too."

Ashlyn stares at me and shakes her head. I hear her mumble, "OMG."

I turn on the charm. "College is special. I never had a chance to go myself, but you do. Senior year is supposed to be the best. We can worry about all this business stuff after you graduate. I'll keep everything at EventCo under control. Sound good? Nothing works if my momma shows up here. Do you understand me? That would be a bad, dangerous choice. She'd for sure bring this whole place down."

Her mouth moves as if she wants to say something but can't. Poor girl. I wonder what's running through her little entitled brain.

"I don't believe you. I don't believe anything you say." She opens the door to my office. "You are not my parent. You never have been, never will be. Stay out of my life."

How dare she? She thinks she has power here. Calling my momma? Calling dentist Ron? She shouldn't be stirring up trouble she doesn't know how to serve. I'll have

Uncle George handle this. It's his specialty.

I sit down at John's desk. I wonder how long it will take to feel comfortable in my new role. I take a deep breath and look around at this gorgeous space. I think I'm used to it already.

CHAPTER 35
KATE

Sandra finally turns up with Bob by her side. I meet them at the door to my office.

"We have a situation," I say, ushering them into my office.

"I know. Tish is here despite the fact she signed the separation agreement before we launched the IPO," Sandra says. "I don't get it."

"She's delusional and dangerous for our company, and a major distraction. I'll take care of it. I just need proper witnesses. Let's go."

As I walk through the office, my employees wave at me. A few clap their hands. I'm energized. These are my people. I feel like an elite athlete about to enter the ring for the fight of her life. The undefeated champion.

Ashlyn appears as I cross through the atrium. "Mom, I need to talk to you."

"Can it wait?" I ask. "I'm dealing with Tish."

"She says Dad wrote a new will. That she's your equal."

"Impossible." But is it?

What has he done now?

I look at my daughter and realize she's scared.

"Honey, she's bluffing," I say. She must be.

"I hope so," Ashlyn says.

My heart beats rapidly in my chest as I reach John's office. My anger and frustration with Tish build with every step. And now, it feels something like rage. My therapist said rage is a dangerous form of anger: violent and uncontrollable. Maybe so, but I will put it to good use.

Chapter 36
Tish

As I sit and enjoy my office, I allow myself to dream about the future for a minute. Kate and I will settle into a routine here, or she'll leave if she can't handle it. As for the rest of my life, what will be? I think I'll sell the house, upgrade to a bigger one in a fancier community. I'd like a swimming pool and a tennis court.

That's it. I'll start tennis lessons. And that's how I'll make friends. Because right now, I don't have one. All I had was John, and then he betrayed me. I need to find a life outside of him. I sometimes wonder if I'll always be alone. That's what my momma said: nobody could love me.

But John did. He did. For a moment in time, I found true love.

I look up and Kate stands outside my door, a role reversal from earlier. How fun. I shoo her away with my hand and pretend to be busy with something on my desk. She is on my last nerve. Fact is, I found true love, but then she took it away.

Well, I guess I sort of did the same, but that's not important now.

Kate flings open my door and steps inside with Sandra and boring Bob nipping at her heels. It's suddenly a big old party in my office. I don't like it.

"You all need an appointment to see me. Come back later!"

Sandra holds up her hand and says, "Tish, please, take a deep breath. We don't tolerate yelling at EventCo."

I laugh and shake my head. I focus on Kate. "And what exactly do *you* want?" Although I can guess, I want to hear her say it. They'll all be so sorry.

Kate places both hands on John's desk, and leans forward. Bob closes the door and follows Sandra's lead, taking the seats across from me. They're so dramatic. I feel like they're trying to be intimidating, but they look ridiculous.

I drum my fingers on the desk. Impatient and irritated. If only I could get a good night's sleep, I would be much sharper, better equipped for all of this. My house hates me.

"What do you want?" I ask.

My phone lights up. George is fifteen

minutes away, stuck in traffic. I need to stall them.

I type Hurry before returning Kate's stare.

I focus on Sandra. "Actually, it's good you're here. I looked for you earlier. I need a job posting for an executive assistant." I smile. "I can see from the look on your face that you realize I'm a tough cookie to replace. But try. It wouldn't hurt if he were nice to look at. I mean that in the most professional way. Sort of like how John thought about me at the beginning."

"You are crazy, young lady," Bob the troll blurts out.

He needs to get out of here. "I don't even know why you're in my office. I didn't invite you."

Kate stands rigid, fists clenched at her side. "You have exactly five minutes to pack up whatever belongings you have and get out of EventCo. Do you understand me?"

Sandra moves to Kate's side and holds up her hand like a cop directing traffic. Why does she do that? "Tish, look, we know you've been through a lot and that you're still in mourning. But you need to go. You resigned, remember? I have all of the paperwork right here. Your employment was terminated by mutual agreement."

Sandra sounds like a kindergarten teacher.

251

I am tired. I'm frustrated, and it shows. "You are so right, and thanks for noticing. I am exhausted, but I think it's important after a loss like this to get back to work, back to the routine," I say. "The fact of the matter is I resigned my assistant position, but now I'm co-president."

Kate exhales. "What? You're an executive assistant. You don't have a job. You resigned your only position with the company. Get out."

"No." I say it calmly. Professionally. "Things have changed, and I'm not going anywhere."

"Get out of my office or I'll call the police to escort you out. Do you want that? Stop pushing me or I'll —" Kate looks a little menacing, I'll admit. It's hard to look menacing in dusty rose, but she's achieved it.

And why is she talking about police? She'd never call the cops. "Or what, Kate? I always win when it's the two of us. Don't you know that by now?"

"Young lady, that's enough." Bob points his old crooked finger at me and looks like he's the one who is about to have a heart attack. "I'm calling the police."

"Bob!" Sandra yells.

I thought we weren't allowed to yell at

EventCo? "Sandra. Inside voices. You know that."

Sandra says, "I am here to collect your keys and escort you out of the EventCo offices. I assume you don't have anything to pack up? Perhaps out there, at your real desk? But I believe you took everything with you when you resigned."

She should not be messing with me. None of them should be. "I'm not packing up anything. As for this office, my new office, I'm leaving it as is, to honor John. If you keep pushing me, I'll also take his title, CEO of EventCo, although as a nod to Kate, I was offering to be co-president. Maybe I just need to start over with a new human resources executive. There must be a million who are more qualified."

"Stop the nonsense!" Kate is glassy eyed, with a creepy-looking smile. "You will leave immediately. Do you understand?"

Poor Kate. "You seem to think this is your decision." I'm surprised she doesn't accept that John, my husband, gave me half of the company. Too bad.

"Young lady." Bob looks like he's having a stroke. Good. "Leave this moment."

"Old guy," I quip back. *Tish, take a breath.* "I'm not going anywhere."

Kate says, "Upon John's death, the company transferred to me and Ashlyn. It's all well documented in John's will. You're simply wrong."

Where is my lawyer? We have this all planned. He'd better show up. I take a deep breath. "You are mistaken. There is a new will."

"You've got to be kidding me." Kate turns her back to me and motions for Sandra and Bob, but she's still talking loud enough for me to hear her. "John would never do that. I have the copy of his will in the safe in my office. Bob, can you finish escorting her out? I'm done here."

Bob points a trembling finger at me. "You've caused enough trouble, young lady. There is no new will. I drafted John's will myself. You have no stake in this company. None at all."

That's funny. "Oh, Bob, you're so behind the times. That happens with age."

Kate holds her phone in her hand. "I'm calling the police chief. He's a personal friend. One word from me and he'll be right over."

"That would be a big embarrassing mistake for you, Kate. And such a bad news story for EventCo, am I right?"

A knock on the office door startles my guests, but I've been expecting him. "Come

254

in, George. Meet my lawyer, everybody."

My trusty lawyer trundles into the room like he owns the place, or at least like he's been here before. Which he hasn't. He did slip into the memorial service and give me a quick hug, but I didn't introduce him around. I thought I'd save the surprise of him until I needed it. And now is the perfect time. He's not one to be thrown off by tense situations. He thrives in them.

"Hello, all. Sorry to be late to our meeting, but the traffic coming up the interstate was just horrible. I'm George Price, Mrs. Nelson's attorney." George takes off his fedora and sticks a beefy hand out toward Kate, who shakes it quickly.

I know she wants to wipe her hand on her pants leg. She thinks George is slimy. And she's right. But she also thinks I am stupid. She'll pay for underestimating me. They all will.

"Ma'am," George says, "You must be the one of the founders of the company. Nice to meet you." He turns and shakes Sandra's hand. "And you're HR, as they call it. And you're corporate counsel? Nice to see you, Bob."

George is laying it on thick, full-on country bumpkin. Sandra is speechless. Bob is sweaty. Kate is stunned. I love it.

George turns to me with a wink. "And how's my favorite president doing?"

"Better now that you're here. There seems to be a misunderstanding." I'm acting like an executive now. Measured, serious, confident. "Why don't we all sit down, over there where it's more comfortable."

"Great idea. I'd love a cup of coffee. Double sugar," George says. "Do you have someone who can fetch that for me, doll?"

I almost don't stop myself. But I do. "Unfortunately, I haven't hired an executive assistant yet. That's one of the many things Sandra will handle for me."

"Until she does, maybe she could fetch me a coffee?" George says, looking at Sandra, who simply shakes her head and walks out the door.

"You aren't going to get away with this." Kate stands arms crossed, refusing to join Bob, George, and me on the couch.

"Listen, ma'am, I don't like your tone." George sits, the black leather sighs under his weight. "We're being nice. Why don't you try it?"

"Here's nice. I won't press charges against you, or your client here, if you leave immediately. John's last will leaves this company to our daughter and me. He would never leave our business to her." Kate's words are measured, superior. She thinks she's better than me. Better than George. She thinks she's better than everyone. Her superiority complex is so annoying. I know George agrees. I hope he's as good at his job as I think he is.

I put my hand on George's shoulder. "The only way to work through this little issue here is to show them the will. Go ahead, George."

"All righty, let me get that out." We all watch in silence as George fumbles around in his beat-up briefcase. It's probably pleather, I realize. I need to get the man some more professional pieces for the future. Just in case I need him to appear in person again.

"Here you go. You can keep this copy. You are the corporate attorney, correct?" George is so helpful.

"I am one of the corporate attorneys, and I'm Mrs. Nelson's attorney. The first Mrs. Nelson, that is." Bob takes the document and skims to the last page.

"Well, I'm the second Mrs. Nelson's attorney, so glad we could sort all of that out," George says. "You'll find everything is in order, sir. John made sure Tish was provided for. He was so very generous because he loved Tish here so much."

George has all the answers, and he's killing them with southern kindness. The proverbial honey drips from his tongue. As for me, I relax just a little. I finally have someone on my side. George is very convincing when he wants to be, and it appears he really does know what he's doing.

He points to the document. "You'll see it's all witnessed and the like. It's all buttoned up, and it supersedes any other wills. It's the *last* will and testament of John Williams Nelson."

Kate has been reading over Bob's shoulder. Her words are ice. "This can't be real. I don't believe it. That doesn't even look like John's signature."

George chuckles. "Oh, it's real all right, ma'am. You can bet your bottom dollar on that."

Sandra walks into the room carrying his coffee and hands it to him with a proper napkin.

"You aren't going to get away with this, Tish. This will cost you, dearly." Kate glares at me once more. "Bob, come with me."

"Oh, Kate, one more thing. Just because I want us to get along, for the good of the company, I want to give you a heads up," I say.

Kate's voice is ice. "You want to give me a

heads up? About what exactly?"

My face is flushed with excitement. "Even though the new will doesn't give her a penny, don't worry, I'll take care of Ashlyn."

"No. You won't." Kate walks out the door.

I yell, "If you need me, you know where to find me. Corner office."

George and I watch as they scurry away.

Once they're gone, I walk to the door and gently close it.

George takes a sip of coffee and leans back into the couch, puts his dirty shoes on John's glass coffee table. "Nice digs you've got here, kid."

I want to yell at him to act more sophisticated, to sit up, to stop being a country hick. When we got together last time, a week before the IPO, down at the Franklin County Courthouse, he didn't even wear a tie. I was furious. But I must admit his performance just now was quite impressive, so I bite my tongue.

"I've come a long way, Uncle George. A long way." I lean forward. "You need to make sure my momma keeps her mouth shut. Can you do that? Whatever it takes?"

"Your momma? You all haven't spoken for years. She has no idea where you are."

"Ashlyn called her. They spoke. Just make

sure she doesn't talk to her again. Understand?"

He's laughing. "Didn't think that girl would have it in her. But I hear you." He takes a sip of coffee. "Your momma will be told to keep her mouth shut, or else."

"My momma always did try to ruin my life. I don't care what it takes to stop her," I say as I stand up and walk to the floor-to-ceiling windows.

"She also called Ron, the dentist, the little brat," I say without turning around.

"Ron is irrelevant. Don't worry. Just keep your cool, and stay away from the daughter," George says.

I turn around and take in the incongruity of George sitting in this sleek executive office. I can't believe he's here. We're here. The weight of the situation settles over me as I walk to my desk. This is a big company. I'm now expected to run it. Actually, Kate will run it and I will help, like John did.

"Breathe, sugar," George says. "You look tense."

"I just need to take this seriously. It's a big job."

"From assistant to president is a big leap," George says. "Before you get too comfy as an executive, do you think you could make me another cup of coffee for the drive back?

One last menial task."

"Sure, George. As long as you call my momma while I'm making it."

"I'm already ringing her number, sugar. Don't you worry. I know how to put her in her place."

CHAPTER 37
KATE

As I walk back to my office, I try to keep my face neutral, the anger hidden. I don't want the team to see Tish is winning this little fight at the moment. The staff senses my mood anyway, and people duck into their cubicles and offices as I pass by.

This is unacceptable. I thought Tish would be long gone. I seem to have under-estimated her. A mistake I will not make again. Ever. I saw that man, her supposed attorney at the memorial service. He was the man in the fedora. This is a setup.

"Give me a few minutes, will you?" I say to Bob as we reach my office. "Read the *supposed* will. Come back in ten minutes."

He backs away, likely grateful for a break, and I close my door and walk to my book-shelves. I grab a photo from my display on the bookshelf — John and Ashlyn at a father-daughter campout when she was six. It's the only photo I've kept of John in my office because I wanted to remember this simpler time, at least I tell myself that's why it's here. The frame is wood, and the glass is thick. I stare at the image, trying to find a sign of his duplicity, a hint that everything would go so wrong. But I don't. I walk across the room and put my hand on the window. The glass is smooth and cool under my palm.

There's a knock on my door. "Come in." I don't turn to look at them. I know it's Bob and Sandra.

Bob says, "I'm so sorry. Of course it's a fake. The will doesn't even mention Ashlyn. But until we have a chance to contest it in court, we may need to just go along with them. We're a public company now, and we don't want to tip off the investors that there is an internal battle over control of the company."

I don't turn around. I don't want Bob and Sandra to see my expression when I'm not sure what is showing. "There is no battle. I'm contesting this immediately. Challenge it in court. It's a fraud. Start the filing now."

Sandra says, "Of course. We all know John wouldn't do this. It must be fake."

Exactly. I take a deep breath and turn around. "So, let me get this straight. I am supposed to believe that Tish owns half of

EventCo now, we're supposed to be co-presidents, and Ashlyn has been cut out. No."

I don't say anything else. Sandra leaves my office first, shaking her head. I will get rid of this upstart. Tish will not take any part of my company. Not now, not ever. I will win.

"I'm serious, Bob. I want you to personally direct the entire law firm. Drop everything else. Tell them I'll fight this as long and as hard as it takes. All hands on deck."

He wipes his brow with the back of his hand. "I'm on it."

"You'd better hurry. I'm worried about the value of our stock if word of this gets out to our investors, the employees, or the financial trades. It could be devastating. How did John let this happen? Her happen?" I walk behind my desk. The bookshelves behind me are dotted with photos, mostly of Ashlyn.

I study one from our last Christmas together as a family. My parents joined us in Telluride. The photo is of Ashlyn and me with my mom and dad, standing outside on the deck of our condominium. Snow covers our hair like confetti. John took the photo.

"I'll fix this." Bob is at the door.

"No, I'll fix it. You get me the facts. Now."

He nods and is out the door.

I try to imagine, for a moment, a staff meeting led by Tish and me. It would never happen. She doesn't know the first thing about our business. I only tolerated John because he had institutional knowledge and capital connections. Aside from that, I run things around here.

Once his affair with Tish became known, John and I had maintained some semblance of unity at work, aside from the first few awkward months when John would invite Tish into the meetings. That was something I put a stop to by pointing out those meetings were only for executives. John and I had made it work. I had made it work, for the good of the company. I wasn't happy about it, but I suffered through it.

But this, the two of us here in my offices, this will never work. I won't allow it.

I grab my briefcase, walk to my couch, and open my laptop. I have a new plan.

I search the internet for the law offices of George Price and find it in Pineville, Kentucky. I call the number listed.

"Offices of George Price. If you have a problem with the law, with the man, with anybody, we can help," the receptionist says. "Hello? This is Mary? How can I help?"

"Hello, Mary, my name is Mabel Johnson.

I'm thinking of hiring Mr. Price for a legal case, but I need to be sure he doesn't have a conflict of interest," I say. I'm winging it, but I need to find out more about this creep. "Does he have a niece named Terry Jane or Tish?"

"Oh, he sure does, ma'am, is that who referred you? They're so close, it's sweet. I think he looks after her like a daddy," Mary says.

"That's so nice," I say. There is nothing criminal about hiring your uncle to represent you, of course. My eyes glance at the signature page of the fake will. John's name has been forged, obviously, but I look at the witness names. One of them is named Mary. Mary Loveless. My heart beats faster.

"Mr. Price is out of the office today. Could I leave him a message?" Mary asks.

"Is your last name Loveless, Mary?" I ask. "I have some kin down south with that last name."

Mary takes a moment. "How do you know my last name?"

"Just a lucky guess," I say. I look at the other witness signature: Sarah L. Byrne. "Say, do you know how I can reach Sarah Byrne?"

Silence. I think she hung up on me.

"Mary? Hello?" I hang up. She will be

easy to find again if I need her. I look closely at the signature of the other witness. Mary acted so suspicious hanging up on me like that. For sure she knows Sarah.

I do a Google search and bingo. Sarah L. Byrne is on Facebook, and she lives in Pineville. Her sister, Mary, loves to babysit Sarah's kids. How perfect. The Loveless sisters should be easy to deal with. George didn't search very hard for witnesses for the will. One is his only employee, the other, her sister.

As I begin further research, there's a knock on my door. It's Ashlyn.

"Hey, I'm glad you stopped by. I'd feel better if you went home for the day. Turn on the alarm?"

"I'm fine, Mom. Stop worrying," she says. "Did Dad have a new will like Tish said?"

"Supposedly. But look at this. This is not your dad's signature. We've signed contracts together a million times. And these witnesses and the notary? Well, don't worry, I'll figure it out."

"I know you will," she says. "I do have a lot to do, so I'll head out. See you later."

"See you at home, honey," I say and turn back to my computer. I'm not leaving the office yet. I have things to do.

I call Lance, who answers on the first ring.

"I cannot believe I gave her the key to John's office. I'm an idiot. I thought she was here to retrieve some personal items, but she's sitting behind John's desk right now acting like she owns the place."

"She is under the presumption that EventCo is half hers. It's unbearable."

"John was better than this. He wasn't thinking right." Lance was John's best friend at work, maybe in life, since there wasn't much time for anyone else once Tish arrived.

I take a deep breath. I have an idea, one that had been forming since John's death but has become urgent now that Tish is squatting in John's office. "I am going to buy more shares of EventCo. In the open market."

"I understand why you'd want to, but no one entity can purchase five percent or more without triggering reporting," Lance says. I can hear the worry in his voice. "It's a good idea, Kate, if you can find a way to do it. Let me know if you need my help."

I don't need anyone's help. "I have shell companies. I can handle the purchases through them. And under Ashlyn's name. It's totally legal, but I know it would look bad if it was revealed to investors."

Lance exhales into the phone. "Got it. I

know you don't want an SEC investigation. That's the last thing we need."

I'm not stupid. Not when it comes to my money *or* my company. "The last thing we needed was Tish. But I hear you, I'll be careful. What I need you to do is to keep an eye on the unhinged woman in the corner office."

"I will. Sandra is, too. From my office I can see Sandra watching Tish like a hawk. She's working from the atrium, a direct view into John's office. That will drive Tish crazy."

"If only that would scare her off." If only. "Talk to you later. And let me know if the employees come to you. Tell anyone who asks this situation is temporary. And under no circumstances will anyone speak to the media."

"Got it. On it."

I work fast, buying a controlling share of my own company, just in case. At least I know it's a great investment.

Two can play this game. I stand up and stretch, roll my head from side to side. Only one of us knows what she's doing in the business world, and that's me. With the stocks purchased, I focus on the fake will in front of me. The notary's name is Angie Ball of Columbus, Ohio. Her office is just around the corner from EventCo. Perfect. As I walk past her desk, Nancy asks, "Where are you going? You shouldn't leave with that one still here."

"I'll be right back. I just need some fresh air," I say. "Call me if she tries anything. It looks like she's just hiding out in John's office."

I will not be outplayed. Never. Game on, Tish.

CHAPTER 38
TISH

George has terrible breath, like stale cigar smoke and pickles. I'm standing next to him, and I'm dying.

"I told your momma that she shouldn't take any spam callers. I told her what we said all along. If she tries to contact you, I'll take her house and everything she owns," he says. His voice has lost all the southern charm he used when Kate and crew were in my office. "I suspect she'll listen."

"I guess you can go then. I'm all set here." I smile and extend my hand. "Thanks again for everything. Bill me. I'll be in touch if I need you."

"This isn't over, sugar. That woman isn't going to just give up. She's not as easy to control as your momma. And from the sound of it, neither is her daughter." George shakes his head.

I lower my voice. "Look, I'm a step ahead of Kate. Just go. I need to look like I'm standing on my own two feet here, so you lurking around isn't helping. Stay away unless I call you. Get it?"

"Sure. Got it," George says. "You're going to need me. Be in touch, sugar."

George pushes on the glass door, and I watch him descend the stairs. I hope everything is as he promises. I don't want to need him again.

Because the thing is, some people stick around unless you force them to go away. Maybe Kate feels that way about me, like she was finally finished with me after the funeral and then poof, I appear in John's office. But you see, this isn't really about Kate, not really. I've already won the Kate versus Tish match. No, this is about me. My needs. So I'll stick around long enough for all of my stock shares to vest. Long enough to feel what it's like to be a big-time executive. If I like it, I'll stay for good. Power is sexy.

And besides, it's nice here. Not the work part, but the dressing up and coming to a spacious office and being the president part. That I think I will like very much.

I catch a glimpse of my reflection in the glass door. Not bad. In the mirror's reflection I see stupid Sandra is sitting on the atrium couch, and she's still watching me.

Whatever. Enjoy the view, Sandra.

I wish I had someone to go to lunch with. That's what executives like me do at this time of day.

Behind Sandra, handsome Lance walks into the lobby. I wonder if he's single. His dark skin glows against a white button-down and jeans. I've never dated a bald guy.

"Hey, Lance," I say as I hurry into the atrium.

He sees me, and his face falls into a frown. "Why are you here? What are you trying to do?"

"I'd love to take you to lunch. Discuss the future. Explain everything. How about it?"

"What? No. I have plans," he stammers. Weenie.

I ignore him and walk out the door. The adrenaline rush has subsided, and I'm beyond exhausted. But I need to keep up my charm today. Maybe I'll go home for lunch, get a little rest, and then come back. That way, I can avoid Sandra's never-ending stare. She's been perched like a bird of prey watching me. And if I leave, I'll look important. I have places to go, things to do.

In the parking lot, I see Ashlyn. What a surprise. She's standing next to her car just two spots down. "Hey, Ash."

Her eyes bulge as she shakes her head and

slides into her car, slamming the door. I hear the sound of her lock, too. Of course the spoiled brat drives a BMW, white, fully decked out. She crashed her first BMW at school, so we got her a brand-new one. Because that's what rich people do.

I walk fast, but before I can reach her, she backs out of the parking spot. She stops a few feet away from me. Her driver's side window glides down.

"Tell me what you did to my dad. Did you put something in those margaritas? Maybe the same thing you used to get rid of your stepdad?"

"What? What margaritas?" How would Ashlyn know about the margaritas I made in Telluride? I know how she knows about Ralph. My stupid momma.

"Dad's last night. You made him a big pitcher. He sent me a picture," she says from the comfort of her car.

She's lying. He didn't talk to her that night, did he? "What else did he tell you?"

"Plenty," she says. "I think I should call the police. I have enough to get them interested in you at the very least. A suspicious death in Kentucky, and now one in Telluride. I know you're hiding something. Maybe a lot of somethings." The window slides up, and she drives away.

Ungrateful bitch. She's acting like she has evidence of something. "Come back here," I say to her taillights.

I hop in my car and drive home on the side streets. I'm not following Ashlyn, of course, that would be weird. But I am taking a path that would lead me past her house. Kate's house. I see her car up ahead. She called my mother, and she keeps threatening me. Digging around in other people's business isn't healthy. In fact, it can be dangerous.

As we pass the country club entrance, dread runs through me. I'm not a country club kid, as you've likely realized. Ashlyn is the definition of one.

I push the accelerator and pull up next to her at the stop sign.

She looks like she's seeing a monster, but it's just me.

I wave as she floors it.

Such a scaredy-cat. She needs to be taught a lesson, and fast. As I follow her, I call Uncle George.

When he answers I say, "We've got another little problem. You haven't left the city yet, have you?"

"I knew you'd need me, sugar. Let me turn around at the next exit," George says.

"I guess I do need you for at least a little

while longer," I say. "It's Ashlyn. She's out of control."

"Of course she is. She's cut out of the will, her dad's dead, and she's got you for a stepmother." George laughs as he talks. "What do you need me to do, sugar?"

CHAPTER 39
ASHLYN

My hands shake as I call Seth.

"She's freaking me out. She's following me. Can I come over?"

"Sure, come now," he says. "I'm worried about you."

"Be there in five minutes." I try to think about my next move. Would the police even take me seriously with only a hunch and the photo my dad texted to my mom? There's just something about how sloppy drunk Dad was in the photo that doesn't make sense. He wasn't like that. He'd just launched the biggest deal in his life. That is not how he would celebrate.

Before he'd started drinking that night, he'd called me from the lobby of our Telluride condo building of all places. He told me a lot, but especially that he and Tish had another fight and it was over. He was deciding whether to leave Telluride that evening or stick it out one more night. He

277

told me he loved me and that we'd be together as a family again soon. He decided not to bother the pilots and said that he'd be home the next day. When the elevator arrived, we said goodbye. He sounded sad, but otherwise fine when he called me.

Whatever she gave him once he got to the condo, it hit him hard. I stare at the awful photo. His eyes are half-open, his face blotchy and swollen. It's clear he's sick. She had to know it. She had to be the one who did it.

I stop in front of Seth's parents' house and check the rearview mirror. No Tish, at least not at the moment. I open my car door and step onto the street. I turn around in time to see her driving straight toward me. I freeze, waiting for impact. I see my life flash in front of me, my mom, my dad, Seth. I can't breathe, and I hear a piercing scream that must be my own. I lock eyes with Tish, and she swerves away from me and screeches down the street.

She's gone.

A voice in my head tells me to move. I run up the front walk and try the door. It's locked. My heart races as I push the door-bell repeatedly and bang on the door.

"Hey, it's OK. Calm down," Seth says, pulling the door open. I fall into his strong chest as he closes the door. "What's wrong? What happened? You're shaking all over."

"She's after me," I say as my teeth clatter. My breath is shaky, and I'm dizzy. "I've stirred her up. That means I'm onto something."

"Slow down. Who is after you?"

"Tish," I say.

"Whoa. Let's go sit down. Start from the beginning." He pulls me inside and locks the door before taking my hand and leading me down the hall to the kitchen.

"I called Tish's mom. In Kentucky. She told me her daughter is dangerous, that she may have killed someone."

"What? That's scary. What kind of mom says that to a stranger?" Seth asks, pulling out a chair for me at the kitchen table. "I take it they aren't close."

"No, it sounds like they hate each other. It was eerie, talking to her. And then, when I told Tish I talked to her mom, she freaked. I've hit a nerve, that's for sure," I say.

"Take some deep breaths. You're covered in sweat. Let me get you some water," he says.

"Sure." I try to calm down, but my body is on high alert, like I dodged a bullet but another is heading in my direction, and I can't see it.

"You need to stay away from her," Seth says, handing me a glass of water. "Drink this." He hovers over me, tucks my hair behind my ear. I begin to breathe a little like normal.

"Thing is, I watched Dad and Tish at work this summer. They didn't flirt anymore, no gross PDA like before. Dad told me they had a fight and he was leaving her, as soon as he got back from Telluride. My parents were flirting. This is all so weird."

"Did you know he was leaving Tish, before he told you? I mean, so what if they weren't lovey-dovey? That goes away, I hear. And they had a fight, you said. Maybe it was the heat of the moment talking and they made up later, before he died." He takes a seat at the table, too. I look out at the perfect backyard, much like my own. Nothing bad is supposed to happen here, to us.

But it does. I'm still shaking. And I know I'm right. "No, they didn't make up. There's no way he was staying with her, and she knew it. She killed him."

Seth tilts his head. "We've been over this. Your dad had a heart attack. The coroner did an autopsy." He gives me a quick hug, like I'm losing my mind.

"She cremated the body, doesn't that say something?" I wish I could convince him to see what I see.

"It says she's not a fan of caskets. Taking up all that space. I think it's sort of green of her," he says.

I shoot him dagger eyes.

"I know you miss your dad and you're trying to find answers, but if Tish did something to him, the experts would have found something. That's what an autopsy is for," he says. "You should stay away from her."

"Yeah, I know. You're probably right. But I also know she's hiding something." I drop my head in my hand. No one is going to believe me.

I feel his strong arm around my shoulder. "You know what you need? A little gaming in your life. *Call of Duty.* Come on. To my room. You need to calm down a little. You aren't thinking straight. Let's go kill some twelve-year-olds online," he says. "It will make you feel better."

I can't even get Seth to believe me. I need something more. I will figure out something more. "OK, fine. Let's go kill some twelve-year-olds."

And after that, I'll figure out if my stepmonster killed my dad.

CHAPTER 40
KATE

I push open the door to a rather dingy mail supply store and walk to the counter. Dust covers the shelves where gift wrap and boxes should be.

"Hi. I need something notarized. Do you have someone available?" I ask the woman at the counter. She wears thick glasses and doesn't meet my eye. I almost repeat myself, but she flops a big ledger on the counter.

"I'm the notary," she says, flipping through pages without further comment.

"Angie?" I ask.

"Yes, that's my name. What do you have to notarize?" she asks, hand out.

The store is empty, and I'm glad for that. I pull out the copy of the fake will and slap it on the counter. "I don't need anything from you, but I need you to know you notarized a fake document. You could be in very big trouble."

She glances at the document and sees her

282

notary seal. She leans toward me across the counter, finger stabbing at her signature. "I simply acknowledge the document here, this last will and testament, was signed by this guy and these two witnesses in front of me. That's all. Don't you dare threaten me, honey."

"Do you remember these people?" I point to John's name, and then to Mary and Sarah, the witnesses. "What about him? This guy? John Nelson?" A shiver runs through me as I realize someone had to impersonate my former husband. I wonder who that was? How did he have an ID that worked? And then I realize it was likely George Price. "Did this John have a southern accent and a potbelly? Was he wearing a fedora?"

She finally meets my eye, and I see a twitch of acknowledgment. "You know, it's not my job to remember every person. I just take the ID and fingerprints. And the money, of course."

"Fine. Can I see the ID records for the two witnesses and John?" I ask, but already know the answer.

"A fancy lady like you already knows that's not legal without a court order. Now, if you'll excuse me." She grabs her ledger, slides it under the counter, turns, and walks away.

"This isn't the last you'll hear about John Nelson's fake will. Count on it," I say to her retreating back.

But she's right. There's no way to prove she did anything wrong. As for George Price and the witnesses, well, that's a different story. One I will be happy to pursue myself.

As I walk back to the office, I feel good about my newly strengthened position in the company. I'll have the voting rights as the majority shareholder despite Tish's power play. And soon we'll prove the will has been forged, whipped up to try to steal my company. What a joke. I decide not to go back into the office and instead to head home.

The sun is setting as I drive. I'm ready for Bob to tell me the will is a clear forgery and that they've figured out how to prove it. And I'll tell him what I've learned. Because it is. We all know it. I pull into the garage. My heart thumps in my chest. Ashlyn's car isn't here.

I text her: Where are you? You're supposed to be home.

She answers right away, thank god. I'm at Seth's. Home in a bit. All fine.

I'm glad she has such a good friend. I need that in my life. I fill a glass of water from the tap and chug it. I'm tempted to open a bottle of wine and invite Christine over. But first I need to speak to Bob. He will tell me the will is fake. We'll celebrate good riddance to the second Mrs. Nelson. My mind flashes to a powerful memory, the night John announced his plans at our favorite restaurant.

In retrospect, I realized he'd picked a public place so I wouldn't challenge him. So I couldn't make a scene. So it would be easy for him to deliver the news and exit the stage, leaving me to find emotional support from the waitstaff.

When you work as hard as we do, you come to discover that you only have each other and the people you pay to be your friends. The dry cleaner is a great guy; Jody, our favorite server at Lindey's; my yoga teacher; my housekeeper, Sonja. You have that tribe, and then of course, you have your family, and one or two loyal friends like Christine. That's enough.

John waited until our dinner was served; then he dropped the bomb on our lives. "Kate, it's settled. I'm moving out. I need some time."

"What?" I'd rested my fork at four o'clock on the white china plate. I remember the sautéed spinach and the halibut resting on couscous. "What did you just say?" The restaurant was loud. I must have heard the wrong thing, the wrong words. We'd been agitated with each other, short and unloving. And I knew about his flirty behavior with Tish at the office, their illicit romance, but I was ready to forgive him. It was a phase. All couples go through them — it's normal, typical. I would be the bigger person and welcome him back to us. That's what I'd decided.

John leaned forward and said, "It's over between us. I'm sorry."

"I don't think I understand what you're saying," I said. My mouth had grown dry. Everyone and everything in the restaurant moved in slow motion.

John's face came into sharp focus. I'll never forget the look in his blue eyes. It was a look of pity for me mixed with confidence. A decisive, final heartbreaking smile that burst across his face before he caught himself. I watched as he covered his mouth, brushed imaginary lint from the shoulder of his black T-shirt, and signaled for Jody, making the signing-the-check motion in the air.

"You can't just walk away from us. Everything we've created. What about Ashlyn? The company?"

"Ashlyn will be fine. I've already talked to her."

286

What? "You've spoken to our daughter about leaving me?" My god, he told our daughter first. How long did Ashlyn know the truth? How foolish I'd been. What a joke I was to my daughter. To everyone. What the hell did John think he was doing?

Jody arrived, handed John the check, and turned to me. "You can't be finished, Kate. You've barely touched your meal. Was something wrong with the fish?" It was then she must have noticed the tension. She grabbed the credit card from John and fled.

"Ashlyn will be fine. She's focused on her own life at college. We'll work out all the details. I want you to know this will have no reflection on EventCo, nor will it affect what we've built together there. We'll have the attorneys protect everything. EventCo is on a huge upward trajectory, with lots of investor interest. Soon we'll both be rich beyond our wildest dreams." John stood, reached out to touch my shoulder, but I pushed his hand away. A bolt of electricity shot through me. A jolt of realization.

My husband is leaving me.
For her.

I stood up. "Why?"

"The truth? I've found my soul mate, as corny as that sounds." John shrugged as he shoved his hands in his pockets. And then the diabolical grin reappeared. "I'm in love."

How can you compete with that?

"You're in lust," I retorted as he turned and walked out of the restaurant. I knew about their affair. But I never would have imagined it would come to this.

That he'd pick her over me.

And now he's gone, and Tish thinks she can saunter into his place. But she's wrong. She will not take the company I worked so hard to create.

Never going to happen.

I walk to the kitchen window and try to appreciate the beauty outdoors. The sunset's orange glow, the green grass, the new mom pushing a baby in a stroller along the sidewalk, the privileged peace of the suburbs.

But I'm not at peace.

I take a deep breath as the doorbell rings. That will be Bob. Bob will have good news.

And then none of us will see Tish ever again.

But when I open the door, Bob's face tells me the game isn't over. Not by a long shot.

"I found the notary. She's lying. We need to go after her," I say to Bob as I open the door. "You don't look like you found anything to help us."

"It's going to be tough," Bob says.

288

I remember that look in John's eye the night he left me. And the fire builds. "I'm tough. Tougher than she knows."

CHAPTER 41
TISH

I don't enjoy it when Ashlyn gets out of line. Sure, she's mad I was at the office, in her daddy's office, but she'll get used to it. And what about me? My needs. My grief. And then, she takes it a step further and threatens me. The nerve. Uncle George told me to calm down when I told him what I wanted him to do. Said it was a mistake. I told him to handle things or I'd find another lawyer. I predict he'll handle it.

I pull into my garage, but I'm restless. And hungry. I hurry inside the house, into the kitchen, and yank on the refrigerator door. I am greeted as usual by empty shelves. I need to learn this work-life balance thing now that I'm an executive. I need someone to do the grocery shopping for me. As I stand staring at the empty shelves, I feel the heat start pumping from the ceiling. I know what's next. Music will blast from the speakers any minute.

I slam the refrigerator door and remind myself to stay calm. *Heat is good for the skin,* I tell myself as I push open the kitchen windows. This situation makes me furious. I don't believe in letting ghosts get the upper hand. I believe in winning, and I will outlast this hot haunted house, and all of these people who are out to get me.

Nobody better try to mess with me. Not Kate, certainly not Ashlyn. I'm a step ahead, and I just may have a few more tricks up my little old sleeve.

CHAPTER 42
ASHLYN

I know Seth doesn't believe me about how dangerous Tish is, but he still walks me out to the car. I also know he wants to kiss me, and I'm starting to think that might be a good idea, despite the fact I'm going back to college in the next couple of days.

"Thanks for calming me down this afternoon," I say and reach for his hand. It's dark outside, and crickets chirp like crazy.

"You've been through a lot," he says. "I'm here for you. One of the benefits of going to Ohio State."

I wrap my arms around his neck, and the next thing you know we share a heart-tingling kiss. I pull away. "Let's take it slow. We've been friends forever."

"You're right." He opens the door to my car. "Hey, this isn't good. You left your door unlocked. Lock the doors. All the time. I'm worried about you."

"Yes, sir," I say, and I know he's right. In

my hurry to get inside his house, I forgot. I look around the front seat, and everything seems fine. "I'll text when I get home."

Seth stays at the curb as I drive away. I push my new confusing feelings for him away and focus on the drive, constantly looking in my rearview mirror. I don't trust Tish, but I know I'm being paranoid and I'm imagining things. Seth is right. She's crazy, but she's not dangerous. I need to let it go.

As I pull onto Lane Avenue, my car starts freaking out. My fried emotions go into overdrive, and my hands shake on the wheel. What is happening? My dashboard has crazy lights everywhere. I'm going forty miles an hour, but my car isn't responding to anything I do. I pump the brakes but nothing happens, the steering wheel won't turn when I pull on it. Ahead is the highway and a huge intersection. On my right is a shopping mall parking lot. I use all of my strength to yank the steering wheel. I close my eyes so I don't have to watch as I feel my car fly over the curb and crash into a parked car.

The last thing I remember is the sound of crunching metal, the airbag muffling my screams.

CHAPTER 43
KATE

I escort Bob into the family room, a place that used to be a refuge, but not anymore. Everything has shifted, nothing is as it seems. I need to focus. I shove the will, the real will, across the coffee table as we sit facing each other. I still don't like the worried expression on his face. But I'm not backing down. Bob should know that by now.

"I know one thing for sure — the John I married, the John I built a company with, and the John who is the father of our daughter would never do this. He wouldn't. This is his will. The only will." I slap the paper with my hand for emphasis, and Bob jumps. "He never went to that notary. He never sat down with George Price. He would have used you to execute a new will."

"I agree. There's something I need to tell you." He shakes his head and places the new will on the table. "This was filed with the

294

state one week before John's death."

"What? Just a week before John died. What are you trying to say?" I ask, and pull my cardigan closed to fight a sudden chill.

"I think it's suspicious. I mean they file a new will, they even added in a no-contest clause of all things. It's buttoned up, and then, conveniently, John dies a sudden death a week later." Bob stands and paces the room as my mind struggles to take in his words.

Oh my god. I place my hand over my heart and lean back into the couch. "What has she done?"

Bob stops pacing and stands in front of me. His suit is rumpled, his hair is, too, and there's a dark five-o'clock shadow taking hold, matching the color of the circles under his eyes. "I just wouldn't put anything past her, would you?"

"No," I answer. My voice is shaky.

"The timing is suspect. They could have filed the will and then set the plan in place to kill him." Bob stares at me.

My hand covers my mouth as I shake my head. Everything is in slow motion, like I'm watching Bob on a movie screen. "Tish is a killer? Tish killed John?"

Bob nods, unblinking.

This isn't a joke.

"You're serious, aren't you?" I manage, the words coming out slow and thick.

"It's possible, I'm afraid."

The realization that John may have been murdered by Tish is overwhelming.

"I need a minute. Can you excuse me, please?" I hurry from the room and run up the stairs to the privacy of my bedroom. What was once our bedroom. I sit on John's side of the bed and try to imagine his last evening. His last night on earth. I force myself to imagine Tish murdering him.

Oh, John, I wish you could tell me what happened that night.

And then I remember. Maybe he did tell me. His last words spoken to me were on a voice mail he left me after I'd fallen asleep. The night he died. I haven't listened since the morning after, since he was gone. I reach for my phone and press the voice mail from John. I hold the phone to my ear as I listen to his last words.

When I heard this message originally, I didn't think anything of it. But now, in this context, with what Bob has told me about the will? Holy shit.

I fall back onto the bed, cradling the phone on my chest. Now I know the truth. John doesn't sound drunk in his message to me on the night he died, he sounds drugged.

I'm sure of it. I need to tell Bob. I sit up slowly, push myself off the bed, and stand on shaky legs. I hurry back downstairs to the family room.

Bob sits on the couch where I left him. "I'm so sorry to have upset you."

"Oh my god, I'm so glad you figured out the timing, and I think you're right. It's just so horrifying. And you're not going to believe this, but I have proof that what you're saying is true. I have a voice mail message from John, the night he died. I really didn't think anything of it. Not until this moment."

Bob shakes his head. "We all were rooting for you two to get back together. I knew you two were talking again."

I am pleased they noticed. "Yes, we were reconnecting."

"I knew it." Bob's such a romantic at heart.

"On the night he died, John texted me. He was miserable. He wanted to come home and couldn't believe she had forced him to leave his own IPO launch party. He only had to make it through Saturday night. He was flying back here Sunday morning. So, when she served him margaritas, he decided to get drunk."

"I would have done the same," Bob says.

"He called me later in the evening. I was asleep. He left a voice mail message. He slurs his words, but I just listened to the message again. In light of the fake will, it's terrifying." I drop my head into my palm. "I should have done something that night to save him."

Bob's hand is on my shoulder. "Do you still have the texts? Can you play the voice mail message?"

"Yes." I hand Bob my phone and show him the text series. He sees John's selfie with the margarita and the "cheers" message. My text back that it looks delicious. And his final text. It's horrible. Usually she makes good ones, but not tonight. I'm just trying to get drunk. It's working.

Bob shakes his head. "I mean that's sad, but not really incriminating."

"I didn't think anything of it, either. Not until now because of the timing of the will."

I find the voice mail message from John. His last words as far as I know. I play his message on the speaker of my phone, causing a sour feeling in the pit of my stomach.

Bob and I stand side by side as John's strange voice says from the grave, "Hey, listen I'm uh, really, really drunk but I uh, just wanted to call and you know, say hi and well, I love you. I'll see you tomorrow as

298

soon as I can get out of here I, uh, I will. I don't feel so good. And, uh —"

"My god. It sounds like he's gasping for air. The poor man."

I look at Bob. "His voice isn't right. That's not a drunk voice. That's a drugged voice. I know him better than anyone else. Oh my god, she killed him. She poisoned him. She forged a new will and then she killed him." I'm shaking with the realization, the revelation of it all. "And I didn't answer his final call."

"You can't blame yourself. You had no idea what she was up to, that she would try to harm him. I mean, they were supposed to be on a romantic getaway. We all should have stopped it somehow. Long before he married that woman."

I have to agree. "But no one did. And now, John's dead."

Bob looks at his hands. "John sounds so sad in that message, and very drunk."

He's infuriating. "I know what John sounds like drunk better than anyone, and I'm telling you his voice is off. It's slurry, he's not right. She did something to him. I know it. You do, too."

I turn away from him and walk to the kitchen, open a bottle of wine, and pour us each a glass. I carry them back to the living room, hand him a glass, and sit facing Bob. I try one last time.

"I mean the will is obviously a forgery. John loved Ashlyn more than anything. And she is cut out. It was filed a week before his sudden death and leaves everything to the person who benefits the most. This isn't a coincidence. It's murder." My voice is shaking. Is it grief? Maybe. John was killed by his young trophy wife. How awful. I take a deep breath.

Bob stands. "You should know that voice mail wouldn't be admissible in court. But I am convinced, as you are, that she had something to do with John's death. That's why I brought this timing to your attention."

Good. "What can we do?" I stand up, too. Let's go, team.

"We move forward against Tish. Legally. It's our best chance for a quick resolution for you and the company and to protect the IPO," Bob says.

"I agree. Let's tackle the fake will first."

Relief softens Bob's features. He is afraid of Tish, I realize. He likes to focus on the paperwork. That's fine. I'll focus on her.

Bob says, "We need to prove John would never write this or agree to it. We take it apart piece by piece to build our case for the probate judge."

I grab the will from the coffee table and read through it again. "There is no stated position for Tish in the company here. It doesn't say she is co-president. She has no official title in the actual company."

"Yes, that's true."

I take a breath and calm myself. "This is all John's fault. He is the one who fell in love with the woman who killed him. And now she's after my company, too. I read will forgery is hard to prove and is more common that you'd think."

All it took was a simple search. According to Google, the people who commit fraud in these situations are the executor, relatives (second wife), or attorneys (Tish's guy looks shady). Abrupt changes to the will are a red flag (what about a completely new one?) and forgery of a will is notoriously hard to prove in court. Great.

Bob clears his throat. "Don't worry. I have a team of attorneys at the firm on this. Tish's attorney has given us notice of administration. We're preparing the objection now."

"What about that attorney? Do you think he was in Telluride the night John died? Did he help with the murder?" I wonder. But of course, we have no way to prove his involvement.

Bob drops into the chair across from me. "I don't know, I really don't. I wouldn't put anything past him. He's a piece of work. Owns a small practice in eastern Kentucky. They seem to go way back."

"He is her uncle, at least that's what the receptionist told me when I called today," I say.

"Kate, let me handle this," Bob says.

"You should focus on proving John's signature is a fake. Get legal to compel a search of the notary's ledger. Someone pretended to be John," I say. "I have hundreds of contracts, and the real will to prove it."

"I have hired experts, we're on all of this."

Good.

"I think Mr. Price printed the will off the internet of all things," Bob says. "We'll outsmart them, don't worry."

I smile. Of this, I'm certain. "I realize she's street smart. But she's not business smart. She won't get away with this."

Bob wipes his face with his hand. "Ashlyn has the best case to challenge her legally. She's a direct heir who should have received something in the will but didn't."

"Now we're getting somewhere."

302

"We'll file a civil action lawsuit with the probate court in Ashlyn's name. Ohio law considers her a 'qualified person.' " Bob pauses at the front door. "I'm not against trying to prove that young woman murdered John. But the first step is the filing. I'll need Ashlyn's signature on this lawsuit, as soon as possible."

"Have a courier bring over the paperwork when it's ready. She'll sign tonight when she gets home. She must be fed up with Tish, too. She sees what we see." I wonder, though, if she'll see Tish as a murderer? Because I do. And she is.

The timing of events makes everything clear.

Bob is on his phone, pacing again. He hangs up and says, "The papers will be delivered within the hour."

I walk to the kitchen, Bob follows behind. What Tish has done is stunning. I pull out a barstool and sit at the kitchen counter. How can someone murder another person? What kind of monster kills her husband for monetary rewards? Couldn't Tish just ask for a divorce? She must have been filled with hate. I can appreciate that kind of anger. I swallow as my imagination jumps to our condo in Telluride, to the deck where he texted me a photo of the drink. He had no idea what she had planned for him, that she would kill him that night. He knew the drink tasted funny, but he drank it anyway. To escape.

Oh, John. What a mess you made, and what a horrible way to die.

Bob looks at me, catches me wiping the tear from my eye. "Are you all right?"

"I can't believe I didn't see what Tish was capable of before now. John reached out to me his last night on earth, frightened, and alone, and dying. My god."

But I did know one thing for sure — he was finished with Tish. But she got to him first. I shake my head and try to absorb the reality of what has happened. And the fact we won't be able to prove any of this without a body or without her confession.

"I'll be fine, we all will be fine, once we invalidate the will. I can't wait to file that lawsuit."

"We just need Ashlyn," Bob says.

I check my watch and as if on cue, my daughter calls me. Thank goodness.

"Hey, honey, I need you home," I say.

"Mom, listen, I've been in an accident. I'm fine. Just some bruises and a maybe-broken arm."

It takes me a moment to process what she's said. "Oh my god. What happened?

Where are you?" Nothing can happen to my girl. She's my life.

"I'm at Lane Avenue shopping center," Ashlyn says. I can hear her crying. "My car is totaled. Chief Briggs is driving me home. Be there in a few."

"Wait, what happened?" I ask, but she's hung up. My head spins, and my heart beats so fast I can feel it lifting into my throat, choking me. I touch my chest with my hand and tell myself to calm down. Life can change in an instant, and does, all the time. I say a little prayer, thanking god that she isn't more injured.

"What is happening?" Bob asks.

"She's been in an accident. Sounds like she's going to be OK. I have no idea what happened," I say as we both hurry to the front door. "She totaled her first car, texting while driving. If she's done it again, I'm going to kill her."

CHAPTER 44
ASHLYN

I've never been in the back of a police car. That's all I can think when Chief Briggs helps me into the back seat. That, and my arm hurts. My whole body hurts but especially my left elbow.

"All set back there?" he asks as we pull away.

"I sort of feel like a criminal," I say. "But yes, all set."

I want to ask Seth to come over, but I need to figure this out first and make sure the coast is clear. I don't want to draw attention to him, point Tish in his direction, although I'm afraid I already have by going to his house. I pull out Dad's phone and open Find My Friends. Tish is at home. I let out a sigh of relief.

"You were lucky no one was out and about in the parking lot," Chief Briggs says. "And you missed that utility pole."

"I didn't have time to think of all of that.

I just couldn't keep going down Lane Avenue and plow through that intersection. Nothing on my car worked. Not the brakes, not the steering," I say, and the tears spill out.

"Oh, we know something happened," he says as we pull into my driveway. "The detectives are on it."

My mom runs out the front door followed by Bob. Chief Briggs opens the door, and Mom gives me a big hug before I warn her not to.

"Ouch, stop, Mom," I say. "My arm."

"What happened, Chief?" Mom asks. Her hand rests on my shoulder. I lean against her and feel safe. For a minute.

"We should go inside," I say, looking around.

We make it to the front door and Chief Briggs says, "It could have been much worse. Looks like the entire electrical system short-circuited somehow. We have investigators on it. They'll work with BMW."

My mom locks eyes with me. I nod.

"I think it was her," I say.

Chief Briggs says, "Do you want to tell me what's going on here?"

Bob clears his throat. "There's been some strife since John Nelson's sudden death. A bit of a power struggle between the first and second Mrs. Nelson. I'm sure it's totally unrelated to what happened to Ashlyn's vehicle. We'll circle back with you in the morning, Chief, if that's OK?"

My mom puts a fake smile on her face. "Yes, good idea. Ashlyn's been through a lot tonight. We'll let her rest and talk in the morning?"

"We've had her car towed to the dealership. They'll give me an official diagnostic report of what happened to the car as soon as possible. You'll all be OK tonight?" Chief Briggs looks at me and then at my mom. "We could have a squad car add extra surveillance."

"Oh, thank you, but we'll be fine. Why don't you call me when you have the report from the dealership and we'll go from there? You have my number." Mom opens the door. "Thank you for taking care of her."

"No problem. You should get that arm checked out, Ashlyn," he says. "Talk tomorrow."

My mom shuts the door and locks it. The look on her face tells me she's as scared as I am. But there's something else. Rage. I can feel it pouring out of her, I can see it in her eyes. I guess I can feel that anger as well.

How dare Tish do this to all of us?

Mom yells, "Get that paperwork here,

Bob. Now!"

What is she talking about? "Mom, calm down. We don't know for sure if she had anything to do with my car. What paperwork are you talking about?" I realize how upset my mom is because she never yells. This is not just about my accident. Maybe Mom knows even more than I do about what Tish has done? I saw her eyes when she almost ran me over. I know what she's capable of. She's evil. "Mom, what's happening?"

"She's gone too far," Mom says, her fists clenched at her sides.

CHAPTER 45
KATE

"Go sit down in the family room," I say to Ashlyn. "And I'll get you some Tylenol."

Bob says, "I'm going to give you guys space. I'll be in the front room, waiting for the courier."

I settle Ashlyn on the couch, bring her the medicine and a glass of water. She isn't shaking anymore, but she looks like she may be in shock.

"She did this, Mom," Ashlyn says.

"How do you know that?" I ask, hoping for proof.

"She followed me from the office, to Seth's house," she says. "She swerved at me, drove straight toward me to scare me. She came really close. I thought that's all she would do, but I guess not."

"It would take a lot of nerve to tamper with your car. On a public street?"

"I don't know how, but I know she did." Ashlyn starts to cry, and my heart breaks.

310

I have to tell her the truth, no matter how much I don't want to. She'll be traumatized again, but she must know what I've realized.

"I need to share some things with you about the company, and about your dad. They may be hard to hear." I take a deep breath and exhale, my nerves zinging through me. "I believe Tish had something to do with your father's death."

"I do, too, Mom." Ashlyn stares at me. I take her hand in mine.

"Really? You do? Here I thought I was protecting you. I didn't want to worry you with this, but you are an adult and part of the company now." I pull out the phone and hand it to her. I watch as she reads the text chain from the night John died, including the photo of the margarita.

Ashlyn looks at me. "I've read these."

"What? How?" I feel my face flush. If she's read these, she's read everything I wrote, too.

"I took Dad's phone," she says, and breaks into a smile.

"Well, aren't you a tricky one. How did you get it?" I ask.

"I took it out of Tish's purse during the memorial service," she says.

"You've had it all this time. Wow."

"I had to keep track of her for us, you

311

know," she says. "And I can with Find My Friends."

"That's brilliant, really," I say. All this time Ashlyn has been on my side, helping me. Well, actually, she's been one step ahead of me. I wonder what else she's done? What else does she know? "Have you found anything else helpful on the phone?"

"Not too much, I guess. I know from reading his text messages that Dad was drinking to get through the night. He couldn't wait to get away from Tish, and he told her as much. He should have left that night. He stayed because of loyalty or something."

"I'm convinced she put something in your dad's drink." I won't play the voice mail message for her. Not now, maybe not ever. I don't want her to remember him, his voice, like that.

Ashlyn slumps back on the couch, exhausted.

"It's so scary. I actually can imagine Tish doing that, too," she says. "You should have seen the crazy look on her face this afternoon."

"It is hard to believe, but the truth was right in front of us. She's a murderer." The words spill out of my mouth. "I can't believe I didn't put it all together sooner. And now, she's trying to hurt you."

"So you believe me?" Ashlyn says.

"Of course. We need to be more careful, until we get rid of her for good. Bob and I have something we need you to do."

"Sure, OK, but why didn't you tell Chief Briggs all of this? Maybe have him keep an eye on her?"

"We just really don't have enough evidence, but I will if we can get more proof. In the meantime, I'm focused on getting Tish out of the company, and on nullifying that new ridiculous will. Bob's waiting for the papers. Unfortunately, from a legal standpoint, the best person to contest the will is you, honey."

"Tish is going to love that. Not. Why me?" Ashlyn asks. I hear the fear in her voice. She sounds exhausted.

I hold her hand. "Trust me, I'd do it if I could, but you are your father's only direct descendent. Are you up for it?"

The doorbell rings before she can answer. I expect it to be the courier, and I hear Bob answer the door. He carries the paperwork into the family room. I grab a pen from my purse and hand it to Ashlyn.

"Here it is, honey. Take your time, read it over. And then sign if you are comfortable. This is all about your inheritance."

She lifts her head and nods.

"I don't need to read it," she says, and signs her name on the last page. "I trust you. And we need to get rid of her before she does something else."

I hand the signed paperwork to Bob and follow him to the front door.

"I'm filing immediately. Lock the door and turn on the alarm. Call if you need anything. Actually, call Briggs first."

I return to my daughter. "Once this lawsuit is filed, Tish will know you are the one challenging the will."

Ashlyn wipes under her eyes. "I don't care about that. I want to know if she killed my dad."

"I know. We'll get to the bottom of all of this. Just remember, you meant the whole world to your dad. He would never cut you out of the will. That's when I started thinking about the timing of everything. I remembered the texts. Even I didn't realize how desperate he sounded until I read through them again. Combined with the filing date of the fake will, well, it's undeniable."

Ashlyn's breath catches in her chest. "I could see it, I mean, I can see it now. Oh my god. She thought Dad was leaving her to come back home. And you and Dad were flirting."

"I'm embarrassed you read all of that," I say and pivot to the task at hand. "We need some sort of concrete evidence against Tish."

"I can look around her house. I spent a lot of time over there, remember?" Ashlyn stands up. "I need to move all of my stuff out anyway."

"That's too dangerous. She may have tampered with your car. Once we file the lawsuit, she'll blame you for everything."

"Then I need to go now." Ashlyn takes a deep breath as tears well up in her eyes. "It's going to be hard with all of Dad's things still there. But I need to do it now or who knows what she'll do to all my high school treasures."

"What will you tell her about why you're just showing up?"

Ashlyn leans against the counter holding her arm. I think she needs a doctor. "I am telling her I'm moving out. That she and I don't have a relationship any longer now that Dad is gone. And I'll look around. I just don't know what I'll find, if anything. Or what I'm looking for."

I watch as Ashlyn pulls out her phone and texts.

"Are you texting Tish?"

"No, I'd rather surprise her. I'm texting

Seth. I'll need a ride."

"I don't think you should involve anybody else, do you?" I say.

"He's already involved. I was at his house all afternoon," she says, blushing.

"Seth, huh?" I smile. "I like him. You two are cute together."

"We're just friends, OK?"

I realize something more is developing. "Sure. Friends," I say. "I'm going to see if the doctor can make a house call tonight, what do you think?"

"Bonnie makes house calls? She's your doctor, right? The naturopath?" she asks. "I remember I liked her."

"Well, no, I was going to call an orthopedist. Dr. Bonnie is great for herbs and potions and balancing your chakras. Not sure she can do anything for bones," I answer, wondering why this sudden interest in a doctor Ashlyn hasn't seen for years.

"Dad was taking some sort of pills from her, wasn't he?" she asks.

"Oh, right, for stress. You saw that on the texts on his phone," I say, finally figuring out where she remembered the name. "Bonnie is great. But I'll call an orthopedist for this."

"Doctors can't really do anything for broken elbows. I googled it. Let's give it

316

some time," Ashlyn says. "I feel fine. Just a little sore. Seth will be here in ten minutes."

"I'll follow and park on the street. I'll be there ready to run inside if anything happens," I say. "What if she isn't home?"

"She's home," Ashlyn says holding up John's phone.

"Right, I forgot," I say. My daughter is brilliant.

"I've actually been having some fun with all the apps on Dad's phone. Did you know I can control the lights, the heat and cooling, the music — all from here, at all times of the day and night. It must be driving her crazy, the loss of control," Ashlyn says.

"I can't even imagine how frustrating that would be. She said she'd been having trouble sleeping. Great job," I say, pride swelling in my heart. Like mother, like daughter. "Seriously, though, you need to be so very careful over there."

"I'll be fine. Seth will be there. She thinks she's won. She thinks she scared me away."

"But then you show up on her doorstep, and she'll know the scare tactics didn't work. She might have murdered your father. I can't have anything happen to you. You're my favorite daughter."

"I'm your only daughter. And if you're right about Tish, if she killed Dad, she needs

317

to pay. I need to go before she finds out I filed a lawsuit." Ashlyn takes a breath and walks to the front door, cradling her left arm as Seth pulls up. We watch as he sprints up the front walk.

"What's going on? Did she do something? What's wrong with your arm?" Seth says, looking between Ashlyn and me.

"I'll fill you in on the drive," she says.

"Take care of her, Seth," I say.

"I will, Mrs. Nelson."

Ashlyn and Seth are out the door. I hurry to my car and follow my daughter.

Bob calls as I'm driving.

"I want you and Ashlyn to keep away from Tish. She's a dangerous young woman." Bob doesn't need to know we're headed to her house.

"We're fine. We know who she is now." I keep my eyes on Seth's truck, careful to not let anyone come between my daughter and me. No one will, not ever again.

"I wouldn't put anything past her," Bob says. "I filed the lawsuit. Her attorney will receive electronic notification of that soon. I just wish we had enough to talk to Briggs."

"We're working on that," I say. "Thanks for getting the filing in."

"No problem. We will get this sorted out," Bob says, and hangs up.

So far, this feud between Tish and me over the will has been private, a she said, she said. If I get the police involved, people will start talking. I could lose the company. So no, I will keep this quiet and handle her myself, with Ashlyn's help.

I take a deep breath as I turn onto her street. I pull to a stop two houses down, across the street, and watch Seth turn into the driveway. I hope this is the right move. He stays in his pickup as my brave daughter walks up to her front door.

Ashlyn steps inside Tish's home, and my palms sweat as I grip the steering wheel. The door closes behind her.

Now, all I can do is watch and be ready to run inside if Ashlyn needs me.

CHAPTER 46
TISH

I'm glad I didn't go back to the office this afternoon. It gave me a chance to spend some time at home, take stock of everything I have. I have my own house. It's mine. All mine. That brings a smile to my face. It's remarkable. Beautiful. Quiet. Cool. Large. Filled with expensive things.

I concentrate on my love language — money. My love language was in short supply until I met John. Now I'm flush with love. How grand. I pour myself a glass of wine and watch the bright-orange-and-red sunset. Fabulous. I wonder briefly how long Ashlyn will stay at her boyfriend's house? Long enough, I hope.

Ooh, I have a phone call to make. I'm so proud of myself for coming up with another way to be in charge. Surprise, Kate! I know it's risky, and it could be self-defeating if it hurts the stock value, but I need to keep her off balance. I need to focus her attention elsewhere, away from little ole me.

"*Investor Times* tip line. What do you have for us?" a male reporter asks. Young. Eager.

I swallow. I wish I had fake accent options I could use. Instead, I default to sweet southern, my go-to. "Hey, hi there. I have a tip about a company I know of. They just had an IPO. It's called EventCo? I'm an employee."

"Go on. We cover that company. The IPO is doing well."

"It's not about the IPO, not really. You see it's about control of the company. There is a first wife and a second wife of the CEO, and they both work here. He just died suddenly."

I hear a computer keyboard clicking. "Right. John Nelson had a heart attack, the day after the IPO. So, there's trouble between the two wives?"

You could say that, sonny. "Why don't you get a copy of the will? The second wife is co-president, but the first wife doesn't like it. Quite a story."

"It's only a story for us if it affects the business."

"There's a lot of infighting. Employees are taking sides. It's hard to get work done. I'm traumatized. If the investors find out, they could lose confidence."

321

"Want to go on the record?" he asks. I'm sure he knows the answer already. I called an anonymous tip line.

"Oh, it's a great story, and I'll just leave it to you to tell it," I say, and hang up. As far as the press goes, who do you think is more photogenic? Sympathetic? Me, that's who. I'm the grieving widow, the young, gorgeous wife. Kate has pushed me too far, and now, she'll have a little scare when the reporters start to call, circling their prey. It'll be hard for her to bury this story, that's for sure.

Now what? Out the front window I see Ashlyn trotting up my front walk. Someone is sitting in a pickup truck in my driveway. Hmmm. Has she come here to confront me? I haven't done a thing. Been home all afternoon and evening, so there.

I duck away from the window and walk into the kitchen. I'm not in the mood to talk to her. Not now. I've had a long day. I'll ignore the doorbell, and she'll go away.

I wait for the doorbell to ring, but instead I hear the front door open — the locked front door.

"Hello? Who's there?" I call, tamping down the fury. When John and I bought this house, he insisted Ashlyn have a copy of the key. She was "always welcome here because it's her home, too," he said. I make a note to change the locks.

"Hey, it's me, Ashlyn. I didn't know you were home. I just need to grab my things. Seth is going to help." She waves at me as she heads down the hall to the stairs. Odd, she didn't mention anything about her car. She must not have driven it yet. Her good old boyfriend saved the day apparently.

I hope she's not up to something, coming here. I mean, she's not clever. Maybe she wants to talk, you know, kick back and have fun like the good old days. No, that's not what she wants. She thinks I hurt her dad. She's just here for her things, with muscle waiting in the driveway. Ha.

As I stand in the kitchen waiting for her to leave, admiring her boyfriend's biceps as he carries her stuff out to his car, oppressive heat pours from the ceiling vents. My house is out to get me again. I pull out my phone and find the icon for the app I downloaded last night. I thought I'd finally reset all of the thermostats. How can it be blasting heat again?

"Wow, it's hot in here." Ashlyn joins me in the kitchen. "Feels like hell."

I push open the window above the kitchen sink and take a moment to conceal my frustration. "Yes, my thermostats have been on the fritz. And you know your dad. He wanted the smartest of smart homes. I guess it's just outsmarting me." I keep the tone light, but I'm seething. And then I get an idea. I'll put this home on the market. I want a place that no one else has the key to. A place that's all mine.

"Dad did love technology. You know he has all the apps on his phone. I may be able to help you." She tilts her head. "Where's his phone?"

Good question. Where is his phone? I don't remember seeing it, or thinking about it, since the horribly long and boring memorial service. "It's probably in my black Gucci. I haven't used it since the funeral." I assure myself as much as Ashlyn that I have it. "Do you know the password?"

"Of course." She leans against the kitchen counter. "Don't you?"

As a matter of fact I do, how else would I read all his texts? But I'm not telling her that's the reason. "Of course I do. I'm just talking about the stupid apps, you know, the lights, the temperature, all the smart home stuff. I don't have those passwords." Why didn't I think to find his darn phone sooner? I've been busy, and tired. So tired. My stupid house keeps me up all night.

"I know how to get into all the apps. You can go on his phone and turn down the heat. I'll show you how. Where is it?" She's persistent, I'll give her that much. But why would she want to help me?

I'm trying to ignore the fact that his daughter has his app passwords, but his wife doesn't. Moot point now, I know, but still.

"Let me go search for that purse. I'll be right back. Is that Seth outside? Do you want to invite him in?"

"No. He's fine in the car." She seems to be favoring her left arm.

"Is something wrong with your arm?" I ask.

Her eyes narrow, and she shakes her head. "Nothing time won't fix. My car freaked out while I was driving home."

I keep my expression neutral and say a silent thank you to George. "Wow, that's scary. You're lucky you're not really hurt. Electrical failures are so dangerous."

"How did you know it was electrical?" Ashlyn asks. I'm not afraid of her. She's a weenie, with empty threats.

"Just a lucky guess," I say. "I'll be right back."

As much as I hate leaving her alone in my kitchen, I need to be able to control my house, and if she can show me how to do it, it's worth it. I hurry upstairs and pull open the door to my purse closet. Yes, an entire closet just for my purses. Can you even?

I grab the black Gucci and shove my hand inside. It's empty. Maybe it was the black Chanel? I yank each and every black purse out of the closet and search them. Nothing.

I'm certain the memorial service was the last time I saw it. I've been so distracted by other things. Where is his phone? Did someone take his phone?

The familiar anger is beginning to build. I don't need his damn phone. I'm selling this place soon. Good riddance.

Downstairs Ashlyn stands where I left her. Even if she searched my kitchen, she wouldn't find anything. I'm not stupid. She's texting and smiling. Is she making fun of me?

"No luck."

"What do you mean no luck? You can't find Dad's phone?" Ashlyn asks.

I don't really care where his phone is. I mean, the trade-in value is nothing. Why do I need an old phone around?

"I have no idea. I must have misplaced it. No big deal." She needs to leave. I'm so tired of her right now. The way she's looking at me is bothersome.

"He could have EventCo business on that phone, you know, and other secrets." Ashlyn blinks at me. "At least all of his photos are on the cloud. He was such a great photographer." Her voice cracks, and her eyes fill.

I need to be sympathetic. I need to be sad, too. "I'm glad you can get to his photos." I pretend to dab under my eyes as I wonder if he took any photos that last day in Telluride. Or that last night? I need to check. But I don't know how.

"How do I get to those photos? I'd love to print out some of the best ones of us and frame them." I am lying, but it sounds good.

Her eyes dart around the kitchen, no doubt noticing there isn't a single photo in here. None in the other rooms, either. I never took time to print out any of the two of us, although the funeral home did a good job of framing a few for the service. Never really thought it was that important — and I still don't. But I do wonder if there are any photos from that weekend.

"You go onto iCloud. If he shared his albums with you, you can find them there. I have to go, but um, Tish?" Ashlyn wipes away a tear.

"Yes?"

"Is there anything you want to tell me about my dad's death?" She takes a shaky breath. "I'm just trying to understand how it could happen. I know you two weren't getting along. He was going to dump you the night he died."

"This again? You're being ridiculous. And I don't appreciate it. We were enjoying a romantic getaway when his heart attack happened. Sudden cardiac arrest. End of story. Period. Got it?" Ashlyn is on my last nerve.

She sighs. "He was under so much stress, and yet you took him to the mountains, a place where he never felt well." She shakes her head. "It's just odd."

I hate bitchy girls. "We were getting along perfectly fine. He was under a lot of stress, that's true, but he loved me more than anything or anyone. Including you."

"You know he sent texts to people that night. Photos, too." She pulls open the trash bin and spits her gum into it.

"Your dad loved to text." I smile at her. It's fake.

"I'm just going to take all the things I care about from my room. I'm moving out. I won't be coming back here ever again," she says.

"Good. Good riddance. You can leave your key by the front door." This chitchat makes me realize I need to find John's phone and look at his photos. Read through all of his texts.

"No way. This is my house," she says,

328

which is odd because it's clearly mine.

"What do you mean this is your house?" I ask.

"Oh, you'll see. Anyway, will you do me a favor?" Ashlyn turns serious.

"Sure, anything for you." I lie. The little brat thinks everything is hers. Nothing is.

"Leave my mom alone. Leave the company alone. Leave me alone. Just go away."

I want to tell her it's the reverse. That her mommy should leave me alone, just accept the new world order. They all should. But instead, I say, "Why don't you grab your stuff and get on your way? Now."

"Sure," she says and hurries down the hall. A couple of minutes later, she's carrying a corkboard pinned with photos, concert tickets, memorabilia from a perfect high school life. The spoiled brat doesn't have any idea how good she has it. She should make sure she has everything she wants from this house, my house. I'll destroy anything she leaves here.

Ashlyn heads toward the front door and I follow behind, fuming. Here's the thing — the line between love and hate is so thin. So very precarious. I loved her. I thought we would be a family, the three of us. *Silly dreams, Tish.* I shake my head.

She stops and turns around. "It's so hot

in here. I don't know how you deal."

"I can't control it. I don't know where your dad's phone is. I know there are apps on it. I'm not stupid." I am, however, yelling. I take a deep breath. That outburst made me sound like an idiot.

"Well, then, I guess you aren't dealing." Ashlyn laughs as she walks out the door.

It takes every part of me not to slam the door after her. I march into the kitchen and make a call to Uncle George.

"Hello, sugar pie." George answers after only one ring. "I took care of the little princess's car for you."

"I know, thank you. She's bruised, her arm's hurt, but otherwise, she's fine. I like the warning," I say. "She still had the nerve to come over here tonight."

"Gutsy. What did she want?" George asks.

"She said she wanted her stuff from her room, but I think she also was snooping. There wasn't anything for her to find. Did you deal with my momma?"

"Yes, she understands if she talks to anyone up there again, it won't turn out well for her. She does want to talk to you," George says.

"Never." I shake my head. "I can't find John's phone."

"I don't know why you need his phone

when you have a perfectly good one of your own." George chuckles. "Getting greedy again are we, Tish?"

"I am not greedy. I'm worried he might have texted people the night he died, I have no idea what photos he sent or to who."

"If there was anything, you'd know by now. The wife and the daughter, they would have come after you. But they didn't. You're all good, but actually you're all bad." Now he's laughing, a big-belly annoying sound. I think he just snorted.

"Stop it. This isn't funny. I need to get to the photos on there. They could be incriminating."

George pulls himself together. "Listen, sugar. Forget about his phone. They can't touch you or they would have made a move already. You have everything you need, and then some. Call a tech company, and they'll come sort your house out. You sound frantic. What are you afraid of?"

I'm afraid of being poor again. I'm afraid of being discovered as a fraud. I'm afraid I'm not good enough, just like my momma always said.

"Nothing. You're right. Ashlyn says my house belongs to her. She's wrong, right?" I ask George. I can't believe I let her get under my skin.

331

"I haven't heard that one, sugar," George says.

I let out a breath I didn't know I was holding. "I'm fine. Everything is good. I don't have anything to hide."

"That's not true, sugar." George gives a big laugh. He's known me almost all my life. "I still see you reaching into my office candy jar, taking more than one piece, thinking you were getting away with something. So cute. Anyhoo, the good news is the will was filed before John croaked, so it makes it even harder to contest once the state has put a stamp of approval on it."

Contest? "They can't challenge it, can they?"

"Just got an electronic notification. An attorney for Ashlyn Nelson already filed on her behalf. But don't worry, you're in good shape. Get some sleep. You sound cranky."

"What? That bitch was just here, at my house. That's impossible. She has the nerve to file a lawsuit?" I'm astounded. "How did she do this?"

"Whoa, sugar. You would do the same thing if you were in her shoes. Remember, the new will cuts her out entirely, and she's the only direct heir. I advised keeping her in, but you said no. And you're the boss. I suppose the princess hired herself a lawyer."

George laughs again.

He did warn me I was being greedy. But now that she's shown her true colors, I'm glad. "Screw her. We're still fine, right?"

"You're in great shape." He's still laughing.

I stand in my kitchen, and I know I should be happy. I have an avalanche of money coming my way. I should be filled with my love language. But instead I'm beyond cranky. And my house is pumping out heat like the fires of hell and will likely torture me again tonight. But at least the missing phone isn't a big deal, according to George. I wanted to see what other photos John took when I wasn't watching. But I guess it doesn't matter anymore. He's dead.

"Thanks," I manage. "And George, don't laugh at me again or I'll find another attorney."

"Oh, honey, that's a good one," George says and starts laughing again. "You and me are stuck together like peanut butter and jelly."

CHAPTER 47
KATE

Once we were both home from Tish's house unscathed, I felt a wave of relief.

I'd been ready to charge in there and grab my daughter, but she texted me the thumbs-up emoji telling me everything was fine. That was our agreement, text every five minutes. Nerve-racking. I wouldn't put anything past Tish. I know what kind of woman she is. I see her clearly now. She murdered John.

"Don't worry, Mrs. Nelson. I had the light on in my cab so she could see me watching her every move, even in between trips inside," Seth had said after escorting Ashlyn home. Once he left, Ashlyn was ready for more Tylenol and a good, albeit late, snack in bed.

Ashlyn didn't find anything incriminating lying around the house, but she did tell Tish she never wanted to see her again and to get out of our lives. That had to be a stab in

Tish's cold heart. Is Tish worried? I hope so. Worried enough to leave town? Who knows? I also wonder how long she thinks she can play this game with the fake will. She has to feel the ground crumbling beneath her, because it is.

It's good to keep your enemies off balance. It's true in business — and in life, I'm learning.

I've done all I can for the moment, purchasing stock, getting Bob and the attorneys pursuing our legal recourses. I know who the witnesses were for the fake will, and how to find them when the time is right. For tonight, I'll make sure Ashlyn is comfortable and safely tucked into bed.

"I'm going to miss you when you're back at school," I say as I carry a bowl of granola and a banana over to her in bed. Hot chamomile tea steams on her bedside table.

"Me, too. Need help with anything?" Ashlyn winces as she holds her left arm.

"No, all set. You've done so much. Thank you." She really is lovely. I'm so lucky to be her mom. And she needs to see a doctor in the morning for an X-ray, despite what she says.

"What?" Ashlyn asks.

Did I speak out loud? "I was just thinking I'm so lucky to be your mom. And we need to get that arm x-rayed in the morning."

"Aww, that's sweet. But I told you they don't do anything for elbows, even if it's broken." Ashlyn takes a bite of cereal. "Yum."

"If you want to tell me anything else about your visit to Tish's house, I'm all ears," I say, even though I know I should leave it alone for tonight.

"See, you can't help yourself, Mom. It's in your DNA. You were meant to run a company. I'm proud of you. I am. And I wish Tish would just go away." She takes another bite.

"All of this happened to you, too. I just wish we had some more proof. Proof he was leaving Tish, and even more so, proof she put something in his drink. And of course, the ridiculous new will. I ordered a copy of the autopsy report from Colorado."

"Why? If they had found anything, they would have flagged it," Ashlyn says.

Still, I need to take a closer look. Perhaps hire an expert to review it. "Maybe, but people miss things all the time, overlook what's right in front of them."

Ashlyn covers a yawn. "I looked around when I was there, like I told you, but there wasn't a bottle with a skull and crossbones sitting on the kitchen counter."

336

"Very funny."

"If it makes you feel any better, it was about ninety degrees inside her house, and just about now, the music will start blaring." Ashlyn is holding her dad's phone and grinning.

"You're bad. You probably shouldn't," I say. "But I love it. I do."

"She almost ran me over and messed with my car. She practically admitted it. She knew it was an electrical failure."

"She said that? My god, we should call Bob."

"It's not proof. She's careful, devious," she says, and her head drops with the words. "I don't think Dad realized what he got himself into. And then it was too late."

Ashlyn finishes her granola, and I take the bowl from her.

"Do you need anything else for school?"

"I'm good. I'm almost finished packing. I hate to leave you alone to deal with all of this."

"I'll be fine. Go back to school, to all your friends. Remember all the good times with your dad before she showed up." I'll be able to focus on things here better once she's safely back at school. I have an idea. "Ash, take the plane back to school. The pilots would love to see you, and then I'll know

337

you're safely moved in. Please, I insist." I walk to the sink, stroke her long blonde hair.

Ashlyn reaches for her phone. "Are you kidding? I'd love to. Thank you. You're still planning on coming down for parents' weekend? It's in two weeks."

I smile. "Of course. It's already on the calendar. Can't wait."

"Mom?" She reaches into her bag beside the bed and pulls out a key.

"What's that?"

"The key to Dad's house. It works. I used it today. And the alarm code is still the same as ours. I just thought, if things get worse, you might need it. All of Dad's stuff is still there. All the things he cared about." Ashlyn places the key in my hand.

I am beyond pleased on so many levels. "Thanks, honey. This could come in handy. I'll do my best to save what I can for you. I know it's what your dad would have wanted."

She shrugs. "He would have wanted to be alive, to be here, right now."

True. But you can't always get what you want. John learned that the hard way.

CHAPTER 48
TISH

I had the world's worst night's sleep. The nightmare of John's death haunts me every night. I cannot get his face out of my mind, the frozen expression of terror when I had to ID his corpse at the hospital.

Daylight helps. It is now 7:00 a.m., and I'm getting ready for work. It's a big day. I wouldn't miss it for anything. Who needs sleep? Clearly, not me.

I look at my reflection and note the dark circles under my eyes, the unruly hair, and the pasty skin. I don't look right. I don't look rested, but it's more than that. I look a little crazy. Ha. That's not good. I'll need to get to work on this before heading to the office. At EventCo, I only have a little bit of time to make some changes. To assert myself. I read it online. New CEOs are judged right away. If I don't make a good impression, they'll eat me alive.

Maybe I'll start offering free lunch to all

the employees. They'd like that. Queen Tish, that's who I am. Let them eat cake for lunch, every day.

I'm glad I see Ashlyn clearly now. I thought she was a bitch, but now I know for sure. Who needs her? I don't. No more stupid "Ashlyn time," as John used to call it.

"You understand, don't you?" John asked me after telling me I wasn't invited for her sorority's dad and daughter weekend last spring. "It's her choice, and she just wants to spend time with her dad. Kate isn't going, either, if that helps."

John had tried to pull me into a hug, but I wasn't happy, not at all. "I need to be with you, too. You're always so busy. Can't it be Ashlyn and Tish time?"

"I know, you get jealous. That's so cute." He reached for me.

I slapped his hand away. I think I surprised him with the force of the blow. Turns out, I surprised him with a lot of things. "Not jealous. I just don't like you two talking behind my back, that's all. She should call and talk to both of us. It should be a rule."

John shook his head. "Not smart. You can shut down the communication between Kate and me. That's fine. But not Ashlyn and me. She's got a mind of her own, my daughter does. I love that about her."

"She's a child." I had my hands on my hips, still certain of my power over him.

"She is. My only one. I'm going to spend some quality time with her. Alone."

That had been the first time he'd disobeyed me. The first time he would not agree to play by my rules. My hold was slipping. I was furious.

"If you go without me, don't come back." I stomped my foot.

"Don't be ridiculous, Tish." John began packing.

I looked at his phone as a text lit up. Can't wait to see you, Daddy!

Daddy? Really?

John spotted me with his phone. "You need to calm down. It's two nights, albeit two nights at the Regency. I'll be spoiled. I'll bring you some of their famous body lotion, OK?"

As the memory dances through my head, so does the realization I'm wasting time standing here. I need to take charge of the present.

Back to my face. I look in the bathroom mirror and pinch my cheeks. It doesn't help. The word to describe my appearance is *drab.* That's something I've never been called, ever. That's it. The last straw. Period.

I've got to get out of this house. Maybe with a new bedroom, a new bed, and some cool air, I'll erase the vision of John.

It's time to call the real estate agent. I'm reluctant to move too quickly, what with the suburban gossip mill, and Ashlyn and Kate talking about murder, but I have to get out of here. I wonder if I can sue them for slander or libel or whatever it's called.

Ashlyn is going back to college, so she'll be gone; Kate better watch her step.

Focus, Tish. I dial the number.

"Chris Cort here. Grandville's number one agent. May I help?" His deep voice matches the handsome looks of the guy who has sent postcards and calendars to me since we moved into our love nest. We used one of John's real estate friends to buy the house — I'm using the postcard-sending hunk to find my next home. I need a new place, a city place perhaps, closer to the office.

"Hi, yes, this is Tish Nelson. 902 Coventry." I try to add a lilt to my tired voice.

"Gorgeous home. Stately. I love it." He pauses. "Mrs. Nelson, I'm so sorry for your loss."

"Thank you. It's tragic. And now, I'm afraid, I'll need to sell the house."

I don't need to see him to know he's grinning. "I'd be pleased to represent you. Could I come by and take a look at the property? What is your timing?"

"As soon as possible, really. There are just too many memories here," I say, not adding that the stupid place is torturing me. I don't think he needs to know about that. John's ghost will disappear once I'm gone. It just better not follow me.

"I can be there in twenty minutes. Does that work for you?" He's certainly an eager beaver.

"Yes. That works. Chris, does the fact that John died suddenly taint the price of the home?" I ask in the sweetest, almost southern, voice.

"He didn't expire in the home, did he? I mean that creates a stigmatized property situation, but it's not insurmountable."

Expire? Really? Jeez. "No, not in this one. He died in the mountains. At our condo in Telluride. I need to sell that, too."

"I'm happy to help you with both properties. I have a strong referral network in Colorado. Will we be buying a new residence here and there?" I imagine Chris's green eyes glowing with the promise of multiple commissions. I then wonder if they really are green or just photoshopped. I'll find out in twenty minutes.

"Yes, I will be purchasing a new home. I'm staying in the area. I work downtown, so perhaps a condo? I'm not sure." I'm bored with this conversation. "Let's talk in twenty minutes, shall we?"

"Yes, Mrs. Nelson. I'll be there."

Oh, I know you will, Chris. I just hope you are as cute as your advertising. And as young. Young. I'm young. It's time I find a man my own age. No more old guys. I hang up the phone and turn back to the task at hand. I have a lot of makeup work to do.

By the time the doorbell rings, I'm ready. Hair blown out. Makeup heavily applied. The house is in fairly good shape since Sonja handled the red wine mess. And the thermostat is behaving. I'll make a note to call a tech guy next. Maybe Chris knows someone.

When I open the door, I discover Realtor Chris is even more handsome than his advertising. And fit.

As we shake hands, I feel the tingle. The surge of electricity. I give him a big smile, and he returns the favor. This is going to work out just great, for his business and my pleasure.

"Please, come in," I say.

"Gorgeous," he says as he walks through the door, following behind me. I know he's

344

referring to me and not my living room.

It's been a while since someone has offered me an overt compliment, I mean, besides my husband. But he hadn't even noticed me lately. No, he was back in love with his stupid ex-wife. An unfortunate choice for him. I control everything now — the company, the money, everything but this stupid smart home.

I turn and toss my hair over my shoulder and wink. "Thank you." I could lean in and kiss him right now. But business before pleasure today, I remind myself. I have work to do in the office.

"Do you want to give me a tour of the place? I'll have my team come back this afternoon or whenever you'd like to take the official listing photos, but I'd love to get a feel for the property myself." Chris's light-blue tie brings out the green in his eyes.

"Yes, let's get you a good feel." I smile, and he follows me like a puppy into the kitchen. This is going to be fun. I need a release. It's been tough being a grieving widow. It's tough being one step ahead of everyone else.

I wonder how the investigative journalist is doing. I'm glad I called the tip line at the magazine. I've never read the thing, it's all finance and stuff, but they love juicy scandals, too. Like how a rich old woman is trying to intimidate the young second wife who just inherited half of the company. That should keep the pot stirred for me. Mean old Kate taking advantage of the poor young widow.

I wink at Chris, who is following close behind me up the stairs, so close I can smell his aftershave. "You'll love the master bedroom."

"I already know it will be amazing."

CHAPTER 49
KATE

By the time I make it into the office, I know Ashlyn has been in for a while. She left the house early, just as my alarm sounded. I saw her hop into an Uber, and I watched it pull away.

I wonder what in the world would make my daughter wake up so early on her last day at home and work. I jot a note on my desk to-do list to call her in and ask about her early-morning exploits.

I'm energized. Today's the day Tish will find out the game is over. For good. It will be fun for Ashlyn to watch. I must admit, it feels like it has been a long time coming. Tish has been a surprising opponent. She's much more underhanded than I gave her credit for, and much more ruthless. I still cannot believe what she did to Ashlyn's car. I make a note to call Chief Briggs for the report if he doesn't call me first.

A knock on my door pulls me into the moment. It's Jennifer.

"Come in," I yell, and she does.

Jennifer exhales, shakes her head. "I've been trying to kill the story, but the *Investor Times* got a tip. They say they're running with a piece about Tish inheriting John's shares of EventCo, effectively taking control of half the company. I told them the will is being contested and gave them the facts. They maintain the Class B stockholders and investors have a right to know. I'm assuming we have no comment."

I turn, walk toward my office window, and stare down to the street. This is it. The thing I most feared because I cannot control it — my company being ripped apart by fake news and innuendos. By sleazy lies and sensational journalism. That my EventCo could be ruined by something as inane as John's fling that now has led to a private battle between an ex-wife and a current one. This will not be the end of EventCo. It will not.

"Exactly. We have no comment on their ridiculous story." I take a deep breath and turn to face Jennifer. This is the dreaded hit piece that no one can stop, not even our multitalented marketing vice president. I'm just surprised it took so long. Likely the press stayed away because of John's death.

But it didn't hold them off forever, of course. I wonder if Tish had something to do with it. "I know you tried everything to kill it."

"I did. But they say they have a solid source. An insider." Jennifer shakes her head.

"Tish did this. Damn it." I knew we were on borrowed time. We need to move faster. But for now, I will stabilize the company. "Get me the list of the lead investors. I'll make personal calls to them. Now."

Jennifer hurries out of my office as Lance walks through the door with a purpose. His face is locked in a frown. That's unusual.

"What's wrong?" I ask as he takes the seat.

"Everything."

"Not a word I want to hear from my COO."

"Sorry, but it's the truth. I got a call from the reporter working on the story. You and the second wife feuding. John the peace-keeper is gone, and the company is falling apart. That's the angle. Chaos at EventCo." So, the stories, the rumors, are spreading. I notice the dark circles under his eyes.

He says, "I miss John."

I take a deep breath. So much drama. "We all do. But we need to pull this company through. We've worked too hard to lose

349

everything now. How are the employees doing?"

"They'll be fine until this story drops," Lance says. "What do you suggest?"

What do I suggest? "We go on the offensive. I now own controlling shares of EventCo. In my estimation, about seventy percent of the company with my combined Class A and B shares. I am EventCo."

"Congratulations. That's great." Lance is impressed.

I smile. "Tish has no stated title or position in the new will. Get with Sandra and move her to a back office, out of the way if she insists on staying and pretending to work. Call security in if she gives you any trouble. In the meantime, we'll let it slip to the press that we've initiated an executive search and will hire John's replacement soon. A seasoned president, someone the market will approve of who can help us comfort nervous shareholders. I am now CEO of EventCo, the only CEO of EventCo."

"I'll tell Jennifer to call the *Investor Times* with this." Lance stands up and closes my office door. "I've heard Bob and Sandra think John was murdered."

"None of us know for sure. It's conjecture." I shake my head.

"But think about it. If there's even a possibility she was responsible, we owe it to John to go to the police." Lance is more animated now than when he came into my office.

"We don't have enough proof. Or, for that matter, a body." I watch as his face blanches. "I don't think EventCo can withstand that gruesome of a scandal. A long, drawn-out police investigation could ruin us. The new will is the key to getting rid of her. Prove it's fake, and she's got nothing." This is the way it must be. "We filed a lawsuit last night. She will lose this fight."

"I hope so. I really do," Lance says. "I'll get Tish moved and Jennifer pitching our story."

"Thanks. And you know what else? We need some publicity stills of Ashlyn and me collaborating before she heads back to college. Build up the family narrative, next generation already learning the ropes," I say. There's nothing like a good old multigenerational family story to bolster an IPO. How genuine. How corporate of us.

"I love it." Lance is animated again.

"Send Ashlyn in. I'll explain my idea to her. You talk with Jennifer and come back when you guys have a plan or an interested media outlet."

He hurries out of the office as I wonder how it will make Tish feel when Ashlyn and I have a family business photo shoot together. The thought of her reaction when she finds out is delicious.

CHAPTER 50
TISH

Nothing like a quickie to get the day started right. Fortunately, my house didn't sabotage our little romp, and the temperature actually stayed below eighty degrees in my bedroom. A miracle.

Chris is off to work his real estate magic — he promises to be back tonight with more. For more. The thought prompts a little zing in my stomach. Today is going to be a good day.

As I drive to the office, I'm looking forward to solidifying my power. I'm buoyed by the thought that tonight will be my last night living in my haunted home. I'll move into a downtown hotel, like Chris suggested. I can start looking for a condo right away. Money isn't an issue, at least it won't be once the will clears probate. Thanks to a good marriage, it never will be again.

Today's my lucky day. I find a parking space in front of the EventCo offices and, as I step out onto the sidewalk and look up at the impressive building, a wave of pride washes over me. This is my company now. At least half of it. People have to take me seriously. I've arrived. I'm a co-president. Or a joint CEO? I'm something important. I need to figure out what my title is and order business cards. Oh, and new office furniture, too. I'll create a look more feminine than John's, a look more like Kate's furniture. Maybe I'll just copy Kate's setup. I have to admit I like her office, even though I once thought it was overdone. I realize it's not. Our offices will be indistinguishable. Over time, I'll learn everything she knows. Or I'll pretend to know it. How hard can this be?

I let myself in the first floor and walk past a bunch of offices on my way to the stairs. I don't know exactly what all of these people do all day, but I understand their general categories: accounting, IT, sales. I'm going to need to do a sit-down with the department heads and get up to speed. Sure, I know all their names and what departments they lead, but what do they do? I haven't a clue. I'm going to need someone to take me under his wing. I'm going to need Lance. That thought brings a smile to my face as I climb the stairs to the executive offices.

I'm humming as I push through the large glass door and stand in the two-story atrium where John loved to challenge people to Ping-Pong games. I sort of miss the big guy about now, even though I would not be here if he was still alive. He was going to make me stay home. That remembrance infuriates me. After all I did for him. He was going to make me stay home, and do who knows what, so he could spend quality time at the office with Kate. And then he was going to dump me.

Too bad, John. This is all going to work out much better under my plan. I hurry to John's office, pop the key in the door, and walk in. Some small part of me keeps thinking Kate will have the locks changed again to keep me out, but she's not that strong, or that stupid. Perhaps she knows she's lost?

According to the will, this is where I belong. I wonder how fast I can order new furniture. I have the catalog in my assistant desk. I sit down at John's desk and wake up his desktop computer. I need a new one of these, too, don't I? I want something sleek, new. I suddenly hate all of this masculine furniture, this desk, and this chair. It smells like John, like his car: like my nightmares every night. I want a fresh start. I'm entitled to have it the way I want it.

The screen saver on the computer lights up. It's a photo of me, standing in the kitchen in Telluride. When was this taken? I wonder if John's screen saver is filled with photos of me. How sweet. I wait for the photo to change, but there is no slideshow. And then I realize what I'm looking at. John must have taken the photo of me from out on the deck. It's from our last night. I swallow. I'm mixing a batch of drinks. So what. That's what everyone does on vacation. I push the power button and the computer shuts down, the screen dark and lifeless.

Someone is trying to scare me. It's not going to work.

My hands shake as I pull open the desk drawer to find my notepad. Instead I find a sheet of paper folded in half. I open it. It's a printed photo of John, on the last night, drinking my special margarita. Below the photo someone wrote:

I know what you did.

Get out. Leave town. Or else.

I look out to the hall, but it's empty. Who did this?

And what exactly does this person think I've done?

It's a bluff. It has to be. My heart is pounding. I am so sick and tired of people messing with me. Threatening me. Underestimating me. It's exhausting sometimes, but it does make you stronger. And I am invincible.

On the way to my appointment, I make a call to Tish's mom again. I need to ask her a few more questions. She doesn't answer. I try texting, but it doesn't go through. Tish must have gotten to her somehow. I lean back in the Uber, try to figure out another way to reach her besides driving to Pineville, Kentucky.

The driver pulls to a stop, and I hop out ready to focus on my task at hand. I was lucky my mom's naturopath, Bonnie, agreed to squeeze me in this morning to take a look at my elbow. I wait for my appointment in the front room of her home office, taking a moment to quiet my thoughts.

The door opens. "Ashlyn, dear, it's so good to see you. I haven't seen you since you were a child. Please come in," Bonnie says. Her calm presence is just what I need this morning. She wears a rainbow sweatshirt and jeans, and a large crystal hangs from her neck. "I'm so sorry about your dad. I wish I had met him."

"He was a great guy. I thought he was your patient, too," I say as I follow her inside.

"No, men can be very reluctant to take care of themselves. They often don't go to a doctor until things are very serious. What can I do for you, honey?" she asks as I slide onto the exam table.

"I was in a car accident. My elbow is pretty messed up," I say, and show her.

"Oh dear. OK, let me just take a look at this," she says, gently examining my arm. The wall of the exam room is lined with shelves, and the shelves hold glass jars and vials of herbs. It smells like a garden in here. "Oh yes, OK. I know just what you need."

"Mom said you don't work on bones, but I figured you did," I say.

"Yes, we handle everything, just like those traditional doctors. Tell your mom to come and see me. She hasn't been in for years," Bonnie says.

"I will. So you prescribed the pills for my dad without seeing either of them?" I ask.

"Oh, honey, I don't do that, not even for your family. Whatever he was taking, they weren't from me," Bonnie says. "Come on off the table, and let's get you all fixed up.

And tell your mom she's overdue for an appointment. She must be under so much stress right now."

CHAPTER 52
KATE

I lean back in my desk chair and smile. It feels great to have a plan: overturn the fraudulent will, run Tish out of town, calm the investors, watch EventCo grow. Oh, and I'm going to launch my new Forever product. There's no one around to tell me no. Not anymore.

I swivel my desk chair and find Ashlyn standing at the office door. I wave her in.

"Hi, honey. You were up bright and early this morning. How are you feeling? How's your arm?" I tilt my head, hoping for an explanation.

"I'm a little sore, but I think it's better. Stopped by the doctor on the way to work," she says. "Bonnie told me to tell you hi. She hasn't seen you for years."

"Oh, that's not true. I was just there, to get medicine for your dad."

"That's not what she said," Ashlyn says.

We lock eyes. Will she push me further? I

hope not.

Ashlyn drops into the chair across from me. "I've enjoyed working here this summer, Mom. It's weird, not having Dad here, too, though. Sorry."

"Don't be sorry. You're right." For a moment my anger is replaced with a touch of nostalgia, a glimmer of what if. What if John had been faithful? What if it was the three of us, as a family, celebrating the end of Ashlyn's internship and the beginning of her senior year at college? But that's not the way it turned out. And that was all his choice.

Ashlyn wears black pants and a jacket, a white blouse. She's modeled herself after her mentor, Jennifer, and it's a good look. She just needs to go on back to college, and everything will be fine.

"You look happy. What's up?" Ashlyn slides into the chair across from my desk. She looks around conspiratorially. "I think she's here again, by the way. In Dad's office. Maybe you should have the locks changed?"

I smile. "I watched her walk in from the street. Don't worry, she won't be there long."

"Good."

Lance knocks on the door. "Sorry to interrupt. I just thought I'd let you know Tish is in John's office. And she's demanding to see Sandra. Something about her space being violated?" Lance shrugs. "I've set up the back office for her, the one without a window, next to the restrooms. Sound good?"

"Yes. Perfect." I nod. "Maybe I'll go on over there and set her straight."

We all hear the crash at the same time. It's the sound of breaking glass, topped off by a woman's scream.

"Is that Tish?" I ask.

Lance nods.

"She's lost it," Ashlyn says.

I'm calm as I walk through the office, across the atrium lobby, and down the hall to John's office. Now Tish's office. No, John's office. I can't help but notice the employees watching me, anxious to see how this little show is going to play out. They've had a front-row seat since this sordid ordeal began.

First it was John and Tish sneaking around, flirting in meetings, and creating all sorts of fodder for the rumor mill. And then, once they were "out" as a couple, the pity and speculation surrounding me grew. Would I quit? Be forced out? Really? The brains and the heart of EventCo? Could

John push me to the side as a business partner as easily as he did as a spouse?

The answer to that, of course, was no. Never.

And the answer to Tish is no more.

Sandra stands in the doorway to John's office, hands on hips. She's shaking her head like a disappointed schoolteacher.

I can't see Tish yet, but I can hear her. "I'm telling you, Sandra, someone broke into John's office and is harassing me."

"You need to calm down," Sandra says in a teacher voice.

I touch Sandra's shoulder and she jumps. "I'll handle this." I step into John's office.

Tish glares at me, her face locked in a furious frown. "Are you satisfied? This is all your fault."

I take a moment to view the destruction. John's desk is somehow flipped forward on its side, the glass lamp smashed on the floor, the computer monitor shattered. This was the crash we heard from my office. It's unbelievable. Tish is having a temper tantrum like a three-year-old.

"My fault? You're a wrecking ball. Look at what you've done to this office, to this company, to my family." I am in control. I've dreamed of this moment. "If you choose to work here until I invalidate the scam will, your office is in the back. Sandra will escort you there and get you settled."

"I'm not going anywhere," Tish screams.

I turn to Sandra. "Document this incident and the property damage. It should go in her personnel file. Make certain she understands this is not her office. It is for the new president, who we will hire after an executive search. Make sure Tish understands I'm CEO. I'll decide what title, if any, she'll have, and whether her employment will be continued at all. At this point, that's highly unlikely."

Tish shakes with anger.

"And please make sure she understands I'm the majority shareholder here. I will make all the decisions for EventCo. If she doesn't comply, call the police. I'm sure Chief Briggs will be interested to learn of this destructive, out-of-control incident. He'll be calling soon to confirm Ashlyn's car was tampered with. There's so much more we can share with him."

I turn to walk out of John's office, and I hear Tish gasp. I can't help but smile.

"Get back in here, bitch. You can't do this. I'm the one in the will," Tish yells, but I'm pretty certain she'll comply with my demands. It was a gamble but worth it.

"Mom, that was amazing." Ashlyn walks

beside me. Lance is close behind.

Lance pushes my door open and follows us into the relative calm of my office.

I slide into my desk chair. "That went well."

"You killed it, Kate." Lance leans against my office door, grinning.

"I loved it." Ashlyn drops into the chair across from me. "I want to be just like that when I'm the boss. Rad."

I look up, and Jennifer is at the door. "Did you guys get a chance to talk about the publicity shot? Mother-daughter success and succession story?"

"Yes, I'm in." Ashlyn seems excited about it. "I know Dad would have loved it."

"The photographer will be ready in an hour. We're going off-site," Jennifer says before she leaves my office, Lance following her.

"We'll be ready." I close the door behind them. It's just Ashlyn and me. The way it should be. I've learned a lot about myself in the past three years. From being blinded by work and trust, to believing if you did the right thing, worked hard, played by the rules, and were honest, everything would work out. I know that's not the case, that's not how the world works. I'm not naive. Not anymore.

"Mom, she's still here, though. What do we do?" Ashlyn asks.

"Don't worry. I've got this. She won't know what hit her. Stay here. I'll be right back." I walk out of my office and head to the back of the building to find Tish's new, tiny office. It's a closet, and I love it.

"What do you want?" Tish asks, her voice cold.

I'm not afraid. "Here are some facts for you to consider. I control seventy percent of the company, and there is no place for you at EventCo. Never will be. I suggest you take whatever is rightfully yours after three years of marriage and get out of town."

"You don't scare me." Tish stands up. "Get out of my office."

She just doesn't get it. Stupid is as stupid does, that's the saying, right? "By the way, you look horrible. Killers have trouble sleeping, I've read." A low blow, but it's true. Guilty conscience leads to haunting dreams.

"Get out!"

I'm already down the hall.

CHAPTER 53
TISH

Who is threatening me? Who put that stupid photo on John's computer? And why did I agree to relocate to this bleak office in the back of the building? No windows. I mean, this is not fitting for my position.

John's office is a mess, that's why. I'll let them clean it up, and I'll order new furniture. Then I'll move in. This squalid closet is temporary. I need to call George.

Someone stands in the doorway.

Ashlyn. Why hasn't she learned her lesson yet?

"Why did you tip over Dad's desk?" She looks at me, all innocent, like she's never had a fit of rage in her life. I know she has, though, but her anger is more like her mom's. Hiding away under the surface. She'd never demean herself with a public display like mine. In that sense, she is her mother's daughter.

I drop my head and look at my hands. I

have no one to blame but myself for my outburst. Someone will need to be summoned to clean up glass, to stand the desk back up. That thing is heavy. I know. I'm surprised I toppled it. Adrenaline is a powerful thing. So am I.

"Someone burglarized my office, so I had a little temper tantrum. I guess those Cross-Fit sessions are paying off." I chuckle, an attempt at humor. It falls flat. I remember crumpling the threatening note and throwing it on the floor. I need to go get that. It's evidence.

"Excuse me."

I push past Ashlyn and hurry toward John's office. I turn the doorknob, but it's locked. I gave Lance the key. I can see through the glass door, though. The note I tossed on the floor is gone.

Why is Ashlyn following me?

My phone vibrates. I pull it out of my back pocket. I need to get out of here. I'm not coming back until I have a proper office. Proper respect.

It's a text from George. Have confirmation from court. Motion was filed by daughter. Don't worry. Stay strong.

Oh, I'm strong. That's not a problem, Uncle George.

I turn around and face Ashlyn. I drop my

369

voice to a menacing whisper. "I know what you did. Contesting the will. My will. You'd better stop following me. You better stop getting in my way. Do you understand? Here. And at home. I'm on to you. Don't push me. Your car was just a warning shot. You know what I'm capable of doing. Cheers."

As Ashlyn scampers away, I feel the menial office workers staring at me. I don't know some of their names, never really cared to learn, but they know me. Know who I am.

"What?" I bark at two young women leaning against a wall as I turn the corner. They both jump, and that pleases me.

Sandra appears like a sentry as I reach the front offices. Running interference for Kate, I assume.

"Look, I need to speak to Jennifer. Is she in with Kate? I can talk to both of them." My hands are on my hips. I'm not backing down.

"You'll need to meet with her next week. I'm afraid they've all left for an off-site photo shoot. It's quite exciting. They're posing for a national magazine, a feature about the mother and daughter duo who will lead EventCo into its bright future after the untimely death of the CEO. It's for a big national magazine."

370

How dare they do this without me? I am the second Mrs. Nelson, part of the family. I feel tears fill my eyes and push them away. I don't even understand how Kate can own 70 percent of the company when I got John's half? I'll need to ask George. I need someone to help me.

"I should be in that photo session. I'm leading this company into the future. I'm co-president. Tell me where the shoot is."

Sandra tilts her head. "I can't do that. Why don't you see Nancy, Kate's assistant, to make an appointment?"

"I'll get in whenever I want. I'm co-president." Are people dense? Do I need to print copies of the will and show it to everyone? I don't care what Kate says or what fancy math she's trying to use, I own half.

Sandra speaks again. "Your title is not co-president. The new will didn't stipulate a position. It just provided you with ownership. There really is no reason for you to be here. You don't have a job. You resigned as an assistant, remember? But if you insist on coming in, that's where you'll be. Back in the closet. Understood?"

"Whatever." I am so mad right now, I could punch her. Hard.

"Oh, and I've opened a file on you. An employee has charged you with harassment.

We take those allegations seriously here at EventCo."

"I'm not going to forget this." I can't help it. I'm pointing my finger at her. "Someone threatened me. What are you going to do about that? Nothing, right? I'll go get the proof, and then you'd better do something. Investigate or else."

"Are you trying to frighten me?" She takes a step back.

"I'm simply reminding you that I'm your boss. So, you should be more accommodating, do you understand? And when I'm being threatened, you should care."

Sandra shakes her head. "So now *you're* being threatened?"

"Someone left a note in my desk drawer." I drop my voice. "Was it you? Did you leave that note in John's desk?"

"You need to leave. Go back to Pineville, Terry Jane." Sandra turns and before I know it, she's closing her office door, stranding me in the hallway.

She just threw my past in my face and walked away from me. She doesn't know what she's stirring, the pot she's messing with. This all may be her doing. She is the HR officer. She can rummage through anyone's desk with impunity. But somehow, I don't think she's my only problem. All of these people are going to pay. No more nice Tish. I pull my phone out of my back pocket and call George as I walk back to my tiny closet of an office.

"I'm going to take them all down. I don't care if I lose money, too. I want them all to suffer."

George blows out a breath. "You need to calm down, honeybunch. *Right now.*"

That's the last thing I need. One more person telling me what to do. "Just be sure you've covered everything. Make certain I'm secure in all of this. Make sure there is no crack in that will. Do you understand? Kate can't win." I hang up on George before I hear his reply. He'd better have my back.

I've changed my mind. Instead of running this place, I will ruin it.

CHAPTER 54
KATE

A photo shoot is the last thing I feel like doing, but at least it gets Ashlyn and me away from the menace masquerading as an employee and wrecking John's office. Two can play the media game, Tish, but only one of us has done it before. And I'm good at it, despite being forced into this photo shoot long before I would have chosen to push my daughter into the media spotlight.

But it's fine. If it's good for EventCo, I'm in. We'll prove to the investors that despite John's death, we're stronger than ever. The magazine also gets the exclusive about our new Forever product. I'm beyond excited to roll it out.

Once Sandra had escorted Tish to the back, I went into John's office and tidied up, as much as I could. I found the note I'd left in the desk drawer crumpled up and tossed on the floor. I slipped it into my pocket. Maybe the note did it, or maybe it was the screen saver? Either way, her re-action made me smile.

What are a couple of little threats among friends?

I'm still surprised how well it worked.

It's silly, but every once in a while, it feels good to be a step ahead of your enemy. From the looks of the office destruction, she got the message.

I am back in my office by the time Jennifer and Ashlyn appear outside of my door.

"Ready for the shoot?" Jennifer asks.

"Give me ten minutes," I say. "Ashlyn, can we chat in private?"

My daughter needs to understand the importance of everything that has happened today. I will make sure she does.

CHAPTER 55
ASHLYN

As I look at my mom, really look at her, I realize how strong, how brave she has been. And how much her heart must have broken. I'm filled with a deep sympathy for her I've never felt. And I'm surprised at the new emotion inside me: I'm furious with my dad.

This is all my dad's fault. Tish is his fault. If he hadn't been unfaithful, my mom wouldn't have suffered. She's been so lonely since he left her. And then, he flaunted Tish in front of her people, her company.

And he took all of her friends, except Christine. They all sided with Dad over Mom. I hated coming home, finding her drunk, so sad, mourning for the man she spent her whole life with.

He just up and left. How could he do that? As for my mom, I'm not sure what all she's done, but I know she's done it all for me.

I think she has been in charge of EventCo from its founding. I think she just let my dad think he was for a time to get the IPO money in the door from the boys' club of investment banking. My mom is in charge of everything. Tish just didn't realize it.

Neither did I.

CHAPTER 56
KATE

We sit facing each other across my desk.

"Are you doing OK, honey?" I ask. "You haven't changed your mind about the publicity shoot, have you?"

"I want to do the photo shoot with you," she says. "But I'm worried about Tish. What she'll do to you and to the office."

"She won't do anything to me. Wouldn't dare," I say.

"I hope you're right," she says. "Mom, I know Dad hurt you, so much."

"Thanks for saying that. You're right. We built a full life together. Family. Business. He threw it all away," I say.

"But you were the last person he called, ever. I have the proof on his phone. He still loved you," she says.

"Maybe, but there was a lot of damage done." I swivel my chair back and forth. "All of this is a moot point. It's the past. We need to get going. We need to move forward."

"Mom, one last question. Why did you use the name Mabel to communicate with Dad?"

"Oh, that. You know Tish wouldn't allow your father and me to talk directly, and there was a lot we needed to cover, with the IPO and everything."

She nods. "I get that. But why the name Mabel?"

"It was a nickname, from when we first met. I know, sort of sentimental."

"Tish knew it was you, despite the name," Ashlyn says. "You really got her fired up, that's for sure. Maybe on purpose?"

"No. I was just helping Dad through the stress of the IPO. If she read into things, what can I say, honey? Makes me look smarter than I am," I say.

I can tell Ashlyn is about to ask more questions when a text lights up my phone. It's from Bob. You are right. Mary Loveless and Sarah Byrne will admit, for a price, they never witnessed John sign anything. Congratulations. We have an attorney taking their statements now. Handwriting expert agrees John's signature is a fake, too. We have enough to take to the judge and get this thing invalidated.

"Yes!" I leap out of my chair.

"What is it, Mom?" Ashlyn asks.

"We found our crack in the will. The witnesses were phony, and they'll admit it. The handwriting was faked. It's over," I say.

"That's great news!" Ashlyn says.

Jennifer knocks on my office door. "Ready?"

"More than ready," I answer. Glad for the diversion. "Come on, Ashlyn. Let's go show the world who's boss."

The world should know Kate Nelson is holding all the cards.

CHAPTER 57
TISH

I'm pacing back and forth in my kitchen. The same kitchen I can't wait to off-load onto some unsuspecting new owner. The heating and cooling guy was here earlier and disconnected the thermostats from the app. He says they'll work like regular ones now, thank god. The tech guy Chris called should be here any minute to unlink the music system from that app. I'm getting my damn house under control.

The real reason I'm pacing, truth be told: I'm lonely. Nobody at work will talk to me. I don't have any friends. I need to start playing tennis. Stat. And what was stupid Kate saying about owning most of EventCo? I don't understand. I need to find a way to scare Kate some more. I like it when she's afraid of me. But no one at EventCo would tell me where the lame photo shoot was, and mostly, it seemed, they were laughing at me.

My phone buzzes in my pocket. It's a message from Uncle George. We have trouble, sugar. They bought off our witnesses. Better fold up the con. Move on.

What? No. I text: No way. I don't understand. Call me.

I wait. He doesn't call. I call him, and it goes to voice mail. I fight the urge to throw my phone across the room.

This isn't a con, not really. This was my life. But now it's over. I'm surprised when tears spill over my eyes. I've lost. Kate won. I'm glad I left the office. I can't have anyone seeing me like this. I need a new plan, apparently. I dab at my eyes, careful not to ruin my makeup. Fine, I will forget about the company, I'll forget about this place.

Which reminds me, I haven't heard from that real estate hunk yet. No worries, though. I've decided I'll be in residence at the Canopy by Hilton downtown until I find the perfect place. I won't spend another night in this horrible home. I swear it's haunted. Even as I hope it's not me who is haunted.

A brief yet terrifying image of John as a ghost flies through my mind before I push it away. John died a cheater, and in that sense, he earned what he got. He'd better not be haunting me because he knows I

382

always win. At least he knows that now.

I pull two large suitcases out from the storage closet as the whole house music system begins blaring the song "Who Are You" by the Who.

The windows are closed, and for once, the house is a pleasant temperature. I can outlast a little loud music. I open my suitcase, find my noise-canceling head-phones, and pop them over my ears. One point for Tish.

I toss a few outfits into my suitcase, sexy dresses for evening and a couple of workout and tennis clothes for next week. Shoes and purses, five in each suitcase, are next. I open the safe and put on one of my most expen-sive gifts from John, a long gold necklace with diamonds sparkling every half an inch or so along the chain. It's to die for, dar-ling. I pull out my largest diamond studs, and instead of my travel wedding ring, I'll wear the real rock from John. I will look like the spoiled wife I was when I check into my suite downtown.

I close the safe and realize somehow I need to get all of this out of here and into my new place. The only things I care about are my clothes and jewelry. The rest is all John's stuff. I will pay Sonja to bring the contents of my closet to my suite at the

Canopy. I'll have them set everything up on rolling racks in the adjoining room. And I'll have Sonja organize it all. She'll handle that, and then I'll fire her, too. She seems overly loyal to John and Kate. Overly attached to the past.

I am the future. That's who I am. The music still blares as I make my way downstairs to the kitchen. As I stand in the kitchen, the electric blackout shades on the windows in the house start to roll down. I'm plunged into darkness even though it's sunny outside. My house is a fiend.

I push aside the electric shades and open all the windows in the kitchen before realizing the music will carry to the golf course.

I need a fresh start. I'm not going to hang out in downtown Columbus. No, Paris is nice this time of year. Or London. Or, well, anywhere luxurious. I'll go away for a price. And I know who will be willing to pay just about anything. I pull out my phone.

I text Kate: How about coming over to my house for a discussion. We need to work things out between us. For Ashlyn's sake. I don't understand what you said about owning seventy percent of the company, but I do know I have a right to something for being married to John. Don't you want me gone? Maybe we can make a deal?

I watch my phone, pick it up every minute for the next ten minutes. I check to be sure I sent the message to the right phone number. The contact in my phone is labeled *Old Mrs. Nelson.* Yep, that's her.

Finally, my screen lights up. It's Kate. She texts: I'm busy. Sorry.

I'm so tired of these people. I want out. Kate's my multimillion-dollar golden ticket.

I text. I can be reasonable. Buy me out.

She texts: Out of what? I can prove the will is fake. Witnesses, Mary and Sarah, signed statements. Notary ledger is being subpoenaed. John's signature declared a fake per expert. You're done.

Well, shit. I remember George never called me back. And his stupid receptionist, Mary, has turned on me. I'm alone, as usual. Ok, but I'm still here. I can make your life miserable. I can go to the press. Ruin the IPO.

I watch the bubbles as Kate responds. She must have a lot to say. I'm about to send another text when hers finally comes through. You already tipped off the media.

I text: Yup. But I'll keep quiet from now on, for a price.

Kate texts: You killed John. You sabotaged Ashlyn's car. You tried to take my company with that fake will. You tried to take everything.

Interesting. I wonder what she thinks she knows. She's bluffing. She has no proof. Just Ashlyn's stupid speculations.

Still my hand shakes as I reply, His heart stopped. His fault. Ashlyn is a brat who should go back to school. I don't want the company anymore. I know what you want. You can have it.

I yank up the shade and stare outside at the backyard and the golf course beyond. Those guys out there on the golf course are John's people. They were never mine. These neighbors aren't my type. The whole scene in the suburbs never suited me. This is a place people come to die, the last stop before a retirement home. I'm so glad I'm getting out of here. I'm about to be super rich. I search for flights on my phone and discover several to New York this evening. I book a seat, first class of course, and when the travel site screen prompts me, I decide yes, I would like to add a luxury hotel suite. So I do. From New York, I can go anywhere in the world.

My phone lights up with a notice that there's motion at the front door. Likely it's a golfer coming to complain about the late afternoon noise. Or worse. It's probably the neighborhood security guard writing me another citation for not understanding how to control my house. It's like if you have a dog that keeps running away and digging up your neighbor's yard. Sure, it's not you doing the digging, but still, you're responsible. Until you put some ground-up cherry pits in the dog's food, then you're not. That was a lesson dear old Momma taught me when she killed my puppy.

Kate texts: This is your last chance. I'll be over at 7. You better be telling the truth.

I text: I am.

"Coming," I yell, even though I know the person at the front door can't hear me.

I pull open the door. It's the stupid rent-a-security-guard cop again.

"Mrs. Nelson. Good evening." He's yelling and points to my noise-canceling headphones.

I yank them off. "Good evening, Officer."

"Ma'am, your music. We've had several complaints." He's opening his little citation pad and begins to write.

Who cares? "As I told you, I can't control the house. It's haunted. I'm moving. Tell them all I'm moving. Gone tonight for good. That's going to make all of us really happy."

"You know what, ma'am. You're right. I'll let them know. Have a great evening." He is laughing as he walks down my front path.

I hate them all. I walk back inside and just like that, the music stops. I know something else will happen soon, but for now, I enjoy the silence.

I walk out to the garage, and I find a picnic basket. We only used it once, but it's so cute, I should have used it more. The basket is woven, with a red-checkered lining and a small wooden cheese board. The board has a message stamped on it: BRIE HAPPY.

The message warms my heart as I carry everything inside. I'll make a proper cocktail party for me and Kate. We deserve it after all we've been through. I start whistling and preparing for Kate's arrival. This is the sophisticated way to handle our disagreements. We will come to an understanding. We had better. I make two different batches of margaritas. One in a glass pitcher I'll leave in the kitchen. This one is to celebrate if we strike a deal. I tuck the thermos with the special batch inside the picnic basket and take it to the garage.

This is the batch to serve if we don't. I pile freshly rinsed cherries in a crystal bowl and carry them to the living room. I fluff the couch pillows, and as I do, I dream about Paris. I've always wanted to visit. I thought it would be with John, he promised me we would go see the City of Light.

But like a lot of his promises, it was just another illusion.

CHAPTER 58
KATE

In the dressing room, my pulse is racing as
I slip off the formal gown they had me wear
for the photo shoot.

I'm not sure if it's brilliant, or stupid, or
both, but I am going to see Tish tonight. I
know Bob wouldn't approve, but someone
has to get control of the situation. Despite
the fact she knows we can prove the will is
fake, and we will reinstate his real one, the
problem remains: she is still around. I realize for my life to get back to some semblance of normal, she can't be here.

I need to be the one to deal with this once
and for all.

I walk out of the dressing room with a
smile and hand the gown to Nathan, the
shoot director.

"I wish I could keep this," I say.

"Don't they all."

Ashlyn rolls her eyes. "It's a little fairy
tale for you, Mom."

"I can still believe in happily ever after," I say. My phone rings as we walk out into the late afternoon sunshine.

"Mrs. Nelson. It's Chief Briggs. Do you have a minute?"

I stop walking and put the phone on speaker so Ashlyn can hear.

"Do you have the report?"

"We do, someone poured water in Ashlyn's gas tank," he says.

"Like a water bottle?" I ask.

"No, much more than that. Like someone turned on a garden hose full blast," he says. "So much water. Whoever did it wanted to fry the electrical circuit, and they succeeded. She could have been killed if she was on a highway."

Ashlyn gasps. "I can't believe her. She's out of control."

"Who?" Briggs asks.

I raise my finger to my lips and mute my phone. "I think we should handle Tish ourselves, Ashlyn. It's the only way. I'm meeting her tonight."

"Mom, that's too dangerous," Ashlyn says.

"I'll be fine," I say and unmute the phone.

"Oh, Chief, Ashlyn thinks a boy she broke up with might have done it. We're not going to press any charges. He feels terrible I'm sure," I say.

Ashlyn shrugs but goes along with me. "That's right, Mom."

"Well, you all let me know if you change your mind. You've had a lot to handle, Mrs. Nelson. Call me if you need me," he says and hangs up.

Ashlyn stares at me.

"I've got this. Don't worry." I give her a hug. "I'm going to go visit your dad's grave, if you want to join me. I haven't been there yet, and I need closure." I don't even know where Tish put him. I still cannot believe he isn't in the family plot as we planned. I clench my fists. It can wait, but it needs to be done, if for optics only.

Ashlyn shakes her head. "I'm not ready to do that. It's weird. I'm mad at Dad right now. Really mad at him for falling for Tish. And what he did to you."

"I understand. I do. Feeling angry is completely normal, honey," I say. "I'll be home by eight. And I'll drive you to the airport. I love you."

"Come home after the cemetery, OK? We'll go to Tish's house together tonight."

I lean forward against my car. "There's nothing to worry about. Everything is under control. And I'll handle her myself. Do you need a ride home?"

"No, thanks, Seth's on his way. Don't go

there without me. Promise?"

I shrug and smile. "Sure."

But I'm lying. I will visit Tish alone.

As I slip into my car, I remember the last time I saw John. He needed me, again. He was growing tired of Tish's lack of depth, her attachment to material things, her refusal to read. Anything. John and I, at our last secret rendezvous before the IPO, before she yanked him to Colorado, were both making fun of his wife. We sat at our favorite restaurant downtown, joking about our clandestine get-together.

I'd spotted him in his favorite back booth and waved as I made my way to him. "Hey. Is the coast clear?"

He stood up and touched my shoulder. "Good to see you, Kate, or should I say, Mabel? And yes, the coast is clear. Although I do feel a little terrible about it, the sneaking around."

I slid into the booth. I said, "She made us do it. She's the one who insists I call her to speak to you. It's crazy. That's no way to do business."

"Or anything else. I know. She's over-the-top jealous of you. Of your career, your success. Everything. She comes from a very different place than you and I did. She had a really tough childhood. I don't have many specifics. I only know that she was poor and her mom was neglectful, but I'm starting to believe it was even worse than she lets on. Tish has a really violent temper just beneath the surface. I'm not used to that. You were always so calm, so understanding."

I remember thinking, *How nice.* I was so considerate you decided to leave me. I said, "We built everything we have. It wasn't easy for us, either. She has it really good now, but she's acting like a toddler having daily temper tantrums," I said, grabbing the menu before I said any more. I wanted to keep our line of communication open, the relationship growing again. "I'm starving. You?"

"Yes. Lately, my blood pressure medicine makes me famished. I'm just feeling off. It'll be good to get this IPO out of the way and deal with other things. I want to be happy again, Katie." John kept his eyes on the menu.

And that's when I knew. He would get the IPO done, and then he'd get rid of Tish.

"What will make you happy again?"

"I don't know exactly. It's exhausting. I understand why it frustrates you, just trying to get business done. I'm sort of sick of the whole situation, too. She's always glancing at my phone, trying to see my messages. It's funny you need a special name just to talk to me. Funny, and sad. I think she's figured out Mabel is you, by the way. I'm tired of all of it. I miss this. Us." John pushed a hand through his hair before waving for the waiter.

As for me, I spent the rest of our lunch relishing the notion that Tish's time, Tish's hold over our family, was coming to an end.

I was wrong then, but I'm not now.

I turn onto the road to the cemetery with mixed feelings. I do want to visit John's grave. For many reasons, not the least of it is the sense of finality it should provide. The resolve, too. As I drive, I remember something I read about the positive effects of anger. Angry people have a lot in common with happy people. Both tend to be more optimistic. It's true. Take, for example, one study of the aftermath of the 9/11 terrorist attacks. In the study, those experiencing anger expected fewer attacks in the future. I feel certain seeing John's headstone will have the same effect.

It's likely not a wise move to meet with Tish alone, to try to strike a deal. But it is what I need. What my company needs. I'll write up a proposal she can't refuse.

After a quick stop at the caretaker's cottage, I have a map, John's burial site marked with an *X*. It's a quick drive to the rolling green hills of the cremated burial area. The nerve. I find John's simple headstone, a plain marker for an exceptional man, a man who was led astray by a younger version of his wife and suffered the consequences. Yes, a cliché. But my cliché. I take a photo, just to remember this spot. To remember my resolve.

I touch the cold white stone. "John. I'm going to make this right. I'm sorry for everything she did to you, to me, to Ashlyn. But don't worry. She'll be gone soon. I promise."

I bow my head and say a few more words I know John would want to hear.

CHAPTER 59
TISH

I'm going to pack enough for a long, wonderful, luxurious vacation starting in New York City, then Paris, and ending wherever I want to go. The possibilities are limitless.

I've pulled out my two most expensive trunks, Louis Vuitton of all things. When I first bought them, I wouldn't take them anywhere. I was afraid the luggage handlers would steal them, and everything inside. I know *I* would have, at least back in the day.

John had laughed and told me luggage was supposed to be used and enjoyed. He said that I needed to trust people. That most people are good.

He was so wrong about that.

All the windows are open, the shades drawn. My phone lights up with a text. It's from Chris, my hunky realtor. Problem. I ran the title info on your home. You don't own it.

I text back. Yes I do.

Chris responds immediately. No. It's owned by a trust. The Ashlyn Nelson Family Trust. Do you know who that is?

Fuck. My fingers fly over the keypad. Sell the Telluride condo first. I'll straighten this out with my lawyer.

Chris texts: Sorry. That's titled to the Ashlyn Nelson Family Trust, too. So is your Florida property. It's not your Florida property, actually. None of it is. I'll come over tonight. We can mess around and make a plan?

I drop my phone on the kitchen counter.

I need George. George was supposed to protect me. The will was supposed to be ironclad. I'm going to kill him.

I text George. Need to talk now. Property not mine. Kate up to something. Help.

I stare at my phone, waiting for a return text.

But like the last time I called him, there is no response.

CHAPTER 60
KATE

I sit in my car parked outside of Tish's house, waiting for 7:00 p.m.

When my phone buzzes with the alarm I set, I jump.

It's time.

I scan the agreement I drew up once more. I figure if Tish and her shady attorney could download a will off the internet, I could find an official-looking template of my own. I was right.

I start up the walkway to Tish's house. Actually, it's not her house. And I cannot wait to tell her that.

My stomach clenches as I ring the doorbell and knock on the door. I tell myself to relax. This isn't a boxing match. This is a business meeting. I take a deep breath.

Tish and I will come to an agreement. I have what she needs. Money. This is personal. It requires intimacy, talking face to face. I'm the only one who can do this. And I will.

CHAPTER 61
ASHLYN

My mom shouldn't be going there alone. Last night when I was moving out, I left my bedroom window unlocked, just in case I needed to sneak back in for something. The trellis was a handy escape route in high school.

As I make a plan, I think about the last conversation I had with my dad. He told me he'd agreed with mom's idea to put all of his real estate holdings into a trust, for me. He told me it was what my mom wanted, and that he was glad he could make her happy. It's weird to know I own Tish's house. She didn't believe me when I told her, but I imagine she'll find out sometime soon.

I'm pretty sure real estate transactions weren't enough for my mom, not after everything he did to her when he married Tish. Did he really expect Mom to just take him back? Sorry, Kate, here, let's make a trust for Ashlyn as my penance, and I'll just move back in with you.

Like the last five years didn't damage us all to the core. Like the last five years didn't happen? As if he hadn't squashed my mom's big project just when she was ready to launch it this summer. No, Dad, that's not how the world works. You don't always get your way.

And what about me? The damage you did to our relationship was lasting, deep. Once you and Tish hooked up, you barely had time for anyone else. I know you thought we still had a connection, but it was tenuous, transactional. And often, canceled by you. Even the last plans we had, dinner with you, me, and Seth, even that was abruptly called off for Tish. She played you, that's what she did. She got all the power in the relationship and left you looking like a fool to everyone else: to the employees, to your friends, to Mom, and most especially, to me.

Did you ever think about what it was like to have a stepmother who was your own age? Did you think about how humiliating it was for Mom to have to work with both of you every day? Did you wonder how we felt when you dropped a bomb on our lives?

No, you didn't. It didn't matter to you.

Once you found your "soul mate," nobody else mattered. You promised nothing would be different, but you lied. I trusted you, and you let me down again and again. I often wondered if you thought Tish was worth it? I guess you had decided she wasn't. I guess lust doesn't last, but the damage you did to our family certainly does. You don't even know how deep the hurt is, the pain, the anger is. And now, you never will.

Headlights illuminate the front lawn as my mom's car pulls up and parks at the curb in front of Tish's house.

It's time.

CHAPTER 62
TISH

I'm a little nervous anticipating my next visitor.

Thank goodness Ashlyn is out of my life forever. I will never speak to her again. She was the first one contesting the will, and now, it's not worth the paper it was written on. And all along she owned my house? Little bitch.

Focus, Tish. I'm as prepared as I can be for my little meeting with Kate. I'll get as much money as I can, and then I'll get out of here.

The hunky realtor is set to come by for another romp in an hour, but I'm not sure I'm in the mood. I mean, if I can't use him to make some cash, what good is he? I should text him and cancel. I am upstairs finishing packing my large trunks. I wish I could fit all of my beautiful things in these two trunks, but I know Sonja will reunite us again soon.

I imagine the swanky hotel room I'll check into tonight in New York, the crisp high-thread-count sheets, the twenty-four-hour room service, the spa. A hotel John and I have never been to before, a place his ghost can't haunt me. This will all just be a bad dream soon.

I hope Kate has come with a generous offer. I'm young. I should travel, not be chained to a boring corporate job. With me gone, there is no story of a fight between two Mrs. Nelsons. Kate will be pleased. This will be a win-win for both of us. As for Uncle George, he better call and apologize. I can't believe Kate was able to unravel his scheme so quickly. Too bad for him, but I'm not paying the rest of his retainer, no way. And if Kate presses charges, I'll tell them it was all George's idea. I'm just a helpless widow.

George will never know how much Kate pays me tonight. This is my deal, all for me.

I look in the mirror and decide full evening makeup is in order. As I smooth on foundation, I remind myself to transfer the cash from our joint account to the new one I've set up — the one where Kate will make a generous deposit soon. I check out my reflection in the mirror, and my confidence cracks. Who am I kidding? I'm not a step ahead of Kate, I'm not sure I ever was. But I'm about to be free. I'm rich and young and I can go anywhere, do anything, be anyone.

I smile at the thought as I apply mascara and note I need concealer under my eyes again. Because I was haunted as usual last night by John. I know, it's crazy, but he's in my dreams. And not in the romantic sense. Last night, John kept offering me a drink, begging me to take it. Every time I said no, or pushed the glass away, his arm dissolved into the air, only to reappear with the same margarita glass in his hand.

"Come on, Tish. Let's have a little toast," John repeated over and over.

I take a deep breath and add blush to my cheeks. This is almost over. All of it. George kept telling me all would work out as long as I stayed cool, whatever that means. He didn't like the fact I flipped John's desk. That "wasn't cool," as he put it. He doesn't understand the pressure I'm under, or how horrible it is with everyone spying on me at the office.

The last time I talked to him, he asked for more money. That's all this ever was to him.

"I've paid you all you're going to get. The whole thing is falling apart. Quit milking this." Greedy son of a gun is on my last nerve. But he got me this far. Once Kate and I make a deal, I won't need him anymore. She wants me gone. And for once, we agree on something.

The last time we spoke, he'd said, "Behave yourself, Terry Jane. You can't be so angry, so mean all the time." I didn't appreciate George's tone or the use of my hated real name. But he hung up before I could reply. And we haven't talked since. And he won't answer my text messages. As far as I'm concerned, he's gone.

Good riddance. I check the time. Almost 7:00 p.m., and it's still a balmy eighty degrees outside. There's just nothing like Columbus in August. But I can handle the heat and humidity. It's not that different here from rural Kentucky. I take that back — it's a world away from Pineville.

It's so quiet in my house, for once, I almost want to scream. But I don't. Because I've learned to control myself, just like Uncle George says. I've learned to be cool.

I check my outfit in the mirror. I look good. And even though I enjoyed my time with hunky Chris, I won't be jumping into bed with him tonight. No, I need to stay cleaned up until my flight. I slip on my necklace from John. As I put it on, I enjoy the sparkles from the diamonds, the twinkle of the gold chain. I double it so it frames my neck in luxury. My wedding ring glistens in the evening light, too, although I've moved it to my other hand. It's too gorgeous not to wear, but I'm no longer married, so it doesn't feel right on my left ring finger. I'm rich but available, I'm advertising. I search through my jewelry box, shoving everything expensive into my carry-on bag. Sparkly valuables are the best. Maybe I'll meet someone on the flight. I'm in first class, so it should be good hunting. I should rephrase that. I'm not a grifter. I'm not really a con artist. Not really.

I promise I've always been looking for love.

It just seems to be almost impossible to find.

Maybe I've looked in the wrong places. I'm suffocating here, where everyone knows everyone's business and someone like me sticks out like an exotic flower in a field of dandelions. No, thank you. I'm suited for a big city, bigger than Columbus, and I'll be there soon.

It's only a few hours until it's time to go to the airport. This next chapter of life is going to be so fun. I decide to take one last look at all of my fabulous clothes and purses in my closets. Sonja will box everything and send it all to a storage facility where I can retrieve what I want, whenever I want. Until then, I blow my closet a kiss goodbye and turn out the light.

CHAPTER 63
KATE

I slip the key Ashlyn gave me into the lock and open the door. I hurry inside and disarm the alarm.

"Tish! It's Kate. I'm here to talk," I yell up the grand staircase. I know she's here somewhere. I take a few steps up and call her name again.

"Oh, I see you let yourself in. A charming habit your daughter shares." Tish stands at the top of the stairs wearing a super-short skirt and the expensive necklace John bought her when they were engaged. She begged for it, Ashlyn had told me, and he was happy to oblige. He was in love, he told me.

"What's a $30,000 necklace compared to a lifetime of happiness?" he'd asked me when I questioned him at the office.

"Can you just stop flaunting your midlife crisis? It's pathetic," I'd said and turned away in disgust.

410

Tish is looking at me.

"Good evening," I say.

She says, "I could call the cops on you. Breaking and entering."

I smile. "You could, but you won't. You know they're on my side anyway."

"So what? You bought a few squad cars. I can still call them." Tish glares at me.

"I don't think they'd appreciate the fact that you tried to kill my daughter by flooding her car's engine."

Tish laughs. "Not me. She probably was texting while driving again."

"You murdered my husband."

"Your *ex-husband*. And I did not. You're making up stories. You don't have any proof."

"It's over, Tish. You were never going to win. Not in the long run. Not against me. Did you know this house is in a trust for Ashlyn? John and I did that."

"Just found out that charming piece of news. You can have the house. It is haunted." She's gliding down the stairs toward me. "I need a change. I'll leave town tonight, for the right price."

I take a deep breath. I'm not afraid of her. Even if I have allowed her to think I am.

She's a gold digger. A home-wrecker. And I'm convinced it was premeditated. All of it.

411

She's resourceful, I suppose.

It was John who wasn't.

"What do you want?" Tish stands one step above me.

"You will leave my family alone, leave town, and never come back. I'm willing to pay. I just want you gone," I say. Time to drop a few surprises. "John and I weren't getting back together. I was just messing with you. I knew you read his texts."

"What? Yes you were. You wanted what I had." Tish spits the words out but stops. "You didn't want him back?"

I shrug. "That's for me to know. It worked. Your relationship ended as it always was going to. It was a joke from the beginning. Let's get this deal done, shall we?"

"Fine with me. But it's going to cost you. Big-time. Do you understand?" Tish wags a finger at me. "Let's sit in the living room."

I follow her down the hall, and we sit on opposite ends of an overstuffed white couch. I pull out the documents I brought with me and place them on the glass coffee table.

"I have all the money in the world. I can transfer to your account tonight. I have a contract for us to sign, right here. Unlike the fake will you tried to float, this document is real and binding. One of the stipulations is you must never come back to

Columbus. I mean it. This will be the last time we speak to each other. Understood?" I point to clause five of the contract.

"I've made two copies. We'll each sign one. Here are the terms." I point to the numbers and know they look larger than anything Tish has ever seen in writing, bigger than anything she will ever see again.

She smiles and asks, "And what will you agree to?"

"Nothing. I don't owe you anything."

Tish signs on the bottom line, and I sign the contract, too. We each have an executed copy. I slip my copy back into my purse.

Tish leans back on the couch. "He shouldn't have messed around on me. I don't care what you say. Even if it wasn't really an affair, he was going to leave me. That's not OK," she says.

"Oh really?" I say. "That's ironic coming from you."

"Where I come from, we have a way to handle people who aren't true. It's simple, really. Would you like a cherry?" Her tone has shifted. I hear a hint of a southern accent.

She points to a bowl of cherries on the table.

I swallow and try to keep my face expressionless. What is she saying? "No, no thank you."

"John seemed to like them. I always had them around. Even in Telluride on our last trip. The fruit is delicious, you just have to watch out for the seeds," she says with the same creepy southern voice. She takes a cherry and pops it into her mouth.

"I understand what it feels like to be betrayed," I admit. "But killing someone? Your husband? That's diabolical."

"Our relationship was the pits at the end," she says. "You really didn't want him back? You were just messing with him, us?"

"That's what I said." I stare at the bowl of cherries on the coffee table. Did she kill John with cherry pits? Is that even possible? "The coroner ruled it a heart attack. Are you saying something different?"

"I'm not saying anything. John's autopsy didn't find anything. The story is over," Tish says. She pops another cherry in her mouth and smiles. "I made a batch of margaritas. Are you thirsty?"

I fight the urge to run out the front door as a chill runs down my spine. "No, I'm not. You know I shouldn't give you a dime. I'm convinced you really did kill John, and you could have killed Ashlyn."

"I'm not stupid. Ashlyn just needed a little

warning." Tish shrugs.

"You will never contact her again."

She hands me a piece of paper. A deposit slip. "Works for me. Oh, and I need you to make a deposit into this account tonight, before my flight departs at 10:00 p.m."

I take the slip of paper. "It will be done."

Tish smiles and stands up. "Great. So, I need help with my bags. Can you do that or are you too old and feeble? I'm kidding, joking around for old times' sake. Aren't you glad I'll be out of your hair soon?"

Beyond glad, a mixture of emotions but mostly joy. I don't tell her that, of course. I follow Tish up the stairs, the stairs she and John used to climb together up to their bedroom. It's fine. I can handle it. At least this is the end.

"I'm stronger than I look," I assure her. "Did you enjoy the screen saver on John's desktop today?"

She stops at the top of the stairs, and I join her on the landing. She looks momentarily surprised. "No way. That was you? And the threatening note?"

I nod.

"Good job." She nods her head with a smile, appreciating my handiwork, I suppose.

"Thanks, I guess." It's surreal, standing

here accepting compliments from her. But this is what my life's become because of her. And because of John.

At the top of the stairs, Tish sticks out her hand and we shake. She says, "Thanks for coming up with a mutually beneficial deal. I'll hold up my end. Promise."

I follow her down the long hall to the bedroom.

She stops at the doorway. "I can't wait for you to see our bedroom. It was so cozy. We had so many good times here."

Her little dig won't work. I feel nothing. I follow her into the room with a lightness I haven't felt in years. I see two huge suitcases, almost like trunks. She is prepared to leave. This is all working out.

Tish seems almost giddy, like we're girlfriends and this is the start of a vacation together. "Thank you so much for helping me. We can roll the suitcases down the hall, but we'll probably need to carry them down the stairs together."

I start rolling one of the suitcases down the hall. Tish follows with the matching trunk. It's so heavy I have to push it from behind. I'm not sure if we can handle carrying these. We reach the top of the stairs and both stop to reassess.

"I'm not sure about this," I tell her. "I

think we could slide them down, maybe, one at a time?"

"They'll crash into the glass table at the bottom of the stairs," Tish says. "No, we have to carry them."

Tish is bent down, next to the suitcase she's rolled to the edge of the stairs. These trunks are likely worth thousands of dollars with big gold latches and the telltale Louis Vuitton monogram. Each one must weigh over one hundred pounds empty.

I look down the hall, past Tish, and blink. It's Ashlyn. She's running toward us.

"I'll take this one." Tish starts down the stairs, the heavy trunk behind her, and as I watch, Ashlyn shoves her from behind. I see Tish's necklace wrap around the wheel. It's all in slow motion. I hear a guttural scream. I watch in horror as Tish's body flies over the trunk, and they fall together in a terrible tangle to the bottom of the stairs, crashing to a stop under the glass table that shatters and falls on top of the trunk.

We stand together at the top of the stairs. Tish's body twisted and partially hidden by the trunk. I can't process what just happened. All I can think of is protecting Ashlyn. She shouldn't be here. She can't be found here.

"Do you think she's dead?" Ashlyn asks,

her voice a whisper. "I want her to die."

"I understand. She is a bad person," I say. I can't believe this is happening. Did Ashlyn kill Tish? Was this purposeful? And why? I had no idea my daughter felt this type of rage against Tish. I should have realized how much pain she was in, too.

She's looking at me, her eyes shining and wide. "I'm on your side, Mom."

My heart feels the love, but my brain knows we must get in front of this situation. There's no more time to talk. "Ashlyn, go. Now! Leave the way you came. Make sure no one sees you!" I scream.

Adrenaline zips through me as I rush down the stairs to where Tish has landed. Her body is under the trunk, her head at an awkward angle.

Ashlyn disappears down the hall, back the way she came. I run to the living room to get away from the horror and to give Ashlyn time to escape. I'm shaking all over, but I try to breathe. I pace back and forth in the living room, gathering Tish's copy of the contract from the coffee table. I catch a glimpse of myself in the living room mirror: I'm pale, and dark circles shroud my eyes. I turn away and sit down on the couch. The bowl of red cherries glisten in the light of the crystal chandelier overhead.

I don't know how long I've been sitting here on Tish's couch in shock, but suddenly a man walks through the front door.

We stare at each other.

"Who are you?" he asks.

"Who are you?" I ask.

He ignores the question and yells, "Tish? Oh my god!"

He's kneeling on the ground next to the trunk. I rush to his side. "There's been an accident. She just fell down the stairs. I don't know what to do." Tears stream down my face.

"Call 911!" the man yells.

I find my phone in my purse and dial 911.

"What's your emergency?" the operator asks.

"It looks like a woman has fallen down the stairs. It's a terrible accident. Send help, please," I manage in a choking voice. What if she's dead? What if she's not?

"Is she breathing?" the operator asks.

"I don't know."

"The squad is on the way. Stay on the phone. I need you to check for a pulse," the operator demands.

I run to where Tish landed. Sparkling shards of glass decorate the floor. The man who came in the door is kneeling next to her. In my imagination, I watch as she lifts

419

the trunk and stands up, yelling for Ashlyn, trying to blame my daughter and me for her accident. Because, it was, it must be, an accident. But as I reach her side, she's still pinned underneath the trunk.

"Can you feel a pulse?" the operator asks.

"Is there a pulse?" I ask the stranger, but he's shaking his head.

I don't want to touch her. Her neck is at such a terrible angle. I find her right hand and see the excessively large wedding ring from my husband, twice the size of mine. I touch her wrist, but I can't feel a pulse as my own blood rushes through my body at warp speed.

"I don't know. I don't know. Her head, it's twisted," I say, walking away from Tish's body. "She's not moving. I don't know."

"The squad is there, ma'am," the operator says.

And that's when the professionals arrive with calm determination on their faces and I step out of the way. When they lift the trunk off Tish's body, my knees collapse, and I drop to the floor.

I close my eyes, and everything is black.

CHAPTER 64
KATE

When I open my eyes, I'm on a bed, white curtains drawn around me. A nurse leans over me.

"Do you know where you are, Mrs. Nelson?" she asks.

A hospital would be my guess.

"You're at Riverside Hospital. In the emergency room. How are you feeling?"

It's all so shockingly clear in my mind. Tish's fall, the angle of her neck. "I need to see my daughter."

"We've called your daughter. Her flight turned around midair somehow. Looks like she's here now."

"Mom." Ashlyn sobs as she runs to my side.

"Honey." I pull her toward me.

She whispers, "I shouldn't have left you there."

"It was a great idea to take your flight as scheduled. I'm so proud of you." I sit up in

421

the bed, almost like nothing was wrong with me. "Has anyone told you anything about Tish's condition?"

Ashlyn shakes her head. "No."

All the time Tish has been in our lives, I've been waiting for the next terrible thing to happen. That's all she has wrought. Horrible things. Sure, John and I had let our marriage take second place to the business. That made it easy for someone like her to sneak into the gap. But at first, I thought that was all she'd take. John. The love of my life. That was enough.

But once she had John, she moved on to taking EventCo. She tried to take my whole life.

The nurse pops her head in. "Do you need anything in here? The doctor should be by shortly."

"We're all set." I smile.

"Maybe she's dead," Ashlyn says, and starts crying. I hug her tight. "I was so mad, Mom. I wasn't thinking straight. I thought she was going to hurt you. I just reacted. It was an accident."

"I know, I was just as angry."

Ashlyn's face is tear-streaked. She's speaking too fast.

"Take a deep breath. Whatever happened to Tish is her own doing. All of it is." I wrap my arm around Ashlyn. She's trembling. "You have done nothing. Do you understand me clearly? The last time you saw her, she admitted to tampering with your car. You could have died. You were not at her house tonight. Got it?"

She starts to cry again, sputtering.

"Calm down. Listen to me. None of this is our fault. She killed your father. She confessed to me."

"She killed Dad with that drink, right? I saw a pitcher of the same stuff on the kitchen counter tonight when I climbed into my room. She was going to try to kill you, too. I had to stop her."

"Yes, you're right. She used cherry pits. I didn't know they were poisonous and undetectable," I say.

"Mrs. Nelson?" A nurse approaches, and I wrap my arms around Ashlyn, protecting my daughter, who slumps, sobbing, on the bed.

"Yes," I answer, because I am. Always will be.

"I'm afraid the other Mrs. Nelson's injuries are severe. Are you the next of kin? I need someone to authorize treatment, review the options."

Tish is alive. I could have sworn from the way she was crumpled under the trunk that she died of her fall. The nurse stares at me. I am not going to take responsibility for Tish's care, that's for sure. But I would like to be sure she can't harm us anymore. "No, I am not related to her. She's my ex-husband's second wife." I shake my head.

"Where is he?" she asks.

"My husband is deceased," I answer. "You'll need to get in touch with her attorney, a Mr. George Price. He's the only contact of hers that I'm aware of. I'm sorry."

Bob walks into the hospital room and nods in our direction with a finger in the air, signifying one minute. I had texted him as soon as I got to the hospital and had a moment of privacy. I'd feigned fainting to avoid answering any questions. And I needed to get out of here before someone started asking questions here. I told him to get me discharged immediately. He followed orders. "Let's get out of here, shall we? I've signed the papers. Ashlyn, come along."

Minutes later, the three of us walk out of the hospital and into the cool night.

"Mom," Ashlyn says. "We need to go to her house."

"It's a police scene," Bob says.

"She was going to hurt Mom tonight, when she went over there. Kill her, like she did Dad. I know it. She was setting a trap. I saw a pitcher of margaritas on the kitchen counter."

I squeeze her hand so she won't say more. She can't admit she was there, not to anyone, not even Bob.

Bob looks at Ashlyn. And then turns to me.

"She's right. Of course. Tish made another pitcher of her special margaritas, this time just for me," I say, covering for Ashlyn. I'm sure she saw one, though. I wonder why Tish didn't insist I have one? I suppose it's because I came to her home with an offer for a bunch of money, and that's all she really wanted.

"Good god," Bob says, "I'll call the police. Have them search the residence as a crime scene with a special focus on margaritas. Do you know what to test for, what she may have used?"

"Cherry pits. Ground-up cherry pits," I say.

Ashlyn is shaking, and I wrap my arm around her.

"So, she really did poison John?" Bob pulls out his phone. "Yes, this is the attorney representing Mrs. Nelson, the first Mrs. Nelson, and her daughter, Ashlyn. We have reason to believe Mrs. Nelson was trying to poison the first Mrs. Nelson. She was fond of serving it. Yes, she can make a statement. Of course. Thank you."

I don't listen to the rest of Bob's conversation as we stand in the parking lot of the hospital. I just hold on to my daughter. I know the police will want to question Ashlyn and me. But eventually, they'll discover what Tish did.

I'll call Chief Briggs personally and get him involved, if he isn't already. It's wonderful that we finally know what she used. The only thing left to do is be sure she doesn't have a chance to implicate Ashlyn in her "fall" down the stairs.

As we stand outside in the warm night air, I feel my anger dissipating. My shoulders drop, and I take a deep breath. It's true what I read about anger. Anger can benefit relationships, even though society tells us anger is dangerous and we should hide it. Hidden anger in intimate relationships can be detrimental, that's for sure. But it's also true that all emotions have a purpose and evolve to keep us safe. Anger is instinctual. It fuels our primitive need to live and protect ourselves. Anger sharpens our focus, pushes us to fight back when attacked and act to defend ourselves.

It's human nature.

My thoughts drift to my nemesis, Tish. I

wonder who they will find to make decisions about her situation. I happen to know it won't be good old George Price. As his name implies, everyone has one.

Chapter 65
Ashlyn

Mom and I ride home in silence from the hospital, neither of us want to say anything in front of the Uber driver. My whole body aches and trembles, off and on, in waves.

Once we're out of the car and safely inside the house, Mom turns on the alarm and looks at me.

"You thought she was going to kill me, so you made a move. It was the right thing to do," she says, her voice calm, loving. "I couldn't get past the anger, the hurt, with your dad. You understand now, don't you?"

"I think so," I answer, as the shaking starts again.

"It doesn't matter. Tish as much as confessed to killing your father, I have our whole talk recorded on my phone. I even have a photo of the bowl of cherries she served. We'll be in the clear and finally finished with her, once and for all. Thanks to you. You did the right thing. You did."

I wish I believed her. How can almost killing someone be the right thing?

"Mom, you're the one who called and expedited Dad's death certificate. You made sure he was cremated, right?" I ask.

"Everything I did was for you," Mom says. "Tish was a monster. Remember that."

I do know Tish is a monster. But I also know my mom has been manipulating things behind the scenes, like expediting the death certificate. But Mom was flirting with Dad before he died, even though she's told me she'd never welcome him back home. Did she hate Tish so much she simply wanted to sabotage their relationship? Is that what this is all about? Mom lured Dad back to her, but she didn't want him.

Who am I to judge, though? I've been torturing Tish with the apps, and I've been snooping around in her past. She told me to leave her alone, and she'd do likewise. But I kept pushing her, and that's when she lashed out, almost running me over and sabotaging my car. She fought fire with fire.

So, what was I doing when I pushed Tish down the stairs? Was that the result of all the fire, or was I protecting my mom? What was I thinking? I search my memory and the moment is gone, only the feeling of danger and that my mom was going to be

429

hurt. I remember my heart pounding in my chest, a rushing sound in my ears. I'd waited in the shadows on the side of Tish's yard until my mom arrived. When she got out of the car, I ran around the back of the house, ducking under the kitchen windows. That's when I saw it: the pitcher of margaritas just like the one in the photo my dad sent me his last night alive.

I knew I had to save my mom.

I'd climbed the trellis, muscle memory kicking in from all of my high school escape antics. I pushed open the unlocked window and slipped inside my bedroom. When I tiptoed across the room and opened the door to the hall, I heard women's voices from downstairs.

I couldn't hear what they were saying, but I knew it was my mom and Tish. I crept to the top of the stairs and from there could see the white couch where they sat. Tish's back was to me. I couldn't see my mom. They kept talking and then Tish signed something, and before I knew it, they were coming toward the stairs.

My heart raced as I ran back to my room and hid in the space behind my open bedroom door.

Why were they coming upstairs? Did they know I was here? No, that was impossible. I remember feeling angry with both of them. How could they be laughing and chatting after everything that has happened? When my dad is gone forever and Tish killed him.

So when I saw Tish at the top of the stairs, decked out in all the jewelry my dad could buy her, I felt a rage like I've never felt before. Something inside me ignited as I ran down the hall and gave the monster a shove.

Does this mean that now I'm one, too?

CHAPTER 66
KATE

Two weeks later

Chief Briggs came over in person to let me know that investigators found a thermos filled with the poisoned margaritas hidden in the garage, likely ready to serve to me if our meeting went awry. As if I'd fall for that.

"Cherry pits are a deadly way to deliver a fatal dose of cyanide," he explained, sitting across from me in my living room. "Six small pits ground up can kill an adult. The bitter taste easily concealed by a strong margarita mix. Undetectable once ingested, and undetectable in an autopsy after just a few hours, cyanide causes a person's body to shut down, organ by organ. In John's case, his heart stopped."

I remember the bowl of cherries sitting on her cocktail table as a chill runs down my spine. "Poor John. He must have suffered so much. I wonder if she watched him die," I say, taking a deep breath. "No matter how

432

you look at it, John's dead."

"I'm sorry, ma'am, about all of this," Briggs says. "We don't have proof she flooded Ashlyn's car, but it's likely."

"It is," I say. "Tish's quest for money and her need to destroy everyone who was in her way still makes me furious."

"Our experts think she suffers from some form of sociopathy. She had a tough childhood, with abuse, and had run away as a teenager. It's sad, what she went through, but it's no justification for what she put you through or what she did to John. You're lucky you weren't another one of her victims the night she invited you over. You should have called me." His face flushes.

He has been so helpful. "Thank you for everything."

He stands and walks to the front door. "I'm glad things turned out, ma'am. Please let me know if you need anything else."

"You know, I could do dinner this week?" I say. "And, please call me Kate."

He stops in the doorway. "Sounds great. Tomorrow night? I'll pick you up at seven?"

"Perfect," I say before he leaves with a big grin.

"He has a crush on you," Ashlyn says, walking into the living room with Seth close by her side. "You should go on a date with him. He always flirts with you."

"I am. Tomorrow night," I say. I also thought it was a great idea.

"Mom, I'm so happy for you," Ashlyn says.

"Hey, Mrs. Nelson. We're going to grab dinner. Want us to bring you back anything?" Seth asks. The two of them have been inseparable since the night Tish fell. And I'm glad. Ashlyn seems to be doing well with it all, but time will tell. I'll watch her, get her help if she needs it. She could always talk to Dr. Ray. I don't need her anymore.

Thankfully, Tish remains in a coma.

"No, I'm all set. Don't be out too late. You both have class in the morning," I say. Ashlyn's decided to finish her senior year at Ohio State. She'll also keep her internship with Jennifer.

"Yes, Mom. We know. Love you," she says as they depart.

I walk down the hall to my home office to put the finishing touches on the Forever product launch plan. If only John had agreed to it sooner, maybe we'd be in a different place. For me, the project has been a focus, a place to channel my energy after the divorce. Turns out anger can push you to pursue goals others don't think are possible.

On my desk is the latest issue of *CEO*

Magazine featuring me on the cover, and a two-page spread of Ashlyn and me on the inside. The new president starts next week and will take over John's office and report to me. That feels right to everyone.

Tish is out of our lives now, for good.

In fact, she's barely hanging on to hers.

The will she concocted has been ruled a fake, of course. Her witnesses recanted and her attorney, Uncle George, fled the country. Trying to keep one step ahead of the law, I suspect. I know he won't ever be back. I've made sure of it.

It's strange who can come into your life and turn it upside down. And how wrong you can be about someone. None of it is fair, nothing about the situation was right.

John brought Tish into our life, and he paid the ultimate price.

Jennifer's email lands in my inbox. How's the launch plan look?

Perfect.

The next morning, the EventCo staff gathers in the atrium, and I walk alone onto the stage. Jennifer has lured an impressive gaggle of national and regional press, so as I begin to speak, cameras flash and reporters focus.

"Thank you all for coming today. As you know, the last six months have been difficult for EventCo. A day after our IPO, my former husband and cofounder of the company, John Nelson, died tragically in what has now been ruled a murder."

A murmur rolls through the crowd. This isn't a surprise, of course. It's been national news. Some think this whole sordid, sad story will become a movie. I hope not. I focus on the audience. I smile.

"My daughter, Ashlyn, and I were determined to save this company, despite the tabloid fodder our personal lives had become. To that end, I'm proud to announce that the EventCo team has done it again. Today, we revolutionize the way our customers invite their friends to special events, and the way they keep in touch, forever. Introducing EventCo Forever, a lifelong portal of memories and celebrations to keep you connected with your loved ones now, and forever."

The room fills with applause, and I motion for Ashlyn to join me onstage. I tell myself not to dwell on the stock price increase we would have seen at the IPO if John had agreed to launch the Forever product when it was ready. If he'd been focused on the business instead of trying to get out of the mess he'd made by marrying his assistant, just imagine. The anger I used to feel toward him has dissipated some. I've been able to channel it. It made me clear about what I really want. Even Dr. Ray agreed.

Since the magazine article ran, I've enjoyed sharing the spotlight with Ashlyn. Even the tabloids seem to take it easy on us and focus instead on Tish, digging into her past. The police investigation was quick. Chief Briggs had to question me because I was a witness to her fall. He felt terrible for causing me more stress. In reality, he was such a help. He's actually quite handsome, thoughtful, too. I am looking forward to our dinner date.

Tish's fall was ruled a horrible accident that happened to a horrible person. Karma, I suppose.

I shake my head, return to the present. I'm glad Ashlyn and I have a chance to build our bond and build the company together. It was almost too late.

I still have nightmares about what I saw that night when Tish fell. Ashlyn says she's sleeping fine. In my mind, she was never there, and that is how it must be. I tell her that daily.

In my nightmares, Tish doesn't tumble

down the stairs. Instead, she follows me around, offering a glass with some special margaritas. Her head is tilted to the side. It's creepy.

I drink, and she refills my glass.

I always wake up as my body seizes, clutching my chest. I imagine John, gasping for breath, not understanding what Tish had done. I wonder if he knew at the end. I have to believe he did.

I hug my daughter as the cameras flash. I'm so lucky to be alive. We all are.

EPILOGUE:
TISH

Six months later
Shady Valley Care Facility
Newark, Ohio
I hate it here.

I'm trapped at some assisted living place for people in a vegetative state. I hear everything, but so far I haven't mustered the power to keep my eyes open or move my limbs. So, I'm stuck here for who knows how long.

I can't believe my high-priced necklace foiled my plans. And I'm starting to believe Kate had a hand in my accident, too. Because I've had some time to think, and I'm certain she gave me a little shove that night. Yes, that's what happened. When I started to pull the suitcase down the stairs, I didn't realize the Van Cleef & Arpels necklace was wrapped around the wheel of the trunk. The necklace didn't break, and the trunk wheel didn't come off, so my necklace yanked me forward until the trunk and I both hurtled to the bottom of the stairs, gaining momentum as we tumbled. I don't remember anything else, but it must have hurt. The doctors come into my room on occasion, mumble words like "freak accident," "too young to die," and "what a waste" to describe me now. Me. Tish Nelson. I am not a freak or a waste. And I know I didn't get here on my own.

Kate must have had something to do with it.

Somehow, the cops found my little margarita thermos hidden in the garage and tested it. Sure enough, they found cherry pit cyanide. I guess it's not a common mixer up here, not like it was back home when Momma was tired of a pet or I was tired of my stepdaddy. I overheard a nurse say they were going to charge me with John's murder. I think I heard a gasp, some doctor or nurse or someone. How did they look at me when they heard that news? Do they all think I deserve to die now?

No one comes to visit me at the hospital. I'm stuck here in this semiconscious state, unable to move or speak. I don't know how long they'll keep me alive. Apparently, Uncle George, the traitor, is smoking cigars and enjoying island life somewhere that won't extradite folks to the US, leaving me here, all alone, hooked up to tubes and machines, with plenty of time to think. Too much time, actually.

The door opens with the telltale swoosh. It's likely that police chief guy checking to see if I am faking it. I'm not. He comes once a week, sniffs around, pokes my arm. He's itching to put me behind bars. I don't know what would be worse, that or the nonlife I'm living now.

"This is pretty much how she spends her days."

Ah, it's Nurse Retched, as I've become fond of calling her. I don't know what she looks like, but I don't like her voice. It irritates me with its singsong monotone.

"How sad, really. Even after everything she's done."

Oh my god. It's Kate. Maybe she has pity on me? Maybe she didn't really push me. I could be making that up. Maybe she's here to rescue me. Get me out of here. I can forgive her for trying to take John back. I mean, she got the better of me on that one. She doesn't even have to pay me what she promised. I'll take half and get out of town. Promise. I wonder where my signed copy of the agreement is?

I wonder if Kate destroyed them.

"You don't really feel sorry for her, Mom, do you?"

What? It can't be. Is it Ashlyn? Maybe she misses me. Maybe she forgives me. It's not easy being the second wife, I need to tell her

441

that. I made a few mistakes, sure, but every-one does. I'll apologize and all will be forgiven. We'll go shopping. Hi, Ashlyn. I'm in here, I am!

"How long do you plan to keep her like this? It can't be any way to live."

That is Kate's voice. I'd know it anywhere. Is she telling them to kill me?

NO! I'm in here.

"In this case, without next of kin, and without her attorney, we're moving to make her a ward of the state. They'll take it from there. There will be a set time frame for her recovery and milestones. If she doesn't reach them, and she hasn't so far, well . . ."

Well? Wait! No. I'm here.

"Strange to see her like this."

A man's voice. Who is that? Oh, it's Seth, the stupid boyfriend. I don't want him here.

No one is talking. What are they doing? I want them to take me with them, to get me out of here.

But then they'll arrest me.

"She killed my husband." *Kate again.*

"I know. We have the evidence from her garage, all thanks to you, Katie." *The police chief is sucking up to Kate. Shit. Did he just call her Katie? Are they dating? That's what John used to call her. Shit.*

"If she does survive, she'll be left destitute.

The state already has a claim on her clothes and jewelry to pay for her care."

Kate. You promised me money. We had an agreement. How could you? If only I could open my eyes. You should be scared to say such mean things about me. You should know by now who you're dealing with.

I'll tell them all she pushed me. She's the one who should be locked up. That's what I'll do.

Wait, my eyes are opening. I can see. It's bright light. But yes, there's Ashlyn and Kate, and the boyfriend. I need water.

"Isn't this a surprise? Thank you for your help. It was a long shot, but it worked. I'm Chief Briggs. Mrs. Tish Nelson, also known as Terry Jane Crawford, you are under arrest for the murder of John Nelson, and for the forgery of John Nelson's last will and testament. You have the right to an attorney, and the right to remain silent, which you seem very good at."

I close my eyes. Now they know I can hear them. But I can't move. Crap. I feel like screaming, but I can't. Help me, someone?

"Let's step outside, shall we?" *The police chief again. The air shifts and my door closes with a swish.*

Good riddance. Even though I'm trapped here, imprisoned by my own body, at least I'm

443

not in jail. It's peaceful here. I can sleep and dream all day. I will make the most of it.

I feel a hand on my head, breath on my cheek. Who is with me? A kind nurse? I hope she will wash my hair.

"Hello, Tish."

It's Kate. I don't like her tone. I wish I could call for help.

Help me. Someone. Kate's not trustworthy. She's not what she seems.

"Tish, it's possible when you opened your eyes it was some sort of unconscious spasm. But if not, and you're waking up, you'll soon be found guilty of murder and spend the rest of your life in prison. If you aren't, they'll be pulling the plug soon, so you'll be dead."

Her breath is hot on my face. She's standing too close to me. I'm in here, trapped in my own body. I try to open my eyes again, but I can't.

"However it goes, if you live in prison for the rest of your life or you die here in this lovely place, I want you to know one very important thing."

What? Spit it out already!

"I was killing John. You just beat me to it."

My eyes fly open before I can stop them. I try to focus on Kate. She's blurry, but it's her.

444

She has a smile on her face. I close my eyes again.

I just saw her clearly for the first time.

"Do you really think I'd let him get away with all of this, with you, the embarrassment of it all in front of my company, my daughter?" *Kate's voice is cold, deep.* "You see, the pills John took three times a day — the ones he thought were keeping him youthful and stress-free — well those were from me. He thought they were from our naturopath. He thought I cared about him. He was taking potassium. In combination with his blood pressure medicine, potassium chloride causes dangerously low blood pressure, a fatal combination. Perfect, right?"

Kate is laughing. Somebody help me. I try to focus on her, try to make sense of the maniac standing over me. Kate killed John? What?

"Tish, are you scared? Of little *old* me? Remember, I'm the old version, the washed-up version. That's what you told everybody at EventCo, right? But still, you were threatened, I could see it. You hated the launch party on IPO night. Hated seeing John and Ashlyn and me together. As if you had anything to do with our success, as if you belonged there. You are a joke. And you know it. I didn't want John back. I

445

wanted to punish him for leaving me in the first place."

Where is Chief Briggs? A nurse? Anyone? Listen to her. My heart pounds in my chest, it's hard to breathe. I hear a monitor start beeping. An alarm.

"So you took him away to the mountains, to our family's place in Telluride, and finished him off. I'd like to think I would have had it handled, in fact for the longest time I thought my drugs had killed him. But you beat me to it. It was only a matter of time before mine got him."

I'm the one who killed him. Didn't I? All this time, she's been playing me when I thought I was the one in charge. Oh my god.

"And then, for the promise of a few million dollars, you showed me your dirty little secret. The cherry pits. I recorded our chat on my phone. It's almost a confession, according to the experts. Chief Briggs was so impressed by my helpfulness. And thanks to you, I've found love again."

I want to scream. I want to tell someone. Help me! Kate is a murderer. Where's the nurse? I want my money. We had a deal. I can pay for a better place and a better lawyer. She owes me. Where is the agreement we signed?

"Goodbye, Tish. If you're in there, you're

probably wondering if I'm going to honor that agreement we signed the night of your tragic fall."

I didn't fall. You pushed me. I know it. Somebody help me. My monitor is going crazy. Did she unplug me? Help!

"Of course, I won't pay you a dime. Our contract was as fake as the will you concocted. I grabbed both copies and put them in my purse before I dialed 911. I shredded them as soon as I had a chance. There's no record a deal between us ever existed. It's a shame you didn't die that night. But I suppose this is better. I get to say a proper goodbye. I'd pull the plug myself, but it shouldn't be long now. And remember it's always best to be the original, to be the first. Not the next. Never the next. I'll tell you this, though, because of you I did my best work. I channeled a lot of my anger into developing my new Forever product. Not all of it, of course. Some of it I kept focused on John and you."

I've never been so terrified. I've never felt so trapped. So alone.

"Ashlyn was angry, too. At you. At her father. Turns out all along, she was on my side. She knew about the real estate trust in her name and her dad's plan to try to waltz back into our lives as if you never happened.

Ridiculous, of course, because he'd taken this fling with you too far, but John was sure we'd agree to take him back. He told Ashlyn all about it the day he died. She knew more once she took John's phone from you. She even figured out the truth about the pills I gave him. And she understood why. Isn't that wonderful?"

Somebody help me. Blood is thicker than water. Help me!

"I thought the divorce would kill me. But in the end, I guess it killed John and likely, you."

I hear the door swoosh open, and sounds from the hallway momentarily animate my room. And then all is silent except for the beeps of the machines keeping me alive for now.

I told you. It isn't easy being the next wife.

ACKNOWLEDGMENTS

Thank you to Gracie Doyle, Megha Parekh, and fellow authors for welcoming me to the Thomas & Mercer team. Charlotte Herscher, what an honor to have your editorial insights. Thank you for making this book the best it could be.

To Meg Ruley and Annelise Robey of the Jane Rotrosen Agency for being the best agents a writer could ask for, and for your invaluable guidance since we connected. This is the start of a wonderful relationship.

Many thanks are due to so many people who support my books, especially in the fabulous author community, and you know who you are. What a gift. I'd like to say a special thank you to a few people: the real Angie Ball, Andrea Peskind Katz, Tiffany Yates Martin, Ann-Marie Nieves, Nancy Stopper, Colleen Kennedy Sturdivant, and Elizabeth Paulsen. To all the Bookstagrammers and social media fans who help spread

449

the word: you are the best. And to all the booksellers, especially Laguna Beach Books, my local independent bookstore, thank you.

To my friends and family, your love and encouragement mean the world to me. A special thanks to Harley, my partner for the last three decades: We built a company together and raised four kids together, and we're still best friends. It wasn't always easy, but it was always worth it. Your enduring support and belief in me mean everything. To my four kids — Trace, Avery, Shea, and Dylan — you guys amaze me with your creativity, compassion, and team spirit. Not only am I proud to be your mom, I'm so excited to see what the future holds for each one of you. And speaking of building a company, special thanks and love to my team at Real Living, in particular Chris Svec, Alex Butler, and Erin Corrigan. It was real.

Like *Best Day Ever* and many of my other novels, this story is set in the fictional city of Grandville, which as many of you know is actually the Columbus suburb of Upper Arlington. Thanks to my friends there for putting up with another fictional take on our wonderful community.

Readers like you make writing books

worthwhile. I hope you enjoyed *The Next Wife.*

ABOUT THE AUTHOR

Kaira Rouda is a multiple award–winning *USA Today* bestselling author of contemporary fiction that explores what goes on beneath the surface of seemingly perfect lives. Her novels of domestic suspense include *The Favorite Daughter, Best Day Ever,* and *All the Difference.* To date, Kaira's work has been translated into more than ten languages. She lives in Southern California with her family and is working on her next novel. For more information, visit www.kairarouda.com.

The employees of Thorndike Press hope you have enjoyed this Large Print book. All our Thorndike, Wheeler, and Kennebec Large Print titles are designed for easy reading, and all our books are made to last. Other Thorndike Press Large Print books are available at your library, through selected bookstores, or directly from us.

For information about titles, please call:
(800) 223-1244

or visit our website at:
gale.com/thorndike

To share your comments, please write:
Publisher
Thorndike Press
10 Water St., Suite 310
Waterville, ME 04901